The Lament Years

By Nadia Lonnen

Books in this series:

The Lament Years
The Fall of The Walls
A Game's End

Scrap the previous dedication.

I've done it.
And I'm so proud.

Chapter One

Year 79, Month 2, Day 29.
Good morning citizens. As we come to the end of month
2 of our 79th year on 'The Island, I would like to remind
you all of the progress we have made here. Although we
aren't able to venture outside of our walls just yet, we
have come so far with our technology and way of life.
Our population has increased tremendously and the soil
outside of our walls seems to be closer to expansion than
ever before. On this day, I wish those of you with
birthdays to have a lovely day, and ask your spirits to
remain high in the continued efforts to make the world
outside habitable again, so that one day, we can expand
and thrive.
Head leader, Mr Ritton.

My father closes the news update on his bracelet and
smiles warmly at me. I look forward to tomorrow when I
turn 18 and get my own bracelet for becoming an adult,
no longer needing to rely on others. Though I will miss
the extra few minutes I get to sit alongside my father to
read the report in the mornings. I might miss him
entirely if I have to leave home.

"The report is the same as always, I don't think
I've ever seen a different news report come through." I
say to my father as I get up to put our empty mugs in the
sink.

"Well, that's a good thing, don't you think? I
would rather have the same mundane news daily than
bad news, wouldn't you?" He never sees the bad in

anyone or anything, he is happy with the reports never changing. I think there should be more though.

More progress updates, more details, more anything. But I know he doesn't like it when I talk like that. Someone could be listening, and speaking ill toward the leaders could land me in the cage, and no one wants to go in the cage.

"I guess so. I'd just like to read something different for once." I reply with a sigh before quickly changing the subject to avoid being told to be careful what I say, again.

"Anyway, as it's your birthday today does that mean I don't have to go to school? It will be my last day anyway so it's not like I'll learn anything. I want to spend the day with you, it might be my last chance after tomorrow."

In all honesty I'm scared about what tomorrow holds for me. It is the day I officially become an adult and will find out what career I've been assigned, and that'll be it. No change later in life, no choice.

I'll go and start working where I'm assigned, and that'll be my job for the rest of my life. I just hope they give me a good job, an interesting one, though there aren't many of those.

Once I get assigned a job, I'll either stay living with my parents or I'll have to move out, depending on where in 'The Island' I go to work. I won't know until tomorrow, then that'll be it, my life mapped out for me by our leaders.

I love my parents, and if I can spend the day with my father today on the chance I leave tomorrow, then I'll take it. We don't exactly get much time off from our work once it begins, I know I will rarely see them after tomorrow if I move.

We work five out of six days of the week. The sixth day is technically a free day, but we are required by the leaders to go to another Sector and help with their workload. We don't have to spend a full working day where we go, but we are expected to put in a respectable amount of effort. We call this day our sixth.

At least sometimes we get a small choice in what we do.

My mother has already left for work, even though it's her husband's birthday she is not permitted the day off. You only get a birthday off when it's your own.

"You know you can't do that, Talise. As much as I would love to spend the day with my little Pumpkin, I think you should spend your last day of school *at* school. Enjoy being with your friends for your final day of childhood, you know that I'll be here as soon as you get back anyway. Then we can celebrate, okay?" he says, always so reasonable.

"Fine, I'll go. But only because I'm being mature about it and tomorrow I will be an adult." With that he smiles at me, but his eyes are sad, the smile incomplete. I'm an only child. If I leave, my parents will be alone in this house, with no one to care for other than themselves. And I know my father loves our mornings together as we huddle together to read the news update with a steaming cup of tea.

"How about I walk you to school? I do have a free day to do as I please after all," he says with a wink as he gets his jacket off of the back of the chair.

I don't hide my smile or glee at the offer. Me and my father can spend hours talking, discussing and debating topics, reeling off information to one another to try and prove a point. What I love most about those discussions is that he never gives in and that he doesn't let me either. He says, no matter what, you should always stick to your point, trust your feelings and believe in yourself. Never concede if you have heart behind your words, and always be yourself. Most importantly, don't forget to use your head.

"Okay," I beam

"Let's go."

<u>Chapter Two</u>

It's grey out today, it looks like we may get the promise of rain soon, I'd like that.

It only takes us about twenty minutes to walk to school, talking the whole while. It's the one time I wished would be longer. My father stops by the gate and gives me a strong hug, kissing the top of my head.

"Have a great last day Talise, I'll see you at home," he says as he lets me go.

"Thanks Dad. I'll see you later, oh, and have a *lovely* birthday," I reply with a smirk.

He shakes his head at me and turns away, but not before I see the small smile on his face that he couldn't possibly keep away.

Everyone always says that, 'have a lovely birthday'. I feel like I'm the only person that doesn't like how it's said. So repetitive and without any real meaning or emotion behind it.

I walk into the school yard where there are young children running around and playing with their friends. Everyone is happy to be here.

A tall, beautiful, blonde girl sees me and waves, she's standing with another poor soul that will no doubt fall in love with her. That's Jane, my best friend. All of the boys fancy Jane.

She has kissed most of the boys at school that are old enough as well, especially the blonde ones, she likes them best. The boy she's talking to now is no one important, she will get bored with him soon and move on to another. Luckily, she will be leaving school in six months, though she might run out of boys before then.

Next to Jane is Connelly, my other best friend. He smiles when he sees me and tilts his head towards Jane's flirty posture with the other boy rolling his eyes. I laugh as I walk over to my friends.

The three of us have been friends since before I can remember. We have just been in each other's lives from the beginning, as have all of the other kids in our year.

I'm the oldest of the three of us, though I look the youngest thanks to my petite frame. We tend to stick as a group, the three of us. Jane has probably upset all of the girls in school by always having a boyfriend they either want or thought they had first. And Connelly is a quiet kind of guy, he keeps to himself. But it doesn't stop the girls trying to get his attention, though he's never been interested in anyone. If he is, he's kept it quiet.

Then there's me. According to my friends, other kids don't really like being challenged and that's why I don't make many friends. Apparently, I'm too inquisitive, questioning a lot of what we are taught in school, I can't help being curious about the past.

But it works for the three of us, we love each other and we don't need more friends. I leave tomorrow after all, and I may not see my friends more than twice a year after that.

But I don't want to think about leaving and missing them right now, I'll just enjoy my last day with them, even if it is at school.

I stand with Connelly as Jane gives Ben, (at least I think it's Ben, it could be Greg), a kiss on the cheek and walks around him to give me a hug. He stands there for a moment before realising she won't be giving him any more attention and walks off to join his friends.

"I don't know how you do it," I say to her.

"Do what?" she asks as she releases me from her grasp.

"Make all these boys fall ridiculously in love with you in such a short space of time and then crush them weeks later when you get bored. You are a real heartbreaker Jane, you know that right?"

"They're just boys Talise. I'm getting prepared for 'The Island' of men out there waiting for me."

"Guys don't always like girls that kiss everyone they meet Jane," Connelly interrupts.

"Well at least I have kissed someone, unlike you Mr I'm too good for anyone."

"I never said that. I'm just, waiting for the right girl." He kicks at an invisible stone as he says this and I know it's my turn to jump in and save his embarrassment, as always.

"Okay you two that's enough, what are you going to do when I'm gone? You can't spend your days bickering."

"Oh, don't remind us Talise! I want to forget it's your last day today. I'm going to miss you so much!" Jane says, grabbing me for another hug.

A bell rings out signalling for us to go in and start our day of learning. Even though I don't think there will be much for me today, I promised my father I'd be here.

"Come on, we don't want to be late," Connelly says as he walks towards the building with me and Jane trailing behind, Jane rolling her eyes behind his back.

There isn't really much excuse for lateness on 'The Island.' When you get your bracelet, it has the time on it, but in school the bells signal everything for us. They really disapprove of lateness, anytime, anywhere. And Connelly likes the rules, he sticks to them by the letter and would never stray, unlike myself and Jane.

It's just one day though, my last day with my friends. So today, I will follow the rules. All lessons are in the same room with the same teacher every day. We've been with this teacher since we were five, lucky for us Mrs Gamrid is pretty cool and laid back. She's more lenient than some of the other teachers I've heard about, so we got lucky.

Today Mrs Gamrid starts with 'The Island' layout, we don't really get to explore 'The Island' too much other than our sixth if we decide to work far from our homes. That's really the only time you get to travel to a different Sector.

There are three Sectors in total on 'The Island,' covering the three main areas of production. As of this morning, there is a total population of 213,598 people.

One of each of our three leaders lives in each Sector, and it is seen as their Sector to manage and control. This is their main duty, alongside managing the scientists and trying to create a better life for all of us.

We have a large variety of other jobs throughout every Sector, all jobs are equally important, but some just require a larger work force.

Sector One is Farming.

They live furthest north as that's where the sun comes first and leaves last. Sector One is the second biggest Sector, as they have to grow and harvest all of the wheat, grain, vegetables, fruits, and anything else we can possibly grow from the natural resources of the earth. They also have cows and chickens living up in the Farming area so they can accumulate the milk and eggs for us all.

I like to walk through Sector One sometimes and work there on my sixth as it's so green and vast. There is so much land with amazing food growing that keeps us all alive. It really is quite a peaceful treat up in Sector One when you are at the highest point, looking over everything, before the wall blocks the view of anything beyond.

At the far east of Sector One there is also a guard station. Only one in this Sector but we have quite a few in the other Sector's in case of emergencies. It allows the guards to get to the trouble as quickly as possible. But Farming doesn't really have trouble.

We have the baby carers, they look after the newborn babies in the nursing unit, it allows the parents to get back to their work schedule as soon as possible, once the mothers are healed.

I guess it's the most peaceful and quiet Sector due to the lack of machines and animals making a mountain of noise. Thus, making it easier to keep the young ones calm, relaxed and quiet.

Within the nursing unit there are newborn babies as well as toddlers. The young ones stay there until they are five years of age, which is when they will go to school.

Most of the babies stay in the unit for four or five out of six days throughout the six day week, as parents are allowed to spend their sixth with their young one as opposed to volunteering in another Sector.

Parents may not get to see their child together as people have different sixth's, it all depends on when your birthday is, and the work pattern that starts from your 18th birthday. When a child is five years of age and goes to school, they will move back to their original Sector, to be at home with their parents.

Then we have Sector Two which is for Creation.

This is the biggest Sector that we have due to it having the highest demand. People, especially children, are always growing, clothes and shoes are always being recycled. With the large amount of people to provide for, there is such a high demand in Creation that they require a lot of workers, and that's where my mother works.

She comes home a lot of the time with sore, red fingers from where she has been creating materials from scratch. She is very talented, my mother. One summer, when there were a lot of births in our community, I used my sixth to help my mother with some work. Being too young to use the sewing machinery, I helped by delivering out the new clothes to people's homes throughout the Sector.

The leaders weren't too happy about all these births coming at once as it meant certain areas needed extra help, and some people had to change their jobs. The leaders do not like it when they have to change something, and people changing jobs was a big deal.

The births were a problem, but at the same time we also need to ensure our population grows with time so we don't become extinct. Our leaders say we need the perfect balance, and that's what we strive for. We need this as we are slowly rebuilding the world.

It's not just wearable materials they make in Sector Two, they also have metal finders and binders, no one really knows much about what they do in there. Only the people that work with finding the metals know because no one can spend their sixth there

There are jobs producing everything we need for our homes; bowls, cutlery, chairs, beds, and the houses themselves.

We also have wood finders. They go and tend to the trees and plants, cutting down trees when necessary, but always planting another three in it's place. They are always making sure that the resources aren't being used too vigorously as it all contributes towards our survival.

This is why Sector Two is the largest Sector, they need a large workforce. They are the creators.

As it is the largest Sector we have, the hospital is also located there. It is in the middle of the Sector, and next to one of the many guard stations.

There is also a large home nearby for the elderly people to live in when they can no longer work. We call it the 'elders' home'. Sometimes they have the elderly taking care of some of the children in the nursing unit if they are still able, that way they aren't spending all of their time at the home having nothing useful to do.

We have a stage in Sector Two, near to the border with Sector Three, and by the entrance to the bunker.

The bunker runs underneath both Sectors Two and Three.

The stage we have is for large announcements from the leaders, such as important scientific findings, though this doesn't happen often. The stage is also used for weddings, funerals, and rarely, executions.

There are factories and houses scattered in large groups throughout the Sector to make it easier for people to get to work. Myself and my parents live at the very bottom of Sector Two, right on the border with Sector Three.

Sector Three is for Breeding. I have always preferred this Sector, this is where the animals are bred and raised, and it's where my dad works. I know once the animals get on the older side they are put to sleep, and then we use their meat for our food, which is distributed throughout the community equally. I've not yet seen the animals being put to sleep as my dad says I'm not old enough, but maybe if that's my occupation, I will soon learn.

My dad works with the animals outside, so typically I spend a lot of time there with him. We have horses, sheep, pigs, goats, geese, rabbits, and dogs. The cows and chickens from Sector One will be brought down here when they are old, so that they can be put to sleep and their meat can be used.

In every Sector there are houses so that those living there can be close to their place of work. Typically, the children will go to school in the Sector in which their parents work. The schools in every Sector all teach the same curriculum, we all learn the same things and get overseen by the leaders (when they have spare time). They come and observe us to determine where we should work.

Some jobs don't have many employees, like the scientists that are always checking the outside to see if we can expand on our 'Island'. They are limited due to the danger of the role. They go out and check if we can grow any more crops, trees, or resources out there, beyond the wall. They put themselves at high risk and have to wear full body suits to keep them safe from the contaminated world out there.

In 79 years, they have yet to find anything we can build on, but our leaders are hopeful. The world cannot be infected forever, the earth will one day be ready for us again, and we will be there waiting. We just need to work together now, to rebuild the world later.

We have medics, which are important roles, but they aren't required all too often. They are all based at the hospital, and when they aren't tending to patients, they contribute towards creating new and more efficient medicines.

They are always checking for symptoms of infection or anything that might put us all at risk. Being a small community, compared to what the world used to be, if one were to get ill with something deadly, then it would not bode well for the rest of us. Then the human race truly would be gone.

But luckily, we have the bracelets. These monitor our vitals and check our temperature and blood for any signs of illness. If something is found then the bracelet will send a code back to the watchers, and someone will come out to you. The watchers spend their time monitoring computers that display the readings from the bracelets. They are able to see any that have sent out signals for injury or illness.

We don't always notice if we are sick, but the watchers can tell, thanks to the impressive technology our leaders asked to have created for us.

It is hard work for everyone. We work ourselves to exhaustion, because if we didn't, we wouldn't survive. This is what we must do to stay alive, our leaders tell us often enough.

And if we keep going, the scientists will keep checking the earth around us, and one day, it will be habitable again, and we can rebuild the whole world, one Island at a time.

Chapter Three

When the bell rings to signal the end of my last school day, I'm beyond relieved, this day has dragged. Before I can leave, Mrs Gamrid pulls me to one side and asks if she can talk to me for a few minutes. I tell Connelly and Jane to wait outside, I won't be long.

When the class clears, Mrs Gamrid asks if she can give me a hug. It's an intimate thing, to hug someone. Mrs Gamrid has been in my life since I was five, I see her more than my own parents, so I nod.

She wraps me in a warm and silent embrace, rubbing my back and letting out a defeated sigh. She pulls back and holds my shoulders.

"I can't believe this is the last time I will see you, Talise."

"You never know Mrs Gamrid, the leaders may assign me to work here," I say with little enthusiasm. I know it could easily happen, and I'd hate it.

"Talise, for your sake, I hope that doesn't happen. I know this isn't the place for you and I told that to Mr Ritton himself."

I'm shocked by her words. I didn't realise the leaders asked for teachers' opinions on where to send us to work when we are adults, it makes sense though.

"I will miss having you in my classroom every day, Talise. You've been a pleasure to teach."

I laugh at this. With my opinions and defiant attitude, I definitely didn't feel like a star student.

"I wish I could believe that Mrs Gamrid, I think I caused more disruption in your classes than anything."

She smiles widely, her eyes moistening with unshed tears.

"And that has been the greatest gift Talise, you *challenged* me. Kept me on my toes, and I enjoyed every minute of it. Never stop being yourself, Talise, question everything when the rest of us can't, or won't."

I didn't realise how attached she had become to us as her students. Perhaps after all the time together, we feel like her children. I know she doesn't have any of her own.

"I will."

"Promise?" she asks.

I can see fear lacing her eyes, desperation for me to agree with her. It doesn't make sense, but I nod anyway.

"Promise."

She pulls me in for another hug before releasing me and catching a tear with her finger. She signs goodbye to me and waves me out of the door, a smile on her face coupled with tears falling down.

I do feel sad that I won't see her again, I enjoyed her teaching, but I don't think I'm sad enough to cry. I'm very surprised at her tears and attachment to me but I think nothing more of it as I join my friends and walk away from school, hopefully for the last time.

After saying goodbye to my friends, I head back to my house. We didn't have a big goodbye like Mrs Gamrid gave me, luckily my friends will be coming to my house tomorrow after school. They will celebrate my birthday with me and be there when I open my job assignment.

I walk into my house and my dad smiles at me, there's a cup of tea waiting for me on the table next to his. I grin and sit next to him, graciously wrapping my hands around the steaming mug and taking a tentative sip.

We have some time before mum gets home. We talk over our drinks about my last day and my dad's free day. He asks me many questions about my day, my feelings and what I'm looking forward to most about tomorrow. The bracelet, I think.

I'm excited to have a bracelet fitted, to have the freedom of managing myself. Well, as much freedom as is possible on 'The Island' anyway.

"Where did you go?" My father asks and I look up to see his questioning look. My uneasiness about the lack of choice is in the forefront of my mind, but I don't want to mention it. The conversations are always short when I do, with my father telling me not to say that sort of thing and to be careful.

It's frustrating asking a question that my own father won't even answer, that's why I kept to questions at school, where they're meant to be. I have to continuously try and push aside all of the unanswered questions I'll forever have.

"I was just thinking how the thing I'm most excited about tomorrow is also the thing that will mean the end of our morning read together. I'm really going to miss that."

"Me too Pumpkin, me too," he says and sets down his mug, pulling me in for a big hug. My father isn't the tallest of people, it's probably where I get my height from, but he always gives the best hugs.

I start to make dinner, letting my father relax, it is his birthday after all. My mum comes home whilst I'm cooking, I turn as she walks in the door and gives my dad a sweet lingering kiss. She comes into the kitchen and smells the pot in which dinner is boiling and about ready to serve.

"Hey mum, dinner will be ready in a few minutes."

"Great, I'm starving," she says as she grabs a spoon from the side and collects a small amount of the broth to have a taste. She offers me a small smile and heads over to the table to sit with my dad.

We eat dinner and talk lightly; the night seems to be racing away from us. I wash the dishes as my dad has his birthday cake. It's only a small cake that you get a few bites out of, but every year my parents share their cake with each other.

A small treat they always want to have together, I think it's a beautiful thing. I'd love to have someone in my life to share a cake with one day. It's my favourite part of any birthday, I adore cake.

I go to the table and give my dad a kiss on the cheek. It's time for me to go to bed and let them dance in private. They always dance in the evenings, no matter if it's for minutes or an hour. I used to watch them when I was younger. I'd sit behind the wall and poke my head around the corner, watching them hold one another close and move around the tiny room. It's the happiest I've ever seen them.

"Goodnight Pumpkin, we will see you tomorrow, when you are an official adult."

"I hope you've had a great birthday Dad. See you tomorrow." I give him another big hug before heading towards my room. I turn around before I leave the room and look over at my parents.

"Night mum."

"Goodnight Talise."

∞

It's the 30th day of the second month and today is my 18th birthday.

I woke up excited this morning as I knew I would have a break from the routine and get to enjoy a day to myself before learning my new career.

Each birthday you are permitted a present from someone you consider family. For those that have no one, sadly they do not get a present, but they will still get their cake. I wonder what my mother gave my father for his birthday yesterday.

All presents given must be something of use to the person and it must not be a waste of resources. We don't tend to make things here that aren't needed, though occasionally some things do slip through the net unnoticed.

A few years ago, I saw a girl at school that had the smallest, almost unrecognisable, piece of silver chain around her neck. At the base under her shirt, I could see the outline of a heart, such a dangerous yet loving gesture this present was.

It must have been from someone very special to her, I'd never seen anything like it before and haven't seen anything like it since. It's a sad tale though, the girl's parents both died not long after her 16th birthday in a work accident that also affected three other families. She went to live with another family in a different Sector of 'The Island.' I heard that the girl became mentally unstable and tried to leave 'The Island.' She died in the attempt.

The leaders do often remind us of how unsafe it is outside of the walls; they are there for our protection after all. But I'm guessing the grief was too much for that girl.

This year, for my birthday, as I am 18, I will have three gifts. The first being my cake, the second will be what my parents get for me, and thirdly, I will get my bracelet from the leaders.

Each bracelet is powered by our body heat so it's always functioning, a very intelligent design.

When everyone arrived on 'The Island,' all of those over 18 were given the bracelet and since then, all children receive them on their 18th birthday when they are fully grown and ready to start their adult life. It's a sign of trust for us to get a bracelet, it shows we are no longer children and have become part of the workforce saving the human race.

As well as the daily news reports, our bracelets tell us the time, date, and have communication devices inside to contact anyone other than the leaders. They have a different communication network to the rest of us, for safety reasons I'm told, though safety for whom I do not know.

I am looking forward to getting my bracelet today, to get some independence and truly progress into my adulthood. My appointment is at 2:30pm so I have plenty of time to enjoy my day beforehand. Perhaps I'll visit my grandma.

My father assured me there won't be any injections when I get my bracelet, I have a huge phobia of needles and don't think I could have an injection ever again. Last time I fainted and hit my head of the corner of a table, blacking out for three minutes. That was very embarrassing.

There are many exciting things happening today. Once my bracelet has been secured on my wrist, I will have a little time until Jane and Connelly are out of school, and then my parents will finish work shortly after. It will be the last time my parents collect my cake, and whilst they are doing that, they will also collect the envelope in which the details of my job will be contained, along with my new work clothes and shoes in a separate package.

Today is a great day, today I learn what the future holds for me, and today I have freedom.

It's a typical rainy day, it always tends to be on my birthday. It isn't something I mind at all, I love the rain. The day I was born there was a massive thunderstorm, it hammered down with rain and didn't stop for almost thirty-six hours, which happened to be the length of time it took for my mother to give birth to me.

My father would joke that I am a child of thunder and rain, due to the fact that as soon as I arrived the storm stopped, and the rain came to a slow pitter patter, just before stopping completely.

Since I was a baby the sound of the rain has always enabled me to drift off into a deep sleep. If I can hear the soft fall of the raindrops outside, or even the hard pelting of it on our rooftop, it calms me. It always relaxes and eases me into a good night's sleep.

So when I woke this morning to find it raining, something people typically don't tend to appreciate, for me, it was just another birthday gift.

My parents have already left for their day of work, not wanting to wake me when they left, so I can enjoy my only morning of sleeping in a little later. I expect it will be all birthday wishes, hugs and kisses later.

When you wake up at the same early hour every day of your life, you don't tend to sleep in even when given the chance. But I do enjoy the luxury of just lying in my bed, having some time to listen to the winds, the animals, and of course the rain.

I get myself up so I can enjoy as much of the day as possible. I go to my wardrobe and bask in the moment of not having to pull on my school clothes ever again.

I don't have many clothes, no one does. It would be a waste for us to have so many when they are simply not needed.

We have our mandatory school clothes, skirts and a shirt for the girls, trousers and a shirt for the boys, no exceptions. I heard once that a boy was adamant he wanted a skirt, but they refused him because it wasn't normal.

We all have a practical outfit and a social outfit; and the adults have two sets of work clothes. The practical outfit for everyone is some thick water-resistant trousers, a thermal top and waterproof jacket, these are good for the colder and wetter days of the year.

The social outfits for men will either be trousers or shorts and a shirt. For women there is the choice of a top and skirt, or a dress, you get to choose between the two.

Everyone has extra clothing, a few pieces here and there but there really isn't much need for it, the assigned clothing is plenty.

For myself two outfits are more than enough. As it's raining and muddy out, I think I'll go for the practical outfit today, and I'll wear my dress later on this evening when I have my cake and sit with my family and friends.

We all have three pairs of shoes assigned to us. For children there is a pair for school, whereas adults have a pair for work. We all receive a casual pair, and lastly, a pair of boots for when the weather gets bad and we still need to go about our day trudging through the sludge, puddles, mud and whatever else may be blocking up the paths.

I get my boots just in case a storm does come down whilst I'm out. It's really hard to get shoes replaced here, you have to wait for them to be made once you've informed and proved yours are of no use anymore. These are the only cases you are allowed to wear different footwear or clothes, when you're waiting for your replacements.

We recycle all of our materials which is brilliant for our resources but if you really need those shoes quickly there's no way around it. So, I spare my social shoes and wear the safe and sturdy boots for my walk, which I know will end up lasting hours.

My school shoes were taken this morning by my mother to be recycled and I will be receiving my work pair later on this evening. They always start making the work shoes for people in advance of their birthday so that they are ready to start work the next day. The people that make the shoes are just told the gender of the person and the size to make, no one knows of someone's occupation other than the leaders until the 18th birthday.

Just before I step out into the damp morning, I notice a note on the table, it reads 'Happy 18th Birthday Talise, we love you.' The writing is a little scruffy, so I know my dad wrote it, he's the best. This is a great start to the day.

We live at the southernmost part of 'The Island' where the walls are just behind our house, built higher than anything I've ever seen before.

It's a nice home we have. It's small as there is just the three of us now. My brother died shortly after he was born, some type of infection they said. My mother never got to bring him home.

I know his death still haunts my parents. I would have loved to have a real brother, but it wasn't meant to be, and my mother doesn't like to speak of him as it's too sad for her. But I will always remember the brother I never met.

Our home is simple, as is everyone's. We have a kitchen area, two bedrooms and a small bathroom. We don't need any further rooms in the house as we are all out every day, we only spend the evenings together catching up on the day's events.

Everyone is always tired from the long day, so we go to bed early each night. Though my father has always found time to tell me a story as I go to bed, I'll miss those.

There is no need for any 'social' rooms in the house like they used to have. Living rooms and dining rooms. It sounds nice but maybe a little too much when we live how we do. What we have is enough, and we are happy. I do know that the leaders have social rooms though, apparently these are for meetings and work, not pleasure. I'm not sure I fully believe that, but again, this is another thing my father warns me not to voice.

But we all know about it; we know the leaders have lavish things that are definitely a waste of resources. To mention this would definitely result in time in the cage. That's why no one says anything, out of fear.

Where we live is called 'The Island' it was discovered by something that was once called a 'government' as the only safe place left where the disease had yet to infect the water supply.

We have been taught at school that 100 years ago water treatment plants across the world were somehow contaminated and started to produce water that was lethal.

When people around the globe started becoming sick with no explanation, people grew scared. But the more water they drank, the worse they became. It took them three weeks to figure out the water was actually carrying an unknown disease which was the cause of all of the death.

Many of the best scientists in the world worked to try and find a cure, or the source the disease originated from, but they couldn't find anything.

They named it The Lament Disease and advised all those across the world to stop drinking their fresh water supply, though without water people couldn't survive. Gradually over time people started killing each other for uncontaminated drinks, hastily destroying the human race.

The 'government' had started to look for safe places as soon as they discovered the problem. Someone came across 'The Island' and deemed it habitable and without water contamination.

They set to work straight away, using resources from all of the countries to build this safe place. It was kept as a secret at first so that the buildings could be completed in time, though after five weeks of construction, the population's chance of survival couldn't wait any longer.

By this point many of the larger countries had suffered greatly, all of the clean bottled water that had been in full supply at stores and in homes had run out. There were no more resources for people to purify lake or ocean water, and billions of people were getting sick from the contaminated or dirty water.

People were drinking anything they could get their hands on. There were many that had gone days without any liquid at all, their time was limited, it was desperate.

The 'government' released a statement after realising how badly people were struggling and 68% of the world's population had died. They told everyone how there was a safe place to live for anyone without the disease, there was ample clean water. The people were welcomed to build a new future and to be safe until a cure was discovered, or a new source of clean water was found.

They set numerous times and dates, sending their largest ships to save the people around the world. There were many soldiers to protect the innocent, but the innocent also became murderers. In the mad rush to get to safety, people knocked others down to their death. It was a sight of destruction, and they say it was heartbreaking to witness.

Once the ships were loaded, they headed to 'The Island,' although only 8% of the ships made it here. The rest were lost in the journey somehow, all contact was lost. Not every country had someone to come and rescue them either, they were left without any aid. It was brutal.

In total, 14,860 people made it to 'The Island' from the madness. Out of the billions around the world, those were the last survivors.

Once they all arrived on 'The Island' they were directed straight to the bunker for safety. Inside they were met with projector screens on all levels with the leaders on them saying they would be in there for some weeks, just to make sure they were safe and to finish construction.

They declared that they would be in charge on 'The Island' and that they had a plan for survival. Everyone was terrified, so no one argued the point.

On the second day in the bunker, it's said that all they heard were distant sounds, crashing, banging, that went on for weeks. It was as if they were listening to the end of the world happening above them.

At the end of the fourth week, they were told that the 'government' had deployed bombs over 86% of the world in order to remove the people left diseased. It was a kinder way for them to die, rather than allowing the disease to make them suffer for longer.

The following week in the bunker was spent with everyone grieving for those they had lost and left behind. It was a very sombre time and grief hit hard. There were more deaths within the bunker as people couldn't handle the pain and sadness, or what this new world would bring.

On the second to last day in the bunker, the leaders came together to let them all know that the bombs that had rained down to rid the diseased had done irrevocable damage to the Earth, and the government had inadvertently wiped themselves out. 'The Island' and it's population were all that was left.

There was nowhere left outside of 'The Island' that was habitable anymore, they were the only place on Earth that had survived. This was now the only land left with a clean water supply. The rest of the world was left damaged and exposed to radiation.

The leaders explained how they would have three Sectors of 'The Island,' and how they would all work and contribute to a better life. Everyone would be put to work in a day's time, once they had found a house in the right Sector.

Doctors would go around checking on everyone, and the next day everyone would start to get issued with the bracelets so it would be easier to monitor people's welfare, and help with the transition to this new life.

On the last night before their release from the bunker, there had been 403 suicides. When everyone finally came outside, they were met with the rest of 'The Island.'

The bunker was all they knew so far. Built to fit 20,000 people, in there they would always be safe. Outside now, they could see the multitude of houses and factories that weren't there when they had arrived.

They were told that there was a hospital and a school in each Sector, and they say the most shocking of all was to hear that there were animals living on the south end of 'The Island.' At least, that was the most shocking until they looked up and saw the 80ft wall surrounding the land in which they were all now living.

And that was how the world was destroyed and The Lament Disease nearly wiped out the human race. Scientists are still working to find a way to make the rest of the world habitable for us again, but they estimate it to be a long wait for the Earth to heal itself. So, we wait.

We work and we wait for something better. But at least, for now, we are alive.

Chapter Four

Today I have freedom, so it's time for me to do some of the things I like most. I head east, to the animals. The earth is damp beneath my feet, the rain isn't too heavy, but I imagine it will thunder down on me later, and I look forward to it.

It doesn't take me too long to reach the first pen of animals, which are pigs. They are funny things, pigs. They are the messiest animals, so I don't tend to spend too much time with them, I prefer an animal I can pet. So I move off to find the horses.

The horses aren't too far away, there are two that I can see outside the stables. The walkway to the stables is behind the head leader's house, so the others might be hiding back there, I'll have to check.

"Hey Squirt, what are you doing here?" I turn around to see a tall man with messy blonde hair that slightly falls over his warm brown eyes, smiling his half-cocked grin at me.

"Joseph, I'm 18 today, so that means I'm an adult and you can definitely stop calling me squirt.' I smile back at him as I walk over to give him a hug.

"But it is good to see you, how are you?"

"As good as can be expected, work is going to be hard today with this rain getting heavier, I should probably get the horses back to their stables soon," he says this with a heavy sigh and looks over to the stables. I don't know why, but Joseph has never really liked working with the horses, which is strange as he seems to love all of the other animals.

I have known Joseph for about ten years. He has been here ever since I started coming to the Breeding area to help with the work. I like to think of him as a big brother.

He doesn't treat me like a child, he never has. It's one of the reasons I like him so much. We used to play games when I was younger, hiding around by the animals. Though he never liked it when I got near the head leader's house, and told me to be careful not to get too close. He was always looking out for me, making sure I didn't get myself in to any trouble. He's a good guy.

"How about I take the horses to the stable? I have a free day and I do love them." I smile and know he will agree.

"Oh, go on then. Thank you, Talise." His half-cocked smile is warm and reaches his eyes as always.

"Have a great birthday and I expect to see you very soon." He says this as he points at me and winks, walking backwards. He turns around and gets back to his work, whistling on his way.

I love the fact he never tells me to have a lovely birthday, I feel like that's his defiance to the phrase, not that he would ever admit it.

I turn and face the nearest horse to me; I call her Violet. The animals we have here technically don't have names. The leaders say it makes it harder when they were put to sleep, the breeders start to develop attachments to them, which just made the process a little horrific.

I still like to name some of the animals, but only those that I see nearly every time I visit, I guess they are my favourites.

I'm not surprised to see that Violet is one of the two horses out in the rain, she loves it. She has such beautiful white hair and big brown eyes; I think she is the most beautiful of all the animals.

"Hello Violet" I whisper to her ear whilst running my right hand through her mane, my left strokes her nose as I plant a little kiss on it. She is breathing heavily through her nose, as if she's snorting a little, I take this as a sign that she likes me and the name I've secretly bestowed upon her.

As I walk a few steps towards the gate I hear a weird noise that's not quite a bang, but it's loud. It makes me jump and Violet rears back on her legs, clearly not liking the sound either. I right myself and look around me to see if I can spot where the noise came from, but I can't see anything that would make such a noise.

No one else seemed to notice as everyone is continuing with their work like nothing happened. Maybe they didn't hear it over the rain, or it could be that it's a regular sound here, one I've not heard when I've visited before.

Perhaps I will find out for myself soon enough if I am lucky enough to work in Sector Three.

I go through the gate to Violet, stroking her nose to calm her down.

"Come on girl, let's get you inside the stable," I whisper to her.

She stands there enjoying the stroke, as am I. I know I'll have to move first to get her on the go, but I want to stay here and enjoy the rain and peacefulness of stroking her.

After a few minutes the rain gets heavier and that's my cue to get her to the stable. As soon as I head off toward the path she starts to follow me, and we walk side by side, my hand resting up on her neck, gently stroking her.

It isn't much of a walk to the stables even though we are at the opposite end of the fenced off area. We only need to walk past Mr Ritton's house, the head leader, and then we'll be at the mouth of the stable. There's another horse waiting by the house, so I go and give him a little pat and get him to move along with myself and Violet.

One of the windows of Mr Ritton's house is open, and I can hear a gruff voice I've heard only once before, two years ago when there was an announcement of the girl that died.

They told us she tried to escape from 'The Island' by climbing the walls but fell to her death. They say she went mad and couldn't cope with life after losing her parents. It does happen sometimes, rarely, but it happens.

No one can climb over the walls.

I wonder who he is talking to as he lives alone, but I decide it's none of my business and carry on walking toward the stables as quietly as I can with two horses.

"Well I want to know HOW they are getting outside." I stop in my tracks at what he said.

Who does he mean by 'they'? Is he referring to the animals? If so, how are they outside? Outside of their pens, outside of the fences, outside of the Sector?

"Well they could hardly climb over the wall now could they? Are they leaving through the gate?" He is really shouting now, and I know I shouldn't be listening, I can't seem to make my feet move. Questions swarm my mind at the strange things he is saying.

"No Lieutenant. I am telling you now that your excuses are not good enough. What if someone gets out and the others have changed their tactics and decide to ask questions first? What do we do then? The others could ruin *everything*." The emphasis on that last word leads to silence in the air. My body is tense with nerves.

"You need to find them. Find the group that knows about the others, find the people that are escaping, and find out how. If you can't do this Lieutenant, you will be reassigned, and we both know that is NOT something you want to happen. Now sort it before too many people find out. Don't come back to me until you have answers."

It sounds like the end of the discussion and I realise I am still standing here listening, I should definitely get my feet moving now.

I would be in immense trouble if I was found here. I really don't want to be caught eavesdropping on our head leader, especially after what I've heard. I'd like to avoid being in the cage at all costs.

"Come on then, let's get you inside and dry," I whisper to Violet to ensure I'm not heard, and walk off as quietly as possible to the stables with my mind whirring with what I've just heard and what it means.

Who are 'the others?' And how could they ruin 'everything,' what did he mean by 'everything?' Who is escaping, how are they escaping? Outside of the walls is too dangerous, they would die. What is going on?

Just as we are about to round the opening into the stable there is a voice behind me.

"What are you doing?" It's the same gruff voice I heard moments ago.

I freeze and slowly turn around to see that Mr Ritton has come out of his house and he is staring right at me. I'm suddenly filled with a fear that he saw me outside his home listening to his conversation. If he knows I was then I will be made to go in the cage for sure.

The cage is the place where people that break the rules are sent to in order to atone for their errors and to learn not to do it again.

It's a series of containers, with no lights or windows. They put you in there for however many days deemed necessary, and I never want to go in there again.

I went in once when I was ten years old. I had been in the Farming area on a trip with my class when I saw an injured little chick hidden in a corner. I decided to take the chick home thinking my father could fix it.

A teacher had spotted the chick in my hands before we left, and I was told that we are not allowed to take things without permission, they considered it stealing. When we got back to our Sector, they put me in the cage until dinner time. It was the scariest thing that has ever happened to me. I was terrified and alone, surrounded by darkness.

Children are not allowed to be in the cage for longer than a day, but adults, they can be in there for as long as it's deemed necessary. And I'm an adult now.

"Hello Mr Ritton, I am just taking the horses to the stable so they are out of the rain, I think it will be getting heavier soon." I try to sound innocent, like I hadn't just overheard him shouting at someone for things that make no sense to me.

"How long have you been out here for?" He asks.

"Not long sir, I just got the horses and hurried to the stable so we could be out of the rain."

"Is today your sixth?"

"No sir, it's my birthday." I smile with my reply and hope he lets me go; I can't imagine he wants to stand in the rain much longer.

He stares at me for a long moment as if judging whether or not I'm lying. I exaggerate a shiver in the hopes that he will think I'm cold.

"Okay, well, hurry along then, you don't want to be stuck in the rain yourself. It's good of you to help with work on your birthday, the welfare of 'The Island' thanks you." He flashes me his white teeth in a big fake smile as he heads off towards Sector two.

I let out a breath I hadn't realised I was holding as relief floods through me.

I stroke Violet's mane and notice Mr Ritton coming back towards me and he calls out to me.

"I hope you have a lovely birthday young lady." And with that he briskly walks off again. I rush the horses into the stables as my mind races with what happened these last few minutes.

Mr Ritton has certainly never mentioned any 'others' to us. Never once in the updates have they mentioned anything, unless it was at the very beginning, before my parents were even born.

I'm surprised Mr Ritton mentioned finding new work for the Lieutenant, people never change jobs. Whatever he was talking about had really angered him, though I gathered that from the shouting. Where am I going to get answers about what I heard? My father won't let me say anything about it to him. As soon as I start mentioning something like this, he will instantly stop me, scared of the danger my words could bring.

But I can't keep this to myself, not this time. I have too many questions to ask about what I just heard.

"Hey, Harry! Can you come an' help me with this dog mate?" I hear Archie calling to my father and turn to see him rushing over to the wall where Archie is down on his knees next to a black and white dog.

I was so lost in my thoughts I hadn't even realised I'd put the horses in the stables and I was already nearing the other animal pens.

I go over to my dad and Archie just as they are lifting the dog up into a wheelbarrow. I notice it's the little dog that I decided to call 'Scamp.' He's always running around with his tongue flapping out, waiting for someone to give him a scratch behind the ear or throw him something to play with.

"Can I help?" I ask, my father looks up at me and smiles, but it's Archie that speaks first.

"Hey kid, could ya give him a stroke whilst me an' yer dad see if we can't get someone to take the little guy up the hospital." He speaks with such a deep voice, but it's always gentle and kind. I make a mental note to remind him later that I'm not a kid anymore, as of today I am an adult, but Scamp is the priority right now.

I kneel on the floor so I'm level with Scamp and take a look at him. His front left paw is caked with blood and there seems to be some form of wire sticking out of it, hooked under his paw pad. He is whimpering and shaking a little. Just as I look up to ask my father for a blanket, he is already passing one over to me with a small smile.

I wonder how Scamp came to get the wire in his paw, I can't think of anywhere it could have come from other than the top of the wall. That's crazy to think as no one could make it up to the top in the first place, it's too high and we have nothing that could aid us in getting up there. Maybe the wire is worn and old so some of it fell off.

The wire is only there to deflect people from trying to get over the wall, as it's so high, no one could make it up to the top without falling down first anyway. If they somehow managed to reach the top, the barbed wire would prevent them from climbing over. That's why it had been designed that way, to keep people out at the beginning, just in case there were any diseased people left that somehow got to 'The Island' and tried to get in and attack us.

"Dad, do you think he will be okay?" I ask softly.

"Oh, yes Pumpkin, he will be fine, I'm sure of it," he replies, unable to keep out the worry from his voice. I look down at poor little Scamp and do my best to comfort him. I stroke a finger from the tip of his nose to in-between his eyes, he loves it when I do this, it always gets him calm and to sleep.

"Hey, happy birthday beautiful, how do you feel now you are an adult?" I look up at my dad and smile wide.

"I'm excited to find out what career I will be given, I would love to work here with you and the animals," I say. My dad smiles at this, he knows how much I love it over here, even the pigs. I secretly love those weird little pigs.

"Well, let's see what happens tonight, okay? The leaders will know where is best for you."

"I know Dad, I just know where I want to be." I look down at little Scamp, he has stopped whimpering now, but the rain is really picking up, we will need to move him soon.

"What about your cake?" Dad asks, snapping me out of my train of thought, he knows me so well.

"Oh, the cake! I am definitely excited about my cake. It's the best part of birthdays, end of," I grin back. He laughs at me and turns around to see Archie walking back towards us looking slightly deflated.

"Archie, shall I take Scamp to the hospital so you can all continue with your work?" I ask. It makes sense for me to go, seeing as I have a free day and I want to make sure this little guy is okay.

"Oh darlin' that'd be real helpful if you could, love. With the rain a'comin down like this we all gotta put in some extra elbow grease an' we jus' don't have anyone spare to take him up there. You're a star girl." Archie says as he comes over to ruffle my hair smiling, then he's already walking off to get back to work.

"I'll see you tonight, Pumpkin," my dad says as he gives me a kiss on the head. Then he's getting back to work, which is my cue to get going.

It's quite a long walk from here to the hospital, it will take up my whole morning to get him there. If I need to wait around to bring him back, that will be my full day gone, but I don't mind, I want him to be okay. And I think it will give me more time to think about the words I secretly heard from the head leader.

I check my boots are still laced up tightly and brush off some of the muck from my trousers. Once I've tightened my jacket and checked that Scamp is covered properly with the blankets, I pick up the wheelbarrow handles and head off to the hospital.

The further into Sector Two I go, the louder it gets, all of the machinery and buildings, it's all so noisy.

I don't know how these people don't have constant headaches; I wouldn't like to work in this Sector. It was fun to see my mother at work here and to spend more time with her, but I have always preferred the animals in Sector Three, it's where I belong.

It's not often that people see someone as young as me walking around in the day, not at school and with a dog in a wheelbarrow.

I may be 18 today, but because I am a petite person, people just assume I am younger than I am. Firstly, people usually take note of my eyes, they are quite unique, like Archie's. He has one green and one blue eye, but mine are a constant grey. They stand out even more because of my caramel coloured skin and jet-black hair.

No one seems to bother me on my walk, and I manage to get to the hospital quick enough, though I'm unsure how much time has actually passed. Once I get my bracelet later I will be able to know the time without having to ask other people constantly.

When I get inside the hospital, they take Scamp for a quick scan whilst I fill in a couple of forms with as much information as I possibly can.

Once I've filled in the forms, they inform me that the surgery will be quick, as will Scamp's release, so I should wait around to take him back within the next two hours.

It's 1pm and I need to be at the hospital for 2:30 anyway to get my bracelet fitted, just in a different part of the building. So that means I now have less than two hours alone with my thoughts, trying to figure out what Mr Ritton was talking about a few hours ago.

Chapter Five

Rather than sitting here getting lost in my own thoughts and coming up with stupid answers, I decide to go and see my grandma for a short visit. She may even be able to tell me something about what Mr Ritton could have meant when he said 'The others.'

My grandma used to live with us, but she came to live in the elder's home when she turned 73 her legs became too weak, meaning she could no longer walk to work.

My grandma is 81 now, she started to lose her memory fourteen months ago. It was slow at first but is becoming more rapid now. They say she doesn't have much time left with us.

Unfortunately, our doctors and scientists aren't advanced enough yet to stop all illnesses, but they try their best and do manage to create cures for many. My parents tell me that old age is just one of those things that cannot be prevented, and one day, I will lose my grandma.

My grandma always says that what we are doing here is something of great beauty. I never understood this when I was younger, so a few years ago I asked her to tell me what she meant.

"We are rebuilding the world, Talise, what could possibly be more beautiful?" That's when I realised just how smart my grandma is.

Luckily the elder's home is only a fifteen minute walk from this side of the hospital, so I head straight there. This is one of the only buildings with a lot of open space for socialising, as the elderly spend most of their time there. A lot of them are in wheelchairs, so they need the space to be moved around one another.

They have quite a large number of carers that work with the elderly, ensuring they are safe and helping with anything they may need. The social area is the largest part of the building, there are corridors leading off from there in many directions taking you to all of the bedrooms. There is also a kitchen through a door on the right when you walk in, but it's not a room I've ever been in.

Grandma's room isn't far from the social room, so I head off in that direction.

"Hey, Nina's girl, if you're looking for her, she's asleep right now, only just gone to bed as well." I turn to see an elderly gentleman sat in one of the many armchairs, staring at me above his wide framed glasses.

Great. She's asleep.

I can't go and wake her up, maybe I'll just wait a little while and see if she wakes. This is the best place to ask seemingly innocent questions, they are the oldest people on 'The Island,' surely there is something they may have heard before. What's the harm in asking?

"Okay, do you mind if I sit with you for a little while? I have some spare time on my hands," I ask him. I stay standing where I am, not wanting to seem intrusive in case he says no.

"Oh sure, it would be nice to have a bit of company for a change." He smiles when he says this and waves me over.

"Come on now, come take a seat."

I make my way over to the chair he's sat in, jumping out of the way as a man with a guard's uniform and a hard face wheels in an elderly lady, who has a face to match his. They both glare at me, then he wheels her over to a table where he sits across from her and they start to play some type of table game. I try my best not to glare daggers back at them.

"Oh, don't mind them, that's just Dolores and one of her grandchildren, she has three of them, you know. Don't see 'em much mind. That one works at the guard station nearest to us, so he's here often enough, been a guard for twelve years, you know." I get the impression this gentleman likes to gossip, which could either be a good or bad thing for me.

It could have just been a load of rubbish that I heard earlier, but when Mr Ritton said 'the others' I felt a chill that just won't seem to pass. It's bugging me, it confuses me, and I want to know more.

"Are you going to stand there all day and stare or are you going to sit down and have a chat with me?" He asks me almost impatiently.

"Oh, sorry, it's nice to meet you, I'm Talise, what's your name?" I smile sweetly at the elderly man as I sit down across from him.

"Name's Boa, nice to meet you little lady. What are you doing out of school today then, young one?" He asks curiously.

"Today is my 18th birthday, so I am an adult now." I say with pride.

"This'll be the day of your sixth from now on then." He says this so matter-of-factly and I hadn't even thought about it.

As tomorrow will be my first day of work, I will work for five days, and my sixth will be this day of work for everyone else. At least I know that no matter where I end up working, I could spend my sixth working with either of my parents if I wanted.

"Yeah, I guess it will be, I hadn't thought about that. Can I ask you something Boa?" I ask tentatively. I guess there's no harm in just asking, if anything I could play it off pretending I meant the other residents, or something along those lines.

"Ask away my dear, I have big eyes and ears, I hear and see a lot you know," he says this with a gruff laugh that turns into a cough.

I think of how to word this properly, I want it to seem like I actually know some of what I'm asking about.

"Well, I was just wondering what you knew about, 'the others.'" There's a long silence from him after I ask, he seems to be staring right through me. He looks around the room, then leans in close to me like he has a secret to share.

"What do you mean by 'the others' exactly?" He whispers, eyeing me warily.

"Well, you know. Do you know anything about them?" I don't really know where else to go with this now, how much do I elaborate?

"I don't think I know what you're talking about, young one. I've heard everything there is to hear but I've never heard any mention of any 'others.'" He pauses as another little round of coughing comes in.

"I ask you again, what do you actually mean by 'the others?'" He obviously doesn't know anything, he seems confused, and I must admit, I'm confused as well.

Boa seems really out of breath and his coughing has increased. I give it ten seconds, but it doesn't calm down. I look around the room ready to call someone over for help.

"Water," he manages to get out in-between heaves. I jump up and look for a carer, spotting one next to the kitchen. I rush over and ask him for some water. He stares at me intently for a few seconds then seems to shake himself out of it and turns around, going into the kitchen.

I recognise him but I can't place his name, I'm not sure if I've ever known it. He's been here for a couple of years now, I think. He is always kind and says hello if I pass him, though we never engage more than that. My grandma seems to like him though, she calls him the handsome one and then laughs like she's told 'The Island's' funniest joke.

He returns seconds later and passes the water to me with sad eyes and perhaps confusion? Weird. I hastily take the water to Boa, the whole time feeling like I have eyes watching me.

He sips at the water in-between coughs, but it doesn't seem to help him much. Just as I'm about to get up and ask for some help another carer comes over, mumbles something about 'big mouth Boa' and takes him away to hopefully get some treatment.

I'm about to get up and ask someone for the time so I can make sure I don't miss my appointment when a voice from directly behind me says my name.

As I turn around, I notice the guard and his grandma have stopped playing their game. He's speaking to someone on his bracelet, shielding himself from prying eyes and ears, whereas his grandma just stares at me.

The woman that spoke is behind my chair, glaring at me. I'm about to ask if I know her when she speaks.

"I'll tell you now, Talise. I heard everything you just said, and you shouldn't be asking anything about any 'others.' You should be helping 'The Island,' not spreading rumours or getting people worried for no good reason. It's all lies, and you ought to keep your business to yourself before people start thinking you're mentally unwell. They will turn on you just like they did my son before he was killed. Lunatic with his ramblings, just like you. I tell you now, you should stop." Her voice gets louder with each word she speaks until I feel like she is shouting at me.

And just like that she turns around and walks away from me before I can utter a single word.

I stand there a little shocked, not too sure what just happened. What was she saying, her son was killed for asking about 'the others?' That can't be true, our leaders would never just have someone killed like that, it's a disgrace and the people would never allow it.

I do remember hearing of an execution about ten years ago, a raving lunatic they said. Could it have been her son? But she just said her son *was* mentally unwell, so what does that have to do with the 'others?'

This day just isn't making any sense, I'm standing yet again lost in my thoughts, wondering about what I've just heard. I decide it's probably best for me to leave, so I head to my grandma's room first to check on her.

I walk through the door on my left and go the short distance to her room. The door is open so I go inside and I'm unsurprised to see that she is sound asleep in her bed. I go over and give her a kiss on the cheek. I turn to leave but there is someone blocking the doorway.

"Hello Talise." His surprisingly feminine voice sends a chill down my spine, it's the guard I nearly walked into earlier.

"I was just leaving," I say, walking towards the door to leave. He doesn't move.

He stays blocking the only exit. I don't think I could fight my way out of here if it came down to it, so I take a step back and stare at him. I try to look confused instead of scared, but I don't know what my face conveys.

"What are you doing here today? Talking to those elderly people?" He smiles towards me, but his face is calculating, there is a cold look in his eyes that scares me.

"I had to take an animal to the hospital, so I thought I'd visit some of the elders whilst I wait for him to be fixed. I'm sorry but am I in trouble for some reason?" I ask.

"What were you talking to those elderly people about in the social room?" He avoids my question and takes a step towards me; I mirror his actions and take a step backward.

"I was just making small talk, giving them some company and passing time." My legs are now pressed against the side of the bed, I can't walk back any further. He continues toward me, slowly prowling forward, like an animal ready to attack its prey.

I could scream so people could come running to my aid, but that would wake my grandma. The last thing I want to do is wake up someone with memory loss by screaming.

I also have no reason to scream, he is a guard, I would be the one to get in trouble. Maybe I can dodge around him and run out of the room? I could get a kick to his shin and run if I needed to, it's the best plan I have.

Why am I scared? Nothing has happened yet. But I feel it in my gut, his presence here is not a good thing.

"I heard you mention 'the others,' what did you mean by that exactly? Are you feeling unwell?" I don't say anything, he stares at me, the coldness in his eyes growing deeper.

"Maybe I should take you to the hospital to have some treatment, you must be a little unstable in your mind if you can't answer simple questions. Let me take you to the doctor, Talise." He reaches out with his hand as if to grab my arm when a voice speaks out from behind me.

"Are you the doctor? Can you help me? I can't feel my legs." The raspy voice of my beloved grandma asks.

The guard looks over my shoulder at the woman staring at him and lowers his hand from it's reach.

"Are you just going to stand there staring at me or is someone going to get me some medicine?" She practically shouts.

I smile internally at the stern woman I've always known; she knows who she is and who I am. She doesn't take her gaze off of the guard, I know from experience she never breaks one of her fixed stares.

"Of course, I will go and ask for a carer to see you." He smiles widely at her, but he looks less than happy.

"We shall continue our conversation shortly, Talise." He says, a plain threat being delivered there. He doesn't even try to hide it, now I'm even more scared than I was before.

He turns and saunters out of the room, not even glancing back. I know he will be back in a matter of minutes, as hard as it is, I know I have to leave now.

"Talise, who was that man?" My grandma asks.

"I don't know, Grandma, but I don't like him very much. I know I only just got here but I have to go, I'm sorry," I say, then I kiss her hands that I've clutched in mine. She looks up at me and smiles.

"You are such a beautiful girl; do I know you?"

I know it's not her fault, but it still breaks my heart when she doesn't know who I am, especially how quickly it can change. I give her hand a little squeeze and smile at her as a few tears threaten to spill from my eyes.

"Goodbye Grandma, I love you," I whisper.

When I face away from her, I wipe a tear from my eye and see the carer that got the glass of water for Boa earlier today. Now he's standing in the doorway, but he doesn't look intimidating, he looks kind. He isn't looking at me in the weird way he had earlier, now he looks concerned, what's his deal?

50

I've never paid him much attention before, he is a tall and slender man, though he can't be much older than I am. He has jet black hair that's kept short and off of his face with eyes that match perfectly in colour.

He raises his hand to me with a piece of paper in it, scrawled on there are the words *'Don't say anything. They're listening. Come with me.'* I don't know what to make of this guy, what does he mean by 'They're listening?' Who is? And how? This day is making my brain work overtime already.

He points to his bracelet and then to me, is he asking if I have mine yet? I shake my head to indicate no, hoping I don't look stupid. He seems satisfied and gestures for me to go to him. This probably isn't even the strangest thing to happen to me today.

I could go out there and have to go by the guard again, but I don't want to answer any more questions. He asked me what I knew of 'the others,' I have a terrible feeling about what I heard today, and I don't think it's going to get any better judging by the guards reaction. He said I must be unstable and wanted me to get treatment, it didn't sound like it was a choice either.

I could follow this carer, maybe he can give me some answers? He might know something. Or he might be able to take me to a different exit so I can avoid the guard. This guy hasn't done anything to scare me, yet.

My choice is already made. I follow him.

∞

We walk in silence from my grandma's room to the door I came through, but he stops short. I think to ask why he has stopped, then I remember he told me not to say anything because 'they' are listening.

He swears under his breath and turns back to walk the other way. I take a step forward and go up on my tiptoes to peer out of the little window in the door. I'm greeted with the sight of several guards, the scary guard from moments ago is talking to a few other guards and he looks frustrated.

I hear a 'tsk' behind me and remember I'm meant to be following that guy. When I turn around, he's standing there, staring at me, motioning for me to follow him. I'm not sure why but I feel safer with him than the guards.

We stalk the hallways for another few minutes until we come to a wide door at the very back of the building with the word 'EXIT' illuminated above it. He gently pushes the door open and ducks his head when he's met with heavy rain. I'm glad I have my sturdy shoes on, the mud is thick and sludgy now.

He doesn't seem too bothered by it and he steps out into the mud and pouring rain, walking to our left where there are many rows of houses. I hesitate only for a second before I follow him as he picks up the pace.

I wonder how long we will be walking for, it's no secret that some people's houses are over an hour's walk from their work. I hope this isn't the case as I imagine I should be getting back to the hospital to have my bracelet fitted soon.

It's hard not knowing the time for yourself, but I estimate that I should be getting back there in an hour's time for my fitting. I'll make sure to check the time when I'm actually allowed to speak again.

I wonder if this guy is going to get in trouble for just leaving work like that. Does he have an excuse ready? I wonder if he does this often, he could get in real trouble if he did.

I'm pulled from my thoughts as he takes a sharp right and we stop in front of a small brown house. We couldn't have been walking for longer than ten minutes, he is lucky to live so close to work.

He opens the front door and ushers me inside, as expected, no one is here. Everyone will be at work, possibly school if he has any siblings. Even if it's someone's sixth they will be helping at another place of work.

He closes the door behind me then holds one of his palms up facing outwards to me, leaving no spaces between the fingers and thumb. On the other hand, he holds up his index finger and thumb, this is something everyone learnt at school, it's the signal we use for 'wait'.

He rushes off to another room, and I just stand there waiting for him to return. It's interesting he signalled to me instead of speaking now we are in his home; I hardly ever see people signal.

We learnt some basic signals at school, mainly so that when we are with some of the elderly that have lost their hearing, we have a sufficient way to communicate the basic things to them. We all had to learn this because our careers aren't known until we are older, you never know when you may need to signal to someone. I guess because he works at the elder's home he signals a lot, or maybe it's just a habit for him.

"So. What exactly is it that you know about 'the others?'" A smooth and light voice speaks from the room before me. I look up to see the guy staring at me, now with a small circular plate covering the face of his bracelet.

"So, can we talk now?" I probably should have asked who he was first, but I want to sound calm and act like this whole thing isn't completely tearing up my brain.

I'd also like him to think that I have a small idea as to what is going on, though I'm not sure how to do that, because I am utterly clueless.

"Yeah, sorry about that, I couldn't have them listening and knowing that I am with you. It's best no one finds out I helped you back there. But I am interested to know..."

"Excuse me, but how exactly did you help me? Was I in danger with that guard?" At least my voice manages to keep cool and clear as I interrupt him. I had felt scared and threatened, but surely a guard wouldn't have actually harmed me.

The guy starts to chuckle, I wasn't aware I was being funny. When I don't say anything and just stare at him, he soon stops.

"You are joking, right?" He asks, at least now he seems to be a little confused as well as me.

"The guards, they were coming for you because you decided to start asking about 'the others' in front of a room full of people, *including* a guard. If I hadn't have taken you out of there then they would have taken you away for questioning, or treatment and you wouldn't have come back. That's how I helped you, I saved your life." He says this so matter-of-factly that I struggle to doubt his words, but I want to, because it makes no sense.

"Who are you?" I ask.

"My name is Enzo. Now that I've answered a couple of your questions, would you please tell me what you know about 'the others?' And what is your name?" He sounds irritated at having to explain how he'd saved me, but he seems to know more than I do. Should I tell him what I overheard?

"I'm Talise, and I don't know much apart from it's just been a very strange day. I'm not too sure I actually know anything." I look at the floor slightly embarrassed that I don't really have much to tell.

"It's okay Talise, just tell me everything, all of the details, no matter how insignificant you think it might be. If it was out of the ordinary, then tell me, please." He asks calmly.

So, I tell him about the conversation I overheard between the Lieutenant and Mr Ritton, the wire in Scamp's foot, and the loud noise I heard. He probably knows most of what happened at the elder's home already, but I tell him about the conversation I had with Boa, the old lady practically shouting at me, and what the guard had said to me.

It feels good to get it all off my chest, to actually tell someone what I had heard, I'm not sure why, but it had been eating away at me a little.

Once I finish speaking, he is silent, staring down at the small table we have somehow come to sit at.

"Oh, this is bad, this is so, so bad. I need to tell Carlo," he mutters to himself.

"Who is Carlo? And why is this so bad?" He looks up at me, shocked that I had spoken, as if he had forgotten that I was sat right there.

"He's no one, look, you're not safe, you have to hide. I might be able to take you somewhere safe, but I don't know." He gets up and starts looking around for something, I don't know what. He's avoiding my questions and he wants me to go and hide, why? I don't even think I'm in any *real* danger, he's overreacting.

"I don't understand, please can you give me some form of explanation for any of this?" I keep my voice calm and hope it will help, but he is too distracted now.

"I can't, Talise!" He shouts without even looking at me. Why is everyone and everything today so strange?

Enzo is frantic, rushing around the house, I don't understand how he has become so distracted all of a sudden. I didn't think I had any real information, but he seems worried about what I said, and that scares me because I don't understand my own words.

"What are you saying then? I have to go and hide somewhere because I'm in danger? Just for overhearing a conversation I shouldn't have? How am I in danger Enzo? WHO ARE 'THE OTHERS?'"

He rushes forward and puts his hand over my mouth. His whole body is tense, fear seems to radiate from him, his eyes wild.

"Talise, don't *ever* say those words again, you hear me? Never mention 'the others' out in the open like that if you want to live." He says this in such a harsh whisper, but I know he isn't being cruel. He isn't trying to hurt me; he wants me to be safe.

I should just leave this house; run away from this guy I've just met that is acting crazy. But I can't, because I want answers and he can give them to me. I can't lose my temper with him, so I nod, and he moves his hand away from my mouth.

"Enzo, what does all of this mean? I don't quite understand how what I heard has put me in danger. Can you help me understand? Please, explain it to me." I don't care if I sound desperate, I need answers, it's my life that he seems to think is in danger and I need to know why.

He stops and looks at me, he really looks at me as if only just seeing me properly. A girl that looks as young as a child, afraid, confused and alone.

He must take some pity on me because he sits back down at the table and let's out a long sigh. I slide into a chair across from him and sit there quietly, giving him a minute and hoping he will tell me something.

"I can't say much, it's not my place to. But I can tell you this, the lady you spoke to, her son was executed ten years ago by the leaders. They said that he was mentally unstable. He started talking about impossible things, he was making up stories and hallucinating. Or so they said.

"He was doing what you did today, but he was more demanding, he did it on multiple occasions and he was desperate. He would ask countless people if they knew about 'the others.' He said he knew there was more life outside of our walls, said he heard people out there. We needed to open the gates and join them, the other survivors.".". Enzo looks sad as he continues.

"It didn't take long for the guards to come and take him away. They said he needed help, that he was unstable. A week later they gathered people to the stage and the head leader gave a speech about how they tried to help the poor man, but he had attacked them. The man had killed two of their doctors and a scientist, and he hadn't shown any signs of remorse.

"They said it would be with deep regret that they must take his life, he was a danger to himself and to the people. They could not save him; they couldn't do anything to help him.

"They hanged him, right there on the stage, in front of the people that came for an announcement. Everyone else saw it on the projection from their bracelet, his own mother saw it. Everyone believed our leader's lies, they saw him as a monster, and soon after that, so did his own mother. He was 35 years old

"They questioned his sister to see if she was like him, but she had turned her back on her brother and told them as much. She agreed he was unwell and that they had done the right thing by executing him. They offered her a new job as a guard, that was the 748th work transfer approved on 'The Island' since the beginning, other than when we had the influx of births.

"But the thing is Talise, he was never unwell, mentally unstable, or whichever term they used. He was completely sane, he just found out the truth and the leaders killed him for it.

"They took him to a secret prison they had built somewhere on 'The Island,' they questioned him about what he knew and who else he had told. Once he told them everything, they saw the threat he posed, pumped him with drugs and sentenced him to death. He never harmed or killed anyone; he was innocent."

I realise now that I've been sitting on the edge of my seat the whole time, completely wrapped up in the story he is telling.

I wasn't told much due to me only being seven or eight at the time it all happened. But the stories went around, and we were just told a crazy man hurt and killed some people, so he was hanged for it. Simple as that.

If this is the real story, then what else is there to know? This only covers a tiny portion of what happened today. This doesn't tell me anything about 'the others' or who they are. It doesn't tell me if there even are people living out there, it could all be false.

This story sounds very extreme, I should just be honest with the leaders if they question me. I will tell them all that all I heard was the mention of 'the others' on my way to the hospital. I'll definitely be in trouble for eavesdropping, but maybe it won't be so bad.

I won't get killed for asking a question to an elderly man, my parents would certainly never allow it. It's sad what happened to this man, but it wouldn't happen to me. Or would it?

The guard that cornered me was pretty threatening and suggested I might be unstable. What if they do want to kill me?

I need real answers and I am not getting any of them here, I need to leave and think by myself, and I'm guessing it's time for me to get my bracelet.

"Thank you for bringing me here and telling me the story, Enzo, but it's my 18th birthday so I need to go and get my bracelet fitted. I'm probably late already." I stand up ready to leave but he's already in front of me, alarm coursing through his eyes.

"Talise, have you not listened to me? You can't go, you need to hide, I will help you." Now he's the one that sounds desperate.

"Enzo, I'm sorry, but I have listened. You aren't giving me much to go on. You want me to hide somewhere, to leave my family and friends but why should I trust or believe you? You won't tell me anything about what I'm actually asking you, and if I don't turn up to my appointment soon then they will know something is wrong and come looking for me. I am going to get my bracelet." I move for the door.

"Talise, I won't stop you. But you should know, the bracelets, they track you. They also have the audio on all of the time, they hear everything you say, they know everything you do. It isn't for your benefit to have one, it's just a tool they use to spy on us." He sounds so defeated.

"If that's the case then why haven't they come for us both by now? They know we are here, and they would have heard our whole conversation thanks to your bracelet." After I say this, I look at his bracelet and realise he still has that weird plate attached to it.

I look back to his face and he is smiling.

"This plate stops the transmissions of the bracelet; they can't hear anything or locate me whilst this is attached. A friend created it. That's why I asked you not to speak before, this keeps us safe for a little while. But I can't use it for too long otherwise the watchers would notice me missing from the grid." He admires whoever made that for him, he speaks with such pride in his voice.

I don't know how to respond to that. I silently walk towards the door, open it and turn around to look Enzo in the eyes.

I don't know why I feel so bad about leaving him, I've only just met him, yet I still feel guilty.

"I'm sorry, Enzo." And with that I walk out of the door and start a fast walk, zig zagging out of the houses towards the hospital, and I don't look back.

Chapter Six

It's still thundering down with rain; I don't know the time, but I can guess that it's probably time for my appointment. I'm halfway to the hospital already, I think I can get there in about twenty minutes if I pick up the pace, that way I won't arrive too late, I hope.

"Quite unusual wouldn't you say," a stranger's voice sounds just as two guards appear in front of me and I come to a stop. More guards, this is not what I wanted after my last encounter.

I look at the guards watching me. 'Excuse me?' I reply, wary.

"It's quite unusual to see a child running around in the pouring rain rather than staying in the nice dry warmth of her home or a workstation." It's the tallest of the two guards that speaks. She is a well-built woman with a stern face that's on full display thanks to her greying brown hair being pulled back in the tightest bun I've ever seen. She also has a thin red stripe over the right breast pocket of her uniform, indicating she's a Lieutenant.

Even though I knew people would still think of me as a child, it is irritating.

"I'm not a child, it's my 18th birthday today, I have an appointment to get my bracelet attached which I'm already late for, so I should probably get going." I try not to sound too curt, but I just want to get away from the guards for now. I want to try and come up with my own conclusion of today's events.

I move around the guards and start to walk off hastily.

"How about we accompany you the rest of the way. We wouldn't want you falling over in this horrible rain and hurting yourself, especially as not many people are around. Let's escort you there seeing as you don't yet have a bracelet to alert the watchers if you're injured." The guard that's speaking tries to look concerned and smiles at me when she talks, though it's not reaching her eyes. Her eyes are hard and void of emotion.

I'm a little intimidated by this woman but I don't want to show it, especially not in my voice, so I try my best to keep it level.

"Oh, that's okay. I'm nearly at the hospital now anyway so you don't- "

"Oh no, we insist." She interrupts me with ease and continues to speak before I can get any more words out.

"There have been reports of a child around this area today, they say she seemed troubled. We want to make sure we are keeping the people safe, just in case she's still around, we shall escort you. I don't suppose you've seen or heard anything out of the ordinary today have you?"

Boy, have I, but I won't tell her that. I feel like this is more of a threat than anything. The child they are on about is surely me, but troubled, what did she mean by that?

There's nothing I can do about it now, if I refuse, then I'm dishonouring a guard. As I am now an adult, they could detain me for at least a week in the cage for that offence. That is not how I want my birthday to go, none of today is how I've wanted my birthday to go, but I'm certainly not ending up in one of the cages.

"No, I haven't. It's just a normal day." That's all I can come up with right now, so I carry on towards the hospital though I will have to walk now instead of jog. I don't want it to look like I'm trying to run away.

The guards actually stay a little behind me, so luckily, I don't have to answer any more questions from them. I wouldn't hear them over the rain now if they spoke to me anyway.

Just as I'm rounding the corner to the hospital with my two unwanted guests in tow, I nearly bump into a nurse who is in a hurry, probably trying to get out of the rain.

"Oh sorry. I didn't see you there." I try to smile with my apology, but it doesn't quite work.

"That's quite alright. Wait, aren't you the girl that bought that dog in earlier today? The little black and white one?" She asks me this as she eyes the two guards standing right behind me.

"Yeah, that was me. Is Scamp better now and ready to go home?" I realise my mistake as soon as it comes out of my mouth.

"Scamp? You've... named him?" The hardness of her voice shows me that she doesn't approve. Before I can respond though she speaks again, briskly.

"Doesn't matter. He is ready so if you could come and sign for him then we can release him and free up some needed space." She doesn't even wait for my answer as she turns and walks up the side steps to the hospital.

I had hoped maybe the guards would leave me if I had to go and collect Scamp, but I was wrong. I felt bad that I had forgotten about him, the last couple of hours have really gone by quickly.

I go up to the desk to sign the papers and the guards linger back by the entrance waiting for me. The shorter one of them talking on their bracelet whilst eyeing me suspiciously.

A different nurse brings Scamp out and hands him over to me. He seems a lot happier now with his wagging tail, and he gives my cheek a lick. His paw is bandaged but the nurse says he should be fine to walk, so I put him down on the floor and watch as he walks around with only the smallest of limps.

The nurses don't tell me anything about the wire that was in his paw, just that they got it out and repaired the damage. The bandage can be taken off in a day's time and his paw will look as good as new.

It is really impressive how they can mend and heal us so quickly now. We've been told stories of before when it could take six weeks for broken bones to mend, I can't imagine having to wait so long for such a thing.

On 'The Island' our doctors and scientists have come up with ways that make our healing process a lot faster. Broken bones will mend within hours. They can be quite common for those that do heavy labouring, so it means we don't have to go too long with people out of work.

Since the guards insisted on escorting me here to ensure my 'safety,' I think that I may be able to get rid of them now that I'm in the building. Especially if I have witnesses around that could say I did nothing wrong if it came down to it. It's worth a shot.

"Thank you so much for escorting me here through the horrible rain. But now I have the dog I can just walk to my appointment through the building rather than go back outside. It really was kind of you to ensure my safety. I hope you have a pleasant day now that your job with me is complete," I say in my politest tone and try not to lay it on too thick. I smile sincerely at them as the tallest of the guard's eye's me quizzically.

"Very well. Make sure you go straight to your appointment and get your bracelet attached. Oh, and have a *lovely* birthday." She stares at me intently with those last words, gives me a curt nod and they both turn on their heel and leave. The other guard doesn't look too pleased about leaving me, but she knows she can't question her Lieutenant.

It would be quicker to go outside and walk around to the other side of the building, but I want the guards to leave me alone, they've left me feeling uneasy.

In all my life I've never had to speak with guards as much as I have done today, and it's not something I'm enjoying or wish to continue.

I move off down the hall that connects to the main hospital and Scamp comes bouncing after me.

I'm not too sure what to expect now, my dad did give me a brief talk about it and ensured how safe and painless it would be. And there are no needles, I need to remember that so I stay calm.

No needles.

But what about what Enzo said about them being able to track and listen to us all. He could be wrong about that though, surely it can't be true.

Everyone here over the age of 18 has a bracelet, including the leaders. That's hundreds of thousands of people wearing them, I think if we were all being monitored in an intrusive way then that's something people would be aware of.

I reach the waiting room and there is only a small handful of people here. I imagine the few here are also getting their bracelets and they're probably here early because of the rain.

There is one other person at my school I know has the same birthday as me. I guess there are more than a few in the other Sectors, I wouldn't know as we don't meet children from other Sectors. Well, not unless we choose the same place to help with work on our sixth.

I go up to the reception desk and tell the nurse my name and that I'm there for my bracelet. He quickly types a few things on the computer and tells me that I'm in fact twenty minutes late and I will have to wait as the attending nurse is busy.

I take a seat and Scamp jumps up to my lap, we sit there for several minutes. I stare ahead whilst I mindlessly scratch behind Scamp's ear. After a short while a nurse opens the door across from us and calls my name, we get up and follow her into the room.

"Hello Talise, I hope you are having a lovely birthday. Would you like for me to explain to you what is going to happen here?" She has a kind voice and smile, she looks very trustworthy, maybe that's why she was chosen for this job.

"Hi, yeah if you could please, I'm a little nervous." I offer her a smile back, my voice trembling slightly but she's probably used to it if she does this often.

I wonder if she can tell how on edge I am from the day's events, or whether she just puts it to nerves about the bracelet. She gestures for me to sit on the bed whilst she gathers the equipment and begins to explain it all to me.

"So, you obviously know what the bracelet looks like, the face will be just above your inner wrist. On the face you will have the date and time displayed at all times, so you can keep track and get yourself to work and wherever else is necessary. It is important you use your own bracelet to check the time from now on. As you are an adult this means you are solely responsible for yourself. Your parents can't help you if you go wrong, you are your own responsibility." She shows me the face of my bracelet, it's all black just like everyone else's. She flips it over so I can see the other side.

"Now this little pin here, this will pierce your skin when I attach the bracelet, but don't worry, you won't feel anything as we will numb your arm first." She must see the horrified look on my face, sure it's not a big needle, but it's a needle all the same.

"Hey, Talise, it's honestly okay, you really won't feel anything, I promise you." This does ease the tension slightly for me, I give her a small smile, so she knows it's okay to carry on.

"Now, once the pin has pierced your skin it will take your blood into the bracelet. As the bracelet will be stable on your arm it won't move or come off, the pin does stay in your skin. It won't get infected because the bracelet has the ability to administer some medicines into your system, mainly, keeping the area clean and unaffected by bacteria. Are you keeping up with me so far?" She has clearly done this many a time before. She pauses at the right times to let me process the snippets of information, not that I'm sure if my brain is really processing any of this. But I nod and smile again, not quite sure I want to speak yet as I'll just come out with endless questions for her.

"This bracelet will be able to monitor your vitals, it can detect anything within your blood that may be causing a threat to your health. It can read signals from your body if you are injured, even if it's as small as a paper cut, it will notice, and it can process how immediately you need care. That data will be sent back to the watchers, if the injury is quite severe, then doctors will be sent out to you, but if it is minor then you are expected to come to hospital yourself to be seen to. You can send a message to the watchers to let them know if you are coming at any time, you think you may be unwell, or you are injured. This saves them sending doctors out to you if it is unnecessary and will save on time allowing us to treat other patients."

She hasn't said it, but if the watchers see I'm severely injured and they send doctors out to me, surely that means they can track my location, so what Enzo said could well be true. I don't think it would be wise to ask her though, I'll just see what else she tells me first.

"Of course, as well as the ability to communicate with watchers and doctors in case of your own illness, you can also call in an emergency for someone else. You are able to contact anyone directly through your bracelet other than the leaders. So those are the main points of the bracelet for you. Do you have any questions for me at all?"

I think about how I should word it without being rude, as so far, she has been nothing but kind to me.

"I was just wondering, what if the bracelet needs replacing, what if it breaks, I mean?" Surprisingly my voice comes out even and without trembling.

"Well, be rest assured, it won't break. These bracelets can't break. They are powered by your body; they only stop working when someone is deceased. The band of the bracelet has the ability to shape with your body, so if your arm gets larger or smaller, the band will copy and always stay attached with a comfortable fit. You'll be fine, once it's on, it isn't coming off again." She smiles then, more to herself I think, proud at how she handled the question, and delivered her answer. Though again, I feel like there was a threat at the end of her words, but that's probably just my paranoia from today's events.

"Okay thank you, but one last question. What if someone were to rip their bracelet from the arm. Say they had a fight and someone else tried to rip it off, what would happen?" I look at her face whilst I ask this question, because I really don't know the answer. I know that no one has ever taken one off and they are on for life, but I can't help but think what if.

If she was shocked by my question she definitely doesn't show it. She opens her mouth to reply when there's a knock on the door and it opens.

"I'm so sorry to interrupt, but could I borrow you for just two minutes please Melissa?" It's the receptionist. He's walked in halfway through the door and is looking from me to the nurse, who I'd assume is called Melissa. He looks a little pale, and his eyes are wide with worry, maybe someone is injured and needs her help.

"Okay, I'll be back in a minute and we can fit your bracelet." She gives me one last kind smile as she exits the room.

I have a little look around the room and at the bracelet. It's laying on a metal table alongside a little packet that says, 'antiseptic wipes' on it, and next to that a small pot labelled 'numbing cream.' She has it all prepared for me.

Scamp stays sitting at my feet and nudges my foot with his head, I lean down to give him a scratch behind his ear. We sit there for a few minutes, me scratching and him making satisfied sounds until the door opens again.

The nurse walks back in and something feels off, but I can't quite put my finger on it. If I hadn't have met her already, I wouldn't have noticed anything odd, but something has changed about her.

For starters, she won't make eye contact with me, and she's twitchy, maybe even nervous. She walks straight over to the table with the equipment on, stands in front of it with her back to me for a few moments then she turns and looks at me.

"Okay, we should get started now. If you roll up your sleeve to above your elbow, I'll give you the numbing injection." Her voice that was soft and calming is now hard and formal. I start rolling up my sleeve and it takes me a moment to register what she said.

"Wait, you said there wasn't an injection, my dad said it was just numbing cream. Why aren't you using numbing cream?" Now my voice is panicked.

"Not once did I say there wasn't an injection, I told you your arm would be numb and that's what will happen. The needle has been there the whole time we were talking, you just didn't want to see it." She says this all without emotion, like a robot.

I know that it hasn't been there, I know it's not even there right now, I was just looking at the table before she came in. As if reading my thoughts, she steps to the side and gestures to the table, there it is, a syringe filled with orange liquid and a very long needle.   "No. That wasn't there a minute ago, you just put it there. I am not having an injection. Use the numbing cream." But even as I say it I look over at the table and I realise she has also taken away the numbing cream that was there moments ago.

Now I'm really worried about who she went to see out there and what is in that needle. I don't think it's safe for me in here anymore, I don't trust her, and I need to leave.

"Look, there is no cream so if you just let me give you the injection it will all be over in a few minutes. Just calm down Talise, they said it won't hurt you." She is growing very impatient with me now and that made her slip up. Who are 'they,' and why do they want me injected?

This isn't good, I should have listened to Enzo and stayed at his house. My mind is whirring trying to find a way to escape quickly and quietly.

"Okay, can I just get some fresh air before we do this? I'm feeling a little queasy, I'm really scared of needles." I try with an apologetic smile, but she doesn't seem to be having any of it.

"You can't go outside; a lot of other people are waiting. I promise it will be over in minutes, just hold out your arm for me please."

She starts to approach me with the needle when a loud scratching noise comes from the door stopping her in her tracks. We both look over and see Scamp is scratching at the base of the door and then he starts whining. She seems confused by what he's doing, but I could pick him up and kiss him right now, he's giving me my exit.

"Oh no. The err, little guy needs to go to the toilet. Sorry but if I don't take him now, then he will go on your floor."

She looks at me, then back at Scamp who is still scratching and whining. She stands there staring at Scamp as if her gaze will stop him, but he keeps scratching.

"Fine. Be quick. Take him out to the courtyard, it's straight ahead, first door on the left, there's a green area where he can go, leave him out there and then come straight back, I have other patients to see." She says it all with such sharpness and finality. I'm glad she cares more about having to clean up urine from the floor than getting me with that needle.

I hastily jump off the bed, thinking how lucky I am right now to have Scamp with me. I nod and open the door, ready to go straight for the exit.

Just as I step out of the door, I see the two guards that escorted me earlier talking to a nurse at the reception desk. Then I notice that the waiting room is empty even though Melissa had just said she had other patients.

I need to go past the guards to get to the courtyard and make it believable that I'm coming back. They've yet to see me standing here so I could escape if I go a different way and move fast.

I don't wait around; I pick up Scamp and we hastily make our way down the hallway on the right. I know there is another exit this way, but can I get there before the guards catch up to me?

I pick up my pace, not wanting to find out what was in the needle and why the guards are hanging around, no doubt waiting for me. They are probably the ones that gave her the needle so they could take me off for their questioning.

I pass a room on my right that has the door wide open, inside is an empty bed and a large window, slightly ajar. I don't really think about it, I rush inside the room and shut the door behind us.

It's a small room, as they all are, so in a few strides I'm at the window and pushing it open as wide as it will go. If I get out of this window, I will be closer to the elder's home and it means I won't be coming out of an exit that's right next to a guard's station.

Luckily for me I am on the ground floor, so from the window to the ground outside there isn't much of a jump in it at all. It's a little higher for me as I'm short but I can dangle from my arms and drop to the ground with little distance in between.

I unzip my jacket halfway and put Scamp inside; the bottom of the jacket is tight so there's no chance of him falling out. I zip my jacket up a little higher but not covering him completely, otherwise he may try to wriggle out.

I am very grateful that I chose to wear this outfit today, the boots are sturdy and firm, so I can climb out of the window easily. I bring over a chair to stand on first, I lean out of the window and check no one is around. It seems clear so I step on to the window edge and turn to face the room.

I crouch down and grip the window frame base; it's slightly raised so I have a firm grip. The hard part is kicking my legs out and planting them on the wall beneath without slamming myself and Scamp into the wall.

I take a few deep breaths and before I can think twice, I push off with my feet then bend my knees up towards my chest and above Scamp's head. My feet land well and Scamp is unharmed, still in the jacket. The impact isn't too hard on my legs, so I start to walk my feet down the wall until I'm as flat as I can be.

I glance down to my side and see I'm only a foot or so off of the ground. No point hanging here aimlessly so I push myself off of the wall, landing on my feet in the wet mud and grass, but I lose my balance and fall down. I lean into my fall so that I can land on my back and not hurt Scamp in the process.

I manage to angle it correctly. Luckily it was a small fall so my back doesn't hurt too much, though it's definitely going to be sore for a few days. I lay there and breathe deeply for a few moments, unzipping my jacket and checking Scamp is okay. He's none the wiser in there, it's time to get up and move.

It's then I realise I don't really know where I should go. If I go to my grandma there will probably be guards there, and I'm sure some will be at my house now as well. I could go to my mother at work but I'm guessing they will be waiting for me at any place I may go. So that only leaves Enzo.

I get myself up off of the ground and start to run toward Enzo's house. People shouldn't take much notice of me considering the downpour of rain, most people are running in this weather so they can get inside to be dry and warm.

I keep my pace fast, not knowing if anyone is out looking for me yet. I'm hoping Enzo will help me and give me some answers, because I'm still confused as to why I have people trying to either take me for questioning, throw me in the cage or as Enzo believes, kill me. I just don't know what is happening today.

It's easy to remember where Enzo's house is because he's at the very back row closest to the wall on this side of the Sector. I run up to the front door and knock, within seconds Enzo has opened the door, he stares at me, confusion all over his face.

The rain is falling hard and he's just staring at me. I don't want to say anything in case he doesn't have the plate on his bracelet, if it's true what he said about them listening, I don't want them knowing I'm here and that he knows me. Enzo seems to shake himself out of it when I start shivering and he moves aside to let me in without a word.

I wait in the same spot I did only an hour ago. He again goes off to get the plate for his bracelet so that we can talk freely. When he comes back in he almost looks angry, in his hand he holds another plate for me.

I shake my head.

"I didn't get my bracelet," I say as I pull up the sleeve of my jacket just to prove to him I'm not lying.

"What happened? And why is your jacket moving like that?" His voice rises at the end of the second question, clearly baffled.

I look down at my chest just as Scamp wriggles his head out of the top of my jacket and licks my chin. I smile down at the little guy and unzip my jacket further, just then remembering he needs the toilet.

"I'll explain in just a second, someone needs the toilet first." I walk over to the door and open it, popping Scamp outside, he walks over to the wall, cocks his leg and happily does his business. He sniffs around a little then walks back into the house and lays down by my feet.

"Okay. On my way to the hospital two guards decided to escort me there. Luckily, just before I got to the main part of the hospital, I bumped into a nurse who remembered me from dropping off Scamp this morning. She asked me to collect him, once I had him and was inside the building, I openly thanked the guards for their assistance and said I would be okay alone. I thought I had gotten rid of them." I sigh and rub my temples; I think I have a headache coming along and my back is hurting even more after that run.

I take a seat at the table and Scamp instantly jumps up on my lap, I give him a little scratch before continuing.

"Anyway. I got in to see the nurse, she was really kind and explained the bracelet and how it worked, everything was fine. Then she got called out of the room for a few minutes, when she came back in, she behaved weirdly. She was acting the complete opposite to how she had been before, it was really off. That's when she said I needed to pull up my sleeve for the numbing injection-

"But there isn't a numbing injection," Enzo interrupts me before I'm finished. I'm glad he is at least agreeing with me.

"Yes Enzo, I didn't exactly believe her. She said, and I quote, 'they said it wouldn't hurt you.' I don't know about you, but I've only ever heard of nurses referring to doctors by their title. So when she said 'they,' I knew that she didn't mean the doctors. I knew that needle wasn't there until she came back into the room. I was trying to think of ways to get out of there, but she wouldn't let me go. Luckily, I had this little guy with me, he started scratching and whining at the door because he needed to go and do his business. I made her aware he would go on her floor if she didn't let me take him outside. She agreed to let me quickly take him out, so I grabbed Scamp, ran off and found an empty room with an open window. I climbed out and ran straight here." I look at his face to see his expression as I finish telling my story. I'm not surprised to see that he's acting like he knows all of this already.

"I told you not to go, Talise. But at least you got out of there safely. Are you hurt at all?" He's speaking gently to me even though he is probably angry at me for going when he told me not to.

"I'm okay, and I'm sorry I left when you told me not to. But if I'm honest, I didn't know I could trust you, I still don't really. But thank you all the same for helping me again." My gratitude is genuine, and I want him to know that. Then a thought comes to me.

"It's strange though, the nurse said she had other patients waiting, but when I went out to the waiting room there was no one there. Apart from those creepy guards. I'm guessing they gave her the needle and were planning on taking me somewhere, but I've no idea where and I didn't want to stick around to find out."

Enzo just stares at me, pained. I feel he wants to tell me something, but he can't, I don't know why but I think he would be in trouble if he did.

I wonder if he can help me any further, if that safe place he mentioned before is still available for me. I'm on my own, I have no idea what I should do or where I could go. I also don't know why I believe what Enzo tells me, but I do.

I've always thought that there should be more; things that they have hidden from us all this time.

"Enzo, how are you not at work right now? Aren't people going to come here looking for you?" I can't believe it took me this long to think about it, the guards could come for him any minute. He could get in a lot of trouble for not being at work right now, and it would all be my fault.

"No, it's okay. I spoke with my boss earlier and told him I broke my little finger and had to go to hospital. It only takes a few hours for a small bone like that to heal so he granted me the rest of the day off, but I have to go back this evening for a meeting at 8pm." He speaks to me, but I feel like he is in another place. He looks at the time on his bracelet, I can see it from here, it's 3:58pm.

"Okay. But Enzo, what do I do now?"

Chapter Seven

I'm not too sure what our plan is, but I do know Enzo is helping me and trying to get me somewhere safe. He said he couldn't communicate with whoever it is that will hide me as they don't want their cover blown by talking too much. He had already sent this person a message when I unsuccessfully went to get my bracelet.

He says we are just going to have to go to the safe place and hope for the best. The rain is helping our predicament as those that have the ability to work inside will do so, rather than being outside where they can see us.

The schools will keep the children inside until 5pm when they are either collected by their parents or go home by themselves. There shouldn't be many people around other than guards, which doesn't really fill me with hope, but Enzo assures me it will benefit us.

He checks his watch, 4:12pm. It didn't take him long to come up with an idea, he knew we had to move as soon as possible. He will have to get back to work by 8pm so we need to move quickly. Apparently, we have to go a little distance to get to the safe place. Enzo hasn't told me anything about the place he's taking me, he said it would be safer that way, just in case the worst happens on our way there.

All he said was that we should be able to get there in pretty much a straight line. The safe place is about one hour and thirty minutes away, if we jog, we can make good time. Enzo needs to make sure that he is back in time for the meeting, so he doesn't raise any suspicions.

I'm putting my trust in Enzo because I still don't know what's happening. If I go with him, he says I will get answers. That's better than being taken away by guards who want to inject me with a mysterious liquid, that's for sure!

"Remember, Talise, stay close to me. Our best plan is to jog along the wall, we have to be incredibly careful when we are going past the elder's home. I'm counting on the rain to keep us a little hidden as it won't get dark before we get there. Just keep moving forward until I say so, okay?" He speaks quickly and efficiently, like he is going through a check list in his head at the same time.

"Okay, and if anyone sees us and asks why we are next to the wall, we can use the excuse of the rain. Say it's blocking some of the downpour for us as it's coming in from the west," I say. He looks at me like he's impressed.

I pick up Scamp and put him under my jacket again. I look up, Enzo seems like he's about to tell me to leave Scamp but decides against it. He must realise that he can't leave a dog in his house for his parents to come home to, and there is absolutely no way he could get me to the safe place and then get Scamp back to Farming before he has to be at the meeting, it just isn't possible.

He looks me over as if checking I'm prepared, even though I don't have any belongings with me other than Scamp. He throws on his rucksack and says it's time to leave, opening the door and stepping out into the cold, hard rain. I follow him out, closing the door behind me.

We head left around the house, towards the 80ft wall that wraps around us.

The rain pours down over us, there's no escaping it. There's a storm coming, and a big one at that. I'm glad I tied my hair up before we left, it would have been all over my face by now with this wind.

We keep our pace, jogging the whole time. Scamp would be okay to run but I don't want him freezing in all of this rain, especially as he is still limping slightly. I place one arm underneath him, holding him against me under the jacket so he is secure. He seems cosy enough, and even falls asleep!

I ignore the pain that's shooting through my spine as we run and focus on our goal of getting somewhere safe.

We have no problems getting past the elder's home, Enzo was right, there is hardly anyone outside, even the guards are scarce. This makes me love the rain even more, it is helping us get to safety without trouble.

We reach the small fence that separates Sector Two from Three and Enzo jumps over quickly with ease.

I'm too small to get over as easily as Enzo can, so I climb on and straddle the fence. When I lift my right leg over, I catch my knee on a rusty nail that's sticking out in a crooked direction. I have to bite down on my hand, so I don't scream out from the pain, whilst gripping the fence with the other hand so I don't fall and have the nail rip through my knee.

I sit atop the wooden fence, a leg on either side with my knee throbbing in agony. I'm not used to being injured; it must be in me deeply because there is a lot of blood soaking through my trousers.

I try to pull my leg away from the nail, but I can't. It's taking everything I have in me to not faint or throw up right now. I take a few deep breaths and hear a voice nearby swear under its breath. A hand pulls mine away from the fence, while another hand pulls my leg away from the fence in one quick motion.

I'm unable to keep a small scream from escaping my lips this time as the nail catches on my flesh as it comes out. But it's out. It's still attached to the fence, but I am free.

Enzo let's go of my leg, places his arms around my waist and carries me over the rest of the fence before placing me on the floor as I fight off the darkness that threatens my vision.

He grabs his rucksack and rummages around a bit before pulling out a bandage and an antiseptic wipe. He pulls my trouser leg up over my knee and wipes it a few times, but it keeps bleeding, and the rain makes it hard for him to do much. He stops wiping and goes for the bandage, wrapping it around my leg with quick fingers.

I think he has slowed the bleeding down for now. I know we have to keep on going, we can't stay here as someone would surely come over to help us and we definitely cannot go to the hospital.

"Talise, put your arm over my shoulder, I promise we are almost there." I can hear the concern in his voice but also the worry. It will be a lot harder for us to be unnoticed now that I am injured, but he said we aren't far.

I take a moment, tilting my head up to the rain and letting the cold water refresh my face. I stay like that for a minute and let the rain calm me before putting one arm over Enzo's shoulder, the other I put back over Scamp to make sure he stays inside my jacket.

Enzo pulls me up off the floor, gives me a moment to get steady and starts moving again. I limp as quickly as I can, knowing we are losing time now because I can't even walk by myself, let alone jog.

It feels a bit awkward as Enzo is a lot taller than me, he has to crouch down quite low in order for my arm to stay over his shoulder. I'm incredibly grateful for his support, I've never known such pain before and have to focus intently on not passing out.

I can see a barn up ahead. I hope we can get past it without detection now that I've slowed us down considerably.

I spot quite a few people milling around outside to my right. They don't seem to have noticed us yet. I hope we aren't going through the middle of them.

Luckily, Enzo has also spotted the workers and he moves over so we are nearer to the wall again. He holds me in place as he swaps sides to be on my right, blocking me from the workers' view. This means he is walking next to my injured leg, so I try my best to keep my blood off of him.

His pace starts to pick up a little after ten minutes as we approach the barn, though instead of going around it, he seems to be heading toward the entrance. He gets to the wall of the barn, leans me against it then signals at me to wait.

I hope he doesn't take too long; I don't like the idea of standing outside exposed, and I know I can't put any weight on my right leg yet. But I do as he instructed and I wait, pressing myself up as close to the wall as I can whilst all of my weight rests on one leg. Scamp starts to move around in my jacket so I reach in and stroke his nose, hoping he will fall asleep again.

I hear Enzo inside talking to someone. I can't quite make out the voices, or what they are saying over all of this rain, but within a few minutes, Enzo is out of the door and coming to help me inside. We reach the entrance and stand in the large opening of the barn.
I shudder as I come out of the rain. Scamp has luckily been keeping me quite warm from under my jacket and he's stopped fidgeting now, hopefully this means he's asleep.

A short and stocky elderly man is standing in front of me. He's pulling down his sleeves and intently staring at me whilst he does so. I can't tell if he's angry or in pain, his face is hard to read.

"What are you doing here?" His voice is exactly what I expected, strong, firm and unwavering.

"Enzo brought me here, he said I would be safe." I'm a little taken aback by his question, Enzo just told him why I'm here, so why is he asking? My knee is starting to hurt even more now I'm standing still, I need to sit down soon.

"Yes, I can see that Enzo brought you here, what I want to know is why he did it." With that he shoots a glare at Enzo, who lowers his gaze sheepishly to the ground, where it rests.

"So, I ask again, what are you doing here?" He fixes me with an intense gaze, he's waiting on my answer, I don't really know what to say, I don't want him to turn me away. I need this man's help.

I muster all of my strength in my answer, hoping it's enough to get me help.

"I seem to be in danger, and I don't understand why. I overheard a conversation Mr Ritton had, and I asked some questions. Then, all of a sudden, guards want to inject me a mysterious orange liquid, question me, or just throw me in the cage! I was hoping maybe you could tell me why I seem to be in danger, and possibly keep me safe for a little while." I take a deep breath, mainly because I'm trying to stop myself from crying from the pain, but also because the weight of what's happening is attempting to fall down on me, hard.

"So please, can you help me?" I'm past the point of worrying about sounding desperate. I'm in agony and I need him to help me so I can get some answers, and hopefully some form of medical treatment.

The man stares at me for a long moment, then turns his back on me and walks over to a large chicken coop, disappearing behind it. Enzo and I stay where we are. I look to him for an answer but he says nothing.

As we stand there silently, I wonder what the man is doing, or where he went. Will he refuse me and send me back out into the rain injured and alone?

After about five minutes, he reappears with one hand up, palm facing out towards us, the other holding his ear lobe. He is signalling for us to be quiet, then he beckons us over.

We make our way towards the chicken coops, he takes us in-between the first and second set of chickens, it's just about big enough to walk through two at a time.

I'm thankful for this as Enzo is still helping me walk, taking most of my weight as I lean heavily on him.

We walk around to the back of the barn following the wall around and coming to a stop at the large stockpile of seeds and grain. I turn around and see that the entrance is out of sight, we are completely hidden from view.

We stand there for a moment next to the stacks of feed, then the man looks at his bracelet. I try to catch a glimpse of the message on the face, but all I see are the words 'feed now'. The message must have made sense to him as he leans forward and starts to pick up a sack of grain. Enzo leans me against the wall and then copies him by picking from the same pile. I'd follow suit if I could, but I can barely stand by myself, let alone lift heavy bags of feed.

I look up from staring at my knee to see the elderly man is looking at me. He hasn't even mentioned my knee or asked if I'm okay, he just watches me. It's then that I realise Scamp is wriggling his head out of the top of my jacket. Up until now, the man probably assumed I just had some of my belongings in a bag down there to protect them from the rain, I don't think he expected me to have a dog.

I look the man in the eye and try to look apologetic just as Scamp reaches up to lick my chin. I can't help but smile and scratch his ear. The man turns away from me just as Enzo puts the last sack to the side.

I wonder why they needed to move the sacks but something on the floor catches my eye making it clear. A girl that can't be much older than me pushes up a hatch door and looks around until her eyes fall on Enzo and she beams.

Too shocked for words, I just stare at the girl. She has long blonde hair that's been put into two braids that fall to her stomach. Her blue eyes sparkle as she displays a wonderful smile that lights up her face, she is very beautiful.

The girl spots me staring at her and immediately her face changes from happiness to anger. She glowers at me, and after what feels like hours, Enzo goes over and grabs the top of the hatch door, leans it back onto the other sacks and makes a gesture for her to move so he can climb down the hole.

It takes her a second, but she finally breaks eye contact with me and makes her way down and out of sight. I peer down and spot that she's climbing down a ladder, I wonder how far down we are going.

Enzo descends down the ladder until his head disappears from view. I look up to see the elderly man has been watching me the whole time.

He looks like he wants to tell me to hurry up and go down there already. I give Scamp a quick pat on the head and then clumsily limp over to be above the hatch opening. I look down and see that the ladder doesn't lead down too deep, only about twenty steps or so.

I reach down to get my positioning right, which will be really hard now, thanks to my knee. I stumble slightly and have nothing to grab hold of to stop my fall, but I'm quickly caught by a very strong grip. I look up and the elderly man has hold of my arm, stopping me from falling down the open hatch.

I regain my balance and wonder how I'm going to get my way on to and down the ladder, considering the top of it doesn't come out of the hatch.

That's when I feel the hands under my arms. The man lifts me so I'm hanging over the hole, I quickly realise what he's doing and swing my left leg forward and on to a ladder rung. My hands reach out and grab the highest part of the ladder, as soon as I'm gripping the frame and not a second later, he let's go of me.

I use all of my upper body strength to hold on to the next rung down and then hop myself down with my left leg, I repeat this action until I am at the bottom. It's a very awkward experience, especially when I have Scamp tucked in my jacket. I'm lucky he didn't move around too much.

As soon as my feet touch the dusty ground, the light above me is smothered as footsteps start coming down the ladder. Enzo is there instantly and taking my arm over his shoulders again, moving me over so there is room for the man to come down.

We are standing in a small cube room; the floor is all dirt and there is a set of steps going down just to my right. I peer down and see a door at the bottom, seems we are going quite far down after all. This time they are proper stairs though, no ladder, I should be able to manoeuvre this by myself.

I tap Enzo's shoulder with my hand that's draped around his shoulders and then I tug my ear lobe with the other hand - this is the signal for sound. I tap his bracelet.

"It's okay, Talise, you can talk, we all have plates on our bracelets." His voice is quiet, a tone louder than a whisper, but this is a small room, so it was loud enough for everyone to hear. He smiles kindly down at me as he talks to me, which earns me another scolding look from the beautiful girl standing across from us.

"You told her about the plates? What else have you told her, Enzo?" She has a very raspy and somewhat threatening voice, I imagine when she shouts, she is quite fearsome. I hope I don't have to find out if I'm right about that.

"I had to tell her, Scarlett; you know I wouldn't put anyone's life here in jeopardy. But I needed to save her." It's as if Enzo is repeating something he's already said, maybe this is what they were talking about in hushed whispers as I was coming down the ladder.

"Oh, you needed to, did you?" Her voice is rising slightly higher with every word she says.

"How about we take this downstairs. I prefer to talk when our voices can't be overheard and I'm sure we need to get sorted quickly as some of us have a meeting to attend." The elderly man doesn't shout, but his tone of voice is firm, he has a powerful presence, he is definitely in charge here. With this he gives a pointed look at Enzo and waits for us to move over and go down the stairs.

"Excuse me," I say, and everyone turns to look at me. I look directly at the elderly man, so he knows I'm addressing him.

"What's your name?"

He looks puzzled by my question but recomposes his face quickly enough before replying with just another question.

"Do you need to know my name?"

"No, I don't, but it would just make it easier for me. You know my name, and I know theirs." I gesture my head towards Enzo, and then Scarlett, whose name she I picked up from Enzo.

"So, can I have your name. Please?" I ask kindly but I am going to be stubborn on this. I need to know his name, I want to have some information, even something as little as a name.

"It's Carlo. Now, let's make our way downstairs already." His voice has the tone of finality in it, but I got what I wanted. I remember then that Enzo had already mentioned the name Carlo earlier today, but he clearly wasn't meant to say it so I keep quiet, not wanting to get him in any trouble.

We all go down the stairs in the same order as we did the ladder. Scarlett in front, Carlo bringing up the rear with me, Scamp and Enzo all in the middle.

I position myself in the middle of the stairs, the path down is narrow so I can reach out and support myself on the walls with my hands.

I place my hands on both sides of the wall to keep my balance and I hop down the steps one at a time on my left foot. If I fall, Enzo will be the one that needs to catch both me and Scamp, hopefully before we topple all the way down and squash Scarlett. That wouldn't do me any favours, I'm sure.

At the bottom of the stairs Scarlett knocks on the door. Two knocks, a pause, then three more. A moment later I hear bolts sliding on the other side and the door opens. I must admit, they have done really well with their protection here, it makes me wonder how many other people they have hiding, and how long people have been hiding for.

I can tell that this place wasn't just built in a couple of months, to run this deep and have a huge steel door with bolts, it must have taken years to create, especially if it was all done secretly.

<u>Chapter Eight</u>

This underground hideout is the complete opposite to the bunker in Sector Two. I've only been in there once on a trip with the rest of my class, so we had an idea of what it looked like inside, just in case we ever had to go in there during an emergency.

Down here looks a lot smaller, which I would expect, but it must have been built incredibly well, there's not a cracked wall in sight. I wonder who actually aided in building this place.

To my left there is a short corridor with a few doors coming off of it, ahead of me is a large open space with a door at the other end. On my right there are various rooms, some with and some without doors, with open spaces inside.

There are a lot of doors down here. I imagine it's so everyone gets some privacy, especially if they are down here a lot and around one another constantly.

The room directly on my left has it's door open, I incline my head to peer inside, and catch sight of a table in the middle of the room covered in papers. There is a small bed in the corner, it's been made up which contrasts with the messiness of the table.

That's when Carlo steps around me and shuts the door, fixing me with a stern look. It's then that it really sets in that I'm in an underground hideout, with three people I don't really know, one of them who definitely doesn't like me already. There is no way I could defend myself down here, especially with an injured knee.

Maintaining his gaze on me, Carlo starts to speak.

"I'm sure you are about to ask me a list of questions, but first how about you get some dry clothes? Then we can sit down in the kitchen with a hot drink and talk. Enzo, can you stay for a little while?"

Enzo checks his bracelet, whilst keeping his grip on me, which I'm grateful for as I really don't want to try standing without help right now.

"I can stay for thirty minutes but then I have to leave and get back for the meeting, I'm sorry, Talise, but you know I can't stay long."

I smile up at him and know I have to stay here with strangers, but then, he's a stranger too. I keep forgetting I only really met him today.

"I know Enzo, it's okay. I would really like it if we could sit down though, my knee kinda needs a break from standing and my back is still a bit sore." As soon as I finish speaking it's like Enzo remembers why my arm is around him, like he'd forgotten about my knee.

Carlo asks Scarlett to grab me some spare clothes and tells Enzo to take me to the bathroom for privacy to change.

Enzo walks me over to a door that thankfully isn't too far away and opens it whilst helping me into the room.

I'm surprised at how large the bathroom is. It's very pristine and clean, there are some stalls on the left and right side of the room with a few sinks in the middle.

"So, on the left are the toilets, on the right are the showers." Enzo gestures to them as he speaks. Then it hits me, I can't really walk by myself and I certainly won't be able to take off my trousers and put new ones on. He thinks he has to help me, and I definitely don't want him to see me strip down to my underwear.

As much as it would be useful for some help, I can't accept it from him. I tell him to take me over to the sinks in the middle and I'll get myself changed. He doesn't seem sure at first, but he probably understands how uncomfortable it would make me to undress in front of him, so he agrees.

Just as we reach the sink and I let go of Enzo, Scarlett comes in and hands him a pile of clothes before turning and stalking out without even a glance at me. He looks at me apologetically like it's his fault she's being rude to me. I'm not sure if I'm meant to say anything so I just smile back politely. Enzo stays looking at me for another minute then he places the clothes on the sink and leaves the bathroom.

I look around me, of course there aren't any seats in here, so I grab the clothes and put them under my right arm. I place my arm over the front of my body to hold Scamp in place again and I hop over to the toilets.

It's only a small distance to go and I grab the door frame as soon as it's within reach to balance myself. I push the door open and hold the door itself to swivel myself round and sit on the toilet, luckily it has a lid over the top.

That was surprisingly hard work.

I unzip my jacket and allow Scamp to jump down to the floor, he has been stuck in there for hours and he must really need to stretch his legs. He wriggles out under the door that closes as soon as I sit down and I sigh looking down at my legs, wondering how I'm going to do this.

I start with the easy part; I take off my jacket and thermal top. I chuck them on the floor next to me and dry my body off with the small cloth towel that was with the clothes pile. I pull on the new shirt, it's quite a big top and was probably made for a tall man, but it's warm and dry so I'm happy for the comfort.

My right leg is sticking out with only a slightly bent knee, I can't bend it fully otherwise it hurts, and I can't straighten it fully because that hurts too. I shift back as far as I can on the toilet seat and ignore my right leg for a moment. I bend my leg up and place the back end of my boot on the top of the toilet seat and start to unlace it. I manage to get it undone quite quickly and slide the boot off, putting it on the floor with my other wet clothes.

I think the best way to get my trousers off is to wiggle out of them. I undo the button and zip and start to rock myself side to side as I pull my trousers down to my knees. I lean forward and pull the left side of the trousers down as I bring my leg up at the same time freeing my left leg from the trouser.

I lean over and start pushing the trousers further down my right leg but my knee shoots with pain again. I lean back against the wall and breathe deeply through my nose.

I can do this.

I lean over and try again to pull the trousers down, but the movements I'm trying just send more pain to my knee and through my spine, making me breathe heavily and lean back again.

This is proving to be very difficult; I prepare myself to try again when the bathroom door bangs open.

"Hey, what is taking you so long, can you not dress yourself or something?" It's Scarlett, she already seems to hate me, I don't want her to think me weak too.

But I can't kid myself, I need help, otherwise I'll be here all night.

"I'm in one of the toilet cubicles. I can't get my other boot and trouser leg off. Please could you help me?" I try not to sound too pathetic as this is probably the most embarrassing moment of my life, having to ask a complete stranger for help getting undressed.

She's silent for a moment then I hear her walk over to the stall I'm in. She pushes the door open and looks down at me. I think I see a small flash of pity in her eyes, but it's quickly hidden with a scowl that seems to be reserved just for me.

She doesn't say anything but bends down and starts untying my laces for me. She slips off my boot and wet sock then moves to get my trousers off. She is surprisingly gentle with me and takes great care not to move my leg when possible.

Once she has my trousers off, she holds her hand out to me expectantly and I notice I'm still holding the spare trousers so I pass them to her as she rolls her eyes at me. I'm just thankful my underwear is still dry.

She slips the trousers round my feet and pulls them up to just above the knee for me, then I grab the trousers from her and start to shuffle them above my hips. I don't care how stupid I look, I want to show her I'm not completely incompetent, I am still strong.

The trousers are a good fit so far and I get them up and buttoned, hoping they won't fall down as soon as I stand up. She didn't bring me any spare shoes but there are some socks, so I take one and manage to get it on my left foot, before I can say anything, she takes the other one and puts it on my right foot for me.

Without another word she grabs my wet clothes and shoes off of the floor, stands up and leaves. She didn't even comment about Scamp who was laying under the sink watching the whole process.

Moments later the door opens again, and Enzo calls my name. I call out that it's okay to come in and he comes over to help me up and out of the bathroom with Scamp hot on our tail.

Outside of the bathroom we walk over to the room nearest the entrance where Carlo is waiting, holding the door open for us.

There is a small table just in front of us with four chairs situated around it, Enzo helps lower me into a chair first then repositions another chair and props my leg up on it. I try my best not to wince when he does this as I know he is trying to help, but the pain is becoming unbearable.

Enzo takes a seat as Carlo sits himself across from me. I'm glad to finally be seated and elevating my leg is helping slightly. Scarlett mumbles something about drinks and goes over to the side of the room directly behind me.

I look up at Carlo, the anger seems to have left his features now.

"Carlo, please could you explain to me what Mr Ritton meant when he mentioned 'the others,' and how that puts me in danger?"

He acts like he's considering my question for a moment, but he knew exactly what I would ask, so I wonder why he's stalling, then he speaks.

"Let me ask you, Talise, what do you think Ritton meant when he said that? I would like to hear your thoughts first, then I will tell you the truth that I know."

He practically spits out the name of our leader but remains calm the rest of the time. He is being perfectly reasonable; he probably wants to test my intelligence or see if I figured it out myself. I'll give him a quick summary of what I think, but I want real answers, and soon. I hadn't realised how tired I was.

"Okay. I've been thinking about it a lot today. After realising the guards were actually looking for me, I thought it must be something big. Ritton had seen me by the stables but I don't think he suspected me of anything. At first, I thought when he said 'the others,' he could have been talking about the other two leaders, but he wouldn't ask how they are getting outside, it wouldn't make sense. It's when he said that they could ruin everything, that's the part that keeps coming back up in my head."

I look down at my hands and try to remember everything I've heard today, especially what the elderly lady shouted at me and the story Enzo told me about her son. Scarlett places a steaming drink on the table in front of me and stalks out of the room, announcing she will get the medic to look at my knee. I'd forgotten she was in the room.

I grip the mug between my hands to warm them up and notice how I had started to shake slightly. I compose myself and continue talking to Carlo.

"So, with the story Enzo told me and what's been said today, as strange as it's been, I think 'the others' are people living outside of the walls somehow. Now I know that sounds mad, but if someone had told me yesterday that I'd be going to a secret hideaway bunker under a barn today then I would've said that was mad too, but here I am. This is the only thing I can come up with, and it doesn't make much sense, which is why I'm here and asking you to tell me the truth and help me understand."

I look up from my mug as I finish speaking to see Carlo's reaction and I'm surprised to see that he actually looks a little sad, he quickly masks this away, but not before I see it.

"You are quite a smart girl, Talise. Your guess is close to the truth, just not all of it." I'm not really shocked at his confirmation, I guess I kind of knew that I was right. I just didn't want to believe it; it would mean I am in danger and that the leaders have lied to us. I am shocked by the compliment though. But I don't say anything and let Carlo continue.

"There are people living outside of the walls, we believe they live all around us, but at a distance so they can't be seen by our people. A lot of what happens outside of the walls is just speculation to me as I have never been out there, and no one has ever managed to talk to 'the others' in order to give us information."

"If we leave through the gates, or even climb over the wall, 'the others' always shoot first. They don't capture people or ask them questions. If they see people coming out from within the walls, they shoot them. We aren't entirely sure why, but I can take a strong guess that it's because of our bracelets. They're the only things that make us look different."

My mind whirls with this information.

He said *if* they climb over, how could anyone climb over the walls? It's impossible. And the bracelets again have come up. I know they believe that the leaders listen in on us, but how would 'the others' know about that? And what did he mean by 'shoot them?'

My face must be giving away my train of thought because Carlo continues talking to me.

"Talise, I know you are probably finding this hard to believe, but you know it's true. You even heard someone being killed this morning." He actually says the last part with a hint of sympathy in his voice, but I'm shocked by his words.

"What? I didn't... I haven't heard anyone die! Not this morning, not ever." I can't believe he is saying I heard someone die, how would that even be possible. The only place that could make sense would be at the hospital, but I didn't hear anything there, and that wasn't this morning.

"Enzo tells me you heard a strange sound this morning when you were in Breeding, is that right?" He is trying to get me to think of facts and not get lost in my imagination, and I appreciate that.

"Well yes but- "

"That noise you heard was a gun shot. You heard one of our friends being murdered. I guess it's the only thing our leaders haven't lied about. To leave these walls means death."

The horror must be clear on my face, realising that the bang I heard was someone dying. No, it was someone being murdered.

I know I want information, but this is a lot to take in, so I ask Carlo if I can have a bed for the night. I just need to be alone for a little while. I can't take all of this in, and my body is protesting everything.

"Okay, Talise, I know that was a big shock, we can talk more about it tomorrow," Carlo says, though I'm not really listening anymore.

Carlo speaks quickly to Enzo, who takes my arm over his shoulder again and walks me to a room not far away. I can hear Scarlett talking to Carlo as Enzo helps me away, but I'm not really listening, I'm barely aware of my feet moving.

I feel numb. I heard someone get shot this morning. Something I've never heard before, but now know means death.

I need to lay down.

Enzo opens the door for me and there are two beds inside, I hope I'm not sharing with someone. I'm completely exhausted as I sit on the bed that is now mine. Enzo looks like he wants to say something, but I signal for him to be quiet.

I look down at my feet and sigh, realising I have to try and get my legs up on the bed which will be painful and exhausting. All of a sudden, Enzo has bent down and lifted my legs up gently, swinging them round on to the bed. As I lay on the bed it doesn't take him long to leave, he knows I don't want to talk, and he has to go to his meeting.

"Goodnight, Talise. I'll come back to see you as soon as I can. I'm glad you're safe now."

I think over today and how it was meant to be a day of joy and happiness. Finally, my 18th birthday, yet it turned out to be a day full of hiding and fear. I don't think my life will ever be the same again, how have I become a part of this?

I've grown up knowing where I live, knowing that this Island we live on is the whole world. It had never occurred to me that there might actually be more people out there.

How could I have known that we were all wrong? Me disappearing now, it'll be the destruction of my family and I'm subject to this solitary confinement. This has been the worst day of my life by far, and it's all because I overheard a stupid conversation, it's ridiculous.

And I didn't even get my birthday cake.

I close my eyes and let the silent tears fall, wishing harder than ever that this is a horrible nightmare I can wake up from.

∞

It's cold.

It's so cold.

I'm shivering as I open my heavy eyes, but I can feel that my clothes are drenched through with my sweat.

I try to sit myself up, but my upper body just falls back down, why does my knee hurt? It's so dark here.

Where am I? I try to move my legs, to swing them out of bed, but a sharp pain shoots through my knee and I cry out. My whole body goes limp against the bed.

I think I can hear someone say my name but I'm not sure, everything is foggy. I'm so tired, if I could just get warm again so I can go back to sleep.

Some light shines above me and burns through my eyelids, I have fallen asleep again and now someone is shouting my name, why are they shouting for me when I'm right here?

My body starts burning, why am I on fire?

I wish they would turn the lights out again, I'm so tired.

I was having such a great dream, I was standing in the rain, it was trickling down my face, it felt really good. I think it was putting out the fire. I open my eyes to see if the fire is gone but all I see is a face hovering above me.

It's a girl and she's saying my name; her face comes into focus but this must be another dream because she can't be here. Her voice is lovely though, it's soothing me, sending me back to the rain.

I think I'll go back to sleep now; I try to tell her I'm going to go into the rain, but I've fallen into the darkness.

Oh wow, my head and body are throbbing. I know there is a light on above me but my eyes are stinging already, I'll keep them closed for a minute before I adjust.

I had such a strange dream last night. I had the worst birthday and heard some strange things. For some reason I was in the rain all day and running from guards, it was absurd. Then fire, there was so much fire all over my body until I was under the rain again.

There's something wet touching my cheek, a little pressure on my chest and a wet dog smell. I crack my eyes open a little and squint from the light, I'm surprised to see Scamp with his front paws on my chest, licking my cheek.

Why is Scamp in my house? Surely my dad wouldn't let him in here. Confusion sets in so I take a real look at my surroundings, I'm in a bed that isn't mine, what's going on?

It's then that the door of the room opens and in comes that face I could never forget, and I can't help but stare.

Before me stands a girl with the whitest skin I've ever seen. She has striking auburn hair and a small number of freckles spread over her cheeks and on her nose to match in colour. It's the girl from my dreams last night.

Her fierce green eyes are looking right at me, with a look of concern running through them. But it can't be this girl, I know her face, I recognise her.

And I can see the necklace, she isn't hiding the necklace anymore.

How can she be here? She died two years ago.

"I see the little guy woke you up, he's hardly left your side since you've been in bed." She smiles when she talks to me though her eyes are admiring little Scamp perched up on my chest.

I'm just staring at her and I ask the first thing that comes to mind.

"Am I dead?"

She smiles sadly at this and takes a seat on the edge of my bed

"No. You are not dead, Talise." Her voice is just as it was in my dream, though it's very confusing.

I feel like I could ask her anything, she has a presence about her, an openness.

"If I'm not dead then why can I see you? You died two years ago." I know how rude I sound, but my head can't take all this confusion.

"I never died." She delivers this with a sad smile, though her tone never changes.

"But they told us you died. You fell from the wall, I don't understand." It seems to be all I say at the moment, so much is happening that I don't understand. I'm talking to a dead girl right now, a very beautiful dead girl, but dead all the same.

I look away from her and stare at the ceiling exasperated. What is happening to my life? Is this even real, or have I truly gone mad?

Chapter Nine

After a few minutes of silence, I think about the reality of my situation.

It disheartens me when I realise that only part of my dream was false. I was never on fire, but the rest, the running and hiding, that was all true. I am in an underground bunker hiding from the people I thought were keeping me safe.

There are other people living outside of our walls, people that don't have the disease, but they don't allow us to escape. If someone goes outside of the walls they are killed by 'the others,' they don't trust any of us.

So, we are stuck here with leaders that lie to us and apparently, murder us too. Now I'm in danger because I asked about 'the others' in front of a guard, they want to find and question me. Everyone I've met since then seems to think that would mean my death.

None of this sounds plausible, it can't be real. Yet here I am, laying in a bed in a mysterious room with a girl that the leaders told us had died two years ago.

I need to get some more answers from Carlo today. First, I'm interested to hear this girl's story, because up until now I believed she had died trying to escape 'The Island.' So many lies I've been told in my life, how many more can there possibly be?

I shift Scamp down to my lap and sit up in my bed as the girl passes me a glass of water, I hadn't even noticed how dry my mouth was.

How long have I slept for? I have no indication of time and the girl sitting at the end of my bed doesn't have a bracelet. I'd guess it's probably lunch time.

She lifts her legs up onto the bed and crosses them, leaning forward slightly. She seems to be quite tall; her long legs take up a fair bit of space on this little bed.

As soon as she stops moving and is settled in her spot, Scamp jumps off of me and goes over into her lap. She gives him a scratch behind his ear and he starts to groan away happily, I guess he likes her. I notice his paw then, someone has removed his bandage and it does look as good as new, just as the nurse had said it would.

The girl's hair is down and flipped over to the left side of her head. It falls to her shoulders and is such a gorgeous colour of auburn. She has a shaved part on the right side of her head, I can't see how far it wraps around underneath, but it suits her. She has a strong presence about her, but not in a scary way, it's almost calming.

I need to start getting some information so I know as much as everyone else does. I can't get distracted by her face, which is already very distracting.

"Can you tell me what happened? How did you come to live in this bunker, and what happened when we were told you died? Please." I ask.

"Of course, I'm not too sure where I should begin though."

"How about starting with your necklace? Are you wearing it now? Can I see it?" I ask eagerly.

She looks taken aback by this and her hand reaches up to touch the base of the necklace.

She eyes me curiously but doesn't say a word as she pulls the necklace out from under her shirt and rests it on the outside.

She doesn't look at her necklace, she just watches me looking at it. I lean forward to get a closer look and instinctively pick up the small golden heart that's hanging close to her heart. It's just as beautiful as I remember.

I notice how close I am to her right now and how intrusive I'm being. I let go of the heart and sit back again, feeling a burn in my cheeks.

"Sorry. It is very beautiful," is all I can manage to say, not quite making eye contact.

"Thank you. How did you know about it? I've always kept it hidden, even now I still do sometimes, out of instinct."

"I saw it once. I noticed it one day at school, I remember thinking how incredibly beautiful it was, and then you were gone." I look up at her, managing to make eye contact, even though I'm embarrassed about the closeness I had to her.

"That was before I was moved into Sector One. After my parents, I wasn't as careful then, I soon learnt. I'll admit I do recognise you as well.

"The necklace was my gift from my parents on my 16th birthday. My mother and father had sourced the materials from work over a long period of time and they had made it for me. They told me I had to keep it hidden as it was a forbidden gift that had no real use. But for me it was the most useful thing to own as it reminded me of their love every day." She looks down at the necklace that she's fiddling with and grows silent, clearly remembering her parents and feeling the loss of them.

Instinctively I lean forward and put my hand over hers, giving her a little squeeze, hoping she understands my unspoken support. She looks up and into my eyes, I can see her pain burning deep within. Her thumb slowly strokes my hand, and she manages a small smile that turns my stomach into nervous knots.

"It was eight days after my birthday that my parents died in an accident at work. There were three other families also affected by it. They gathered us all together and told us that we had lost our loved ones. Someone lost their wife, another lost a sibling, only one other person lost both of their parents. We were told that there was a problem with one of the machines those people were working with, it exploded and killed them instantly. As I wasn't yet 18, I was told that I'd be moved to another Sector and I'd live with another family until I married and moved out. You should know, the person that lost their sibling in the accident was Enzo." She falls quiet then and gives me a second to process that bit of information.

Enzo had a sibling that died. I'm not shocked he hasn't told me, as I hardly know him. I guess it's not something you discuss with someone you've just met. I smile at her gently and she continues with her story.

"The new family I moved in with were very strict. I often wore my practical trousers to school as I don't really like wearing skirt and dresses. My parents used to let me, but the teachers started sending me home to get changed.

"I went to my first day at the new school in my practical trousers, but they sent me home to change immediately. The teachers there didn't know me and wouldn't listen to my explanation. That day happened to be my foster mother's sixth. She struck me when I got home and told me to never disobey the rules again.

"She took away my practical trousers and said I could have them when she permitted it. She forced me to wear skirts and I was miserable. Anything I would do 'wrong' she would raise a hand to me, always a threat of violence. My foster father did nothing to stop her cruelty." There's an edge of bitterness in her voice now and I can't say I'm surprised. I'm shocked at how this woman treated her, and it saddens me that she had to endure that.

"I started to develop feelings for someone in my class. I didn't tell anyone about it because I knew I was different and feared being punished. I'm not like other girls, and I was scared about what they would say if they knew. I struggled for a year, I told myself I could hold out until I was eighteen, then I could move out if I were lucky enough to work in another Sector. I focused on the future and put all my strength into it, spending every sixth at the hospital in the hope that's where I would work. My feelings didn't change though, I really liked this girl, so I decided to act on it.

"One day after school I walked with her and asked her if she wanted to come to my house for my birthday which was a few days away. I thought she liked me too as she jumped at the chance to come over and it's not like we were friends already. She walked home with me after school on my birthday, we were alone in the house when we got there so we sat down and talked for a while. Then I kissed her.

"It was amazing, and she kissed me back. I don't know how long we sat there for, holding hands and kissing, it was wonderful. It was the first time I'd been happy since my parents died. Until my foster mother came home and saw us. There was a massive argument, she sent the girl home and told me that I was a disgrace and what we were doing was wrong. She said I couldn't be with a girl; it was to end immediately. I refused, telling her I liked girls, and I didn't like boys in that way. She hit me all the way up to my bed, telling me it was for my own good and she would beat the wrongness out of me.

"I cried myself to sleep. The next day I went to school needing to see the girl I liked, hoping to have some secret comfort and apologise for my foster mother's behaviour. When I got there and saw her, she ignored me. She literally turned around and ran in the other direction. In class she moved seats and did everything she possibly could to avoid me. I approached her at the end of the day and asked why she was ignoring me. She told me she didn't like girls and what I did was disgusting. She told me to leave her alone and to never speak to her again.

"That evening my foster mother told me that she had found me a husband. On my 18th birthday we would get married and I would move out. I told her that would never happen, and she said if I didn't do it then she would report me to the guards and let them deal with me." She lets out a small harsh laugh before she continues.

"The next day she did just that and they put me in the cage every day until I was 18. Then I was technically an adult so they could keep me there for a week at a time. It was then, inside the cage, that I realised I could never be myself if I wanted to live unpunished. One day, the cage door just opened, but not by a guard. Wes had managed to find a way to hack into the guard's system undetected and found out about people being kept in the cages. Luckily for me, he saw the information about me and sent a friend to come and bring me into hiding if I wanted it. I couldn't have agreed fast enough, there was nothing for me out there anymore.

"I've been here ever since. Wes told me when I arrived that the guards had been ordered to kill me that night if I refused to marry as they saw fit, that's why he had me rescued. He has kept me updated on everything that's happened up there and he even told me about my apparent death and unstable mind. But no one mourned or missed me, and that girl I kissed, she married a man on her 18th birthday and now she's pregnant." She looks up at me then and breathes out a little sigh of relief, I take that as a sign the story is over.

I process everything she just said, and find I believe every word of it. I can't believe she had to go through all of that alone. I wish I could comfort her and take away the pain, but I can't.

"I'm sorry that happened to you and I'm glad you are here, alive and safe. I have to ask though, who is Wes?"

"Oh yeah, sorry, he is our tech guy. He lives down here with us, you can meet him when you feel up to it. He created the plates for us as well as many other things. He's incredibly intelligent." She talks about him with pride in her voice, just as Enzo had.

"Okay, that would be good. One more thing though. What's your name? I just realised I don't actually know it." I say sheepishly.

"Oh, I thought you knew my name, you said it your first night here when you got sick. My name is Raine, but some people down here call me 'The Medic.'"

Raine. I smile to myself at the perfect name.

I remember trying to say I wanted to stand in the rain, this is probably what she means. She thought I said her name, I guess I did. Why did she say my first night here though?

"Raine. How long have I been sleeping for?" I'm a little worried now, I thought it had just been one long night.

"Well, you had a severe fever that peaked the first night when you went to bed. Scarlett rushed to get me as you were sweating profusely and screaming. I gave you some medicine and treated your knee to avoid infection, but you really struggled with the fever. I've never seen a fever that bad before, you've been unconscious for three days."

I take a few moments to process this. I've lost three days with no memory of it, just lying in bed with a fever. Scarlett was the one that went to get help so I guess that means she is in the other bed in this room, she can't be happy about that. That's three days my parents haven't seen or heard from me; they must be so worried.

I take notice of my body then and my back isn't hurting anymore, the throb I had in my knee has dulled down as well. I was so interested in Raine and her story that I hadn't even taken note of the lesser pain in my body.

I think about her story, how they were going to kill her because she wouldn't marry a man. I wonder if they have killed people before for loving someone of the same sex, even though it's completely ridiculous.

I feel a pang of sympathy for Raine. She lost both of her parents and had to live with someone who wouldn't allow her to be herself and beat her. When she finally got to kiss someone she liked, they told her it was wrong, disgusting and shouldn't be done again. That must have been so hard for her to go through alone.

I look up at her and she's just sitting there, playing with her necklace, allowing me to process it all. She must be so brave and strong.

"Thank you for sharing your story with me Raine, I know that was probably really hard. I think as I've been in bed for three days that I should probably go to the bathroom and clean myself up a little." I lean my head down and get a whiff of myself.

"Oh wow, I stink! I definitely need to have a shower. How could you sit there and not tell me?" I ask her but I'm already laughing. She's instantly laughing along with me, and it feels amazing.

"Come on then, let's get you to the bathroom and then I can fetch you some fresh clothes. There should be some towels in there already for you. You need to leave the bandage on your knee whilst you shower, but afterwards I'll show you to the medical room and take a look at it. Then maybe I can give you a tour and you can meet the other residents." She lays out a very tempting offer and it takes me mere seconds to agree.

She puts Scamp on the floor and helps me off the bed. I'm surprised to notice I can now put enough weight on my right leg to limp myself around, that is a massive relief. I wouldn't want to lean on her when I smell like this, it's not attractive.

∞

The shower brings me such relief I hadn't noticed I needed. I scrub away the dirt and grime, the smell disappearing with copious amounts of soap. I guess I smell this bad because of all of the apparent sweat on my first night.

I think of my parents and what they might think has happened to me. They must be worried and there's nothing I can do to comfort them. Maybe I can get a message to them, if this Wes guy can invent things and hack systems, surely, he could tell my parents I'm okay, it's worth asking.

I know I spend too much time under the water.

Raine said that they have a constant supply here, but we need to keep the usage minimal. There is always the concern that the water usage down here would be noticed if we were frivolous with it.

I reluctantly turn off the water and wrap myself in a towel. I step out of the shower door at the same moment a young boy comes out of the toilet across from me.

He has messy curly brown hair and blue eyes. He looks at me, his eyes widening before he runs out of the bathroom. He must have only been about ten years old. What is he doing down here at such a young age, he can't possibly be hiding?

"Hey, watch where you're going, Rory!" Raine shouts over her shoulder, she walks in with a bundle of clothes just as the boy runs past her. She's laughing at him when she looks over and sees me standing there in my towel.

We stand in silence for a long moment looking at one another. Her eyes look hungry, her gaze seeming to absorb me.

I put my arms over my chest awkwardly realising I am basically naked, and she is staring at me. She seems to snap herself out of it and walks over to the sink, placing the clothes down for me.

"Some clothes for you. I got your boots as well. I'll wait outside and make sure no one comes in so you can get changed without interruption," she says as she backs her way out of the door, still watching me. I swear I can see a small smile tug at her lips.

My cheeks feel like they're burning, I should have said something, but I just stood there like an idiot.

I get changed and dry my hair with the towel as best I can before I braid it and let it hang down my back.

I open the door and she's waiting for me like she said. She smiles and gestures for me to follow her as she starts walking off towards some other doors.

"So, that boy, did you say his name is Rory?" I ask.

"Yeah, he always seems to be in the wrong place at the wrong time. You'll see him running around here a lot, he's actually taken a strong liking to your dog. They play together a lot, I think it's good for him."

"Oh yeah, Scamp is a great play buddy. He loves attention so I'm not surprised they've been together a lot." It makes me happy to say his name knowing I won't get in trouble for it.

"I was going to ask you his name when I first came to your room, but you thought that you were dead, so I thought I'd put the question aside for another time." She has a sad look in her eyes when she says that, and it makes me feel guilty for what I said.

"I'm really sorry about that, it was just a big shock." It's a feeble apology but I don't know what else I can say other than sorry.

"No need to apologise, I probably would have reacted the same way." She turns and smiles at me when she says this, and I get that little knot in my stomach again.

She opens a door on our left and switches the light on, I'm greeted by a large white room. There are five beds lining the far wall, presumably for patients, thankfully they are empty at the moment.

She tells me to sit on one of the beds so she can check out my knee. I go to the nearest bed at the end of the row and jump up, my legs are dangling above the floor, as usual.

There are quite a lot of cabinets in here, presumably filled with medicines and equipment. I wonder if she can perform surgery, though I doubt they would have let her try that whilst she was a child. She must be incredibly clever if she learnt everything about medicine solely on her sixth's.

She puts on some gloves and pulls over a chair to sit on so she's level with my knee. She cuts the bandage and gently peels it away, taking care to be gentle with me. I look down at the wound, which still hurts but it's tolerable, it doesn't look too bad.

It's not a large wound, but it's deep. I remember it digging right into my flesh, and seeing how crooked the nail was when Enzo pulled my leg away from it. The memory of it sends a shiver down my spine. Raine looks up at me and asks if I'm okay, I smile and nod so she can continue, swallowing back the nauseous feeling.

"Well, on the plus side it's not infected. The downside, I need you to keep these stitches in for another day at least, then we should be able to take them out. Unfortunately, we don't have all of the tools necessary to make you heal as quickly as you would at hospital, but I've done the best I can for you."

She sounds so sincere and a little disappointed that she can't heal me any quicker. I place my hand on her shoulder and catch her gaze.

"Thank you for fixing me." I smile at her as the door opens and I snatch my hand back as Rory bounces into the room.

"Hi! I'm Rory, you're Talise aren't you? You live here with us now, don't you? Can I see your wound, is it gross? Can I see it, please?" Before I can even answer him, he has rushed over and is staring at my knee with Scamp hot on his heels.

"Rory, please can you move back a little so I can bandage up Talise's leg? We don't want it to get infected, especially as I'm certain Scamp will be jumping all over her any minute now." She looks pointedly at Rory, who picks up Scamp and holds him so she can work on my knee.

"I think Talise can answer some of your questions while you wait though." With that she looks pointedly at me with a little smirk on her face.

"It's nice to meet you Rory, and yes I will be staying here. How old are you?" I ask.

"I will be twelve in seven days' time! How exciting is that? Mum said I can even have a birthday cake, I'm really excited. If we have a little party in the kitchen will you come? Please say you'll come to my party, everyone will be there, even Wes said he will, and he *never* stops working." He talks so quickly, not even pausing for breath.

"I would love to come to your birthday party, I look forward to it." I say.

"Great! Oh yeah, Mum told me that I should apologise for being in the bathroom when you were washing. But I didn't know you were there, so it's not really my fault, but she told me to say sorry, so, sorry Talise."

I smile at this energetic boy and laugh.

"It's okay Rory, don't worry about it. Now it seems Raine has finished wrapping up my knee so would it be okay for me to give Scamp a cuddle?"

"Oh yeah sure, he is your dog anyway. I like the name Scamp, Enzo told me that was his name, when he came by to see you this morning. But you were still sleeping, super lazy I told him. He told me he would come back for my birthday though." He passes me Scamp in the middle of talking and as soon as my hands are around him, Rory bounces off out of the door shouting something about the kitchen and snacks before disappearing.

Scamp reaches up and gives my cheek a lick, I laugh because no matter how many times he does it, it always seems to tickle slightly. I start to scratch behind his ear and he buries himself into me, hopefully because he's missed me.

Raine has finished tidying up the area and it looks like she is returning things into some disinfectant. I must admit, I am very impressed with the cleanliness of the bunker, and I've only seen a small part of it.

"He seems like a sweet boy, who's his mum?" I ask.

"Her name is Kimya, you will meet her soon when I take you on a tour of your new home." She has a genuine smile on her face at that statement, but I can't help but feel sad, I miss my family. But I smile back, not wanting to dampen the mood.

"Great, could we start in the kitchen? I'm starving," I say, maintaining my smile.

"Sure. But, are you okay? You looked sad." I'm amazed at how she can read me already.

"Yeah, I'm okay, I just miss my parents. But it's alright, I'm grateful to be here and to be alive." I've managed to go this long without crying, I won't start now, especially in front of someone I have a growing crush on.

Raine walks over towards me, she takes my hands and lifts me off of the bed. I'm a fair bit shorter than her, but I like it. She lets go of my hands and wraps her arms around me, pulling me into a hug. It's such an intimate thing to do to someone you hardly know, but it feels right. I return the embrace and her chin rests on the top of my head.

It's such a warm moment and it sends fire through my body. It feels so natural to be like this with her, I don't want it to end.

We stand there, wrapped in each other's arms for several minutes when we are interrupted by a strange sound, my growling stomach.

We both laugh and let go of one another, she walks towards the door and calls for me to follow if I want food.

I can feel my cheeks are flushed with heat again, and hope it's gone down by the time we reach the kitchen.

The kitchen isn't far at all and there's no one else in there. We talk and eat, enjoying each other's company.

Raine stands and says it's about time I have the tour, she shows me around the rest of the hideout, talking the whole time. She makes me feel completely at ease, I could talk to her endlessly.

Chapter Ten

My eyes open but I'm greeted with darkness and the faint breathing of another. It takes a few seconds to remember where I am.

I'm wide awake now, there's no going back to sleep, not after that nightmare. It wasn't the worst I've had these last few days, but it ends the same as they all do, with my parents dying.

I can't stop thinking about them.

I can't help but think about how they could be in danger because of me. If the guards truly want me, they could have taken my parents as hostage, trying to lure me out. And I would never know, being stuck down here without any communication.

I have to know something. I can't wander round this bunker aimlessly, it will truly drive me mad. I think it's already starting to.

I haven't seen Carlo since I came down here and no one can really tell me much more than what I already know. There doesn't seem to be a plan either, no one is actively doing anything to stop the leaders.

I know they have planned some escape attempts that have all ended badly because 'the others' kill anyone that leaves the walls. There doesn't seem to be any other plan at the moment. Surely the people living in this bunker haven't spent all of their time only planning some escapes over the walls. What about showing everyone above ground what the leaders are doing? Or trying to meet with 'the others?'

Everyone just goes about their days as normal, as if this is what life has always been. It's driving me nuts.

I get out of bed, and feel my way to the door, opening it as quietly and slowly as possible, slipping out into the empty corridor.

I head to the bathroom to shower and get dressed. Luckily there are clocks down here. They are very old, but they work, Wes did something to make them run constantly. I get to the bathroom and the clock next to the door reads 3:58am. It's so early.

But now I'm up I carry on. I stand under the hot shower hoping it will wash away the horrible thoughts, but I just can't get rid of them.

Once I'm dressed I head out to see if Wes is up, I've heard he tends to get distracted when he's creating things. He stays up all night and usually sleeps in the day, though not much.

I only briefly met him on my tour, and he didn't really speak to me, I got the impression he is a bit of a recluse. I get to the room and find Wes typing away at a computer.

"Hey," I whisper, not wanting to startle him.

It didn't work. He jumps and spins round to look at me, his eyes bulging. Wes scares very easily it seems. I'm not sure why as he hasn't told me how he ended up here, nor has Scarlett, and I don't want to pry, yet.

"Talise. You scared me," he says, and it sounds like an accusation. But I see his face is nothing but fraught as he regains his composure.

"Sorry, I can't sleep. I had a nightmare about my parents dying, now my thoughts are haunted too." I don't even try to stop the truth from flooding out of me.

"Oh, erm right. Well, did you need something?" He asks.

I think that Wes is quite awkward when it comes to conversations about anything other than tech stuff. This is only the second time I've spoken to him.

He's a very attractive guy, I can imagine Jane would like him, I wonder if he would be interested in her. I miss Jane and Connelly; I wish they were here with me. No, actually I wish we were all together above ground without danger, that's what I truly want.

"Actually, there is, I was hoping you might be able to get a message to my parents somehow. Just to tell them I'm safe, or check they are safe, anything really."

"I can't," he says, turning back to the screen.

"Please, Wes, I need to know they are safe at least. Please, just one message?" I plead.

"It's not that I won't, Talise, I have tried. I've tried many different ways to get them a message for you already, but I can't. They are being watched by the guards, but they are safe. I can tell you that much, they are still working and going about their daily lives, they haven't been taken or put in the cage. It's too dangerous right now to reach out with them being monitored."

I think I knew this would be the answer, it doesn't stop it from hurting though. But I have reassurance, they aren't in the cages, they aren't being treated any differently, just watched. I wonder exactly how closely they are watched.

I'm sure Wes has tried everything, but it's not enough. I need to speak to them, or one of them. I need to see with my own eyes that they are okay and hear it from them.

"It's okay Wes. I know you would help me more if you could. Thank you for trying before I even asked, I really appreciate it."

"It wasn't any trouble, Raine asked me to do it when you got here," he says and again turns back to look at his computer, fingers already flying at the keys.

"Oh, okay. See you later, Wes." I say, not too sure what to make of Raine asking that on my behalf before we even met. I turn to leave; Wes is clearly too busy right now.

On the table by the door there are more of the plates that go on the bracelets to deactivate them. Without thinking I grab a couple and walk out of the room, heading back towards the bathroom.

In the bathroom I grab a small rucksack from my locker and head to the kitchen. I grab some bread, wrapping it up and fill a bottle with some water and put it all in the bag. I don't want to take too much unnecessarily.

Before I know it, I'm at the door that leads out of the bunker, I look around and no one is nearby, so I open the door.

I slip out and shut it hastily behind me, as soon as the door closes, I start up the stairs and then I'm climbing up the ladder to the hatch door.

I really didn't think ahead when I planned this, the hatch is of course shut. I try it anyway, on the off chance the sacks aren't on top of it.

I unhook the bolt locks and push up with one hand whilst keeping my other on the ladder to hold me firmly in place.

It doesn't budge.

I push it again and again, trying each side, nothing happens.

I stay there, holding on to the ladder and stare at the hatch with anger, frustration, and underlying fear. I need to see my parents, I can't stay down here doing nothing, I just can't.

I hit the hatch again, using my palm to thrust up, all the strength I can muster goes into it. The cold metal rings out loudly with each hit getting harder and harder but it doesn't move an inch.

My face is damp with the tears streaming from my eyes. I give up and climb back down the ladder feeling useless and defeated. I look around me and there is no other path, no other way. It's up the ladder or down the stairs.

I sigh and walk down the stairs, just as I'm about to grab the handle to open the door I realise there isn't one.

How could I have been so stupid? I didn't even think about it, that the hatch is weighted shut, and the door only opens from one side. Of course, it can only open from one side, that's why it's so safe.

In frustration I slam my hands on the door, tears spilling down my cheeks more freely now. I kick the giant metal door a few more times before collapsing to the steps. I don't even care about the noise I make or what I look like, I'm exhausted with it all.

My heart is thundering in my chest, from the crying, the kicking, or my anger. I don't know. I try to take a few deep breaths but I can't, I just sob.

Everything is getting to me now. I would have never been here if I could have just kept my mouth shut in the beginning. Why did I have to mention 'the others?' Why couldn't I have just stayed up there, ignoring what I heard like anyone else would have done?

Instead, I had to know an answer, as always, I had to question it. Now I'm stuck underground, not even in the bunker because I was stupid enough to get myself locked out of it. And my parents, my parents could be suffering without me, they could think me a criminal, or dead. I don't know. I don't know enough, and I don't know what to do.

I sit there and sob to myself. Clutching my arms around my body, rocking back and forth until I succumb to the darkness.

∞

The next couple of days go by without anything eventful happening. After my failed attempt to sneak out and my embarrassing breakdown it's been quite muted down here.

Carlo has turned up, but he is still angry with me for my escape attempt. He's probably more annoyed because he is the one that found me curled up in a ball outside of the bunker door, and he had heard my banging from the barn above.

The state I was in though, he didn't say anything. He just scooped me up and carried me into the medical room, putting me on one of the beds and covering me with a blanket before leaving. I woke up to Raine sitting beside my bed, pity in her eyes.

A short while later Carlo came in and spoke with me. He didn't shout or call me names, he spoke calmly, making me aware of the danger I put everyone in. If I had gotten out and been captured and tortured for information, I would have given them all the details about the bunker. Everyone here would have suffered for it.

He couldn't really punish me; he may be in charge, but it's not that kind of place down here. He did give me something to do each day, so I was less inclined to try anything else equally as stupid. He also agreed to speak with me and answer my questions, but after the party.

It's Rory's birthday so everyone is happy, Carlo might even give us a smile. I had my stitches out this morning and my wound has fully healed. I've been in one of the training rooms strengthening my leg, as well as the rest of my body.

Other than the people I have met already, there is one other person living here. He is a quiet man and doesn't talk much, his name is Ajax, and he is an incredible fighter. I don't know how he came to be here, but he is making me the fittest I've ever been.

That is what Carlo tasked me with, training with Ajax.

He teaches us all basic combat and how to defend ourselves. I get extensive training, learning how to fight properly and to read a room. Raine tells me that she's only heard two words from him outside of the training room in the fourteen months he's been down here. He only talks when he trains us, other than that he doesn't speak, and we don't know why.

The training doesn't come without pain though. Since I started, I've had recurring muscle spasms, and I constantly have a sore neck. But I carry on with my training, I don't want to be a weak link if it ever comes down to a fight for our lives.

Raine is our medic, as I already knew. She has a lot of books in the medical room, where she spends most of her time, reading and learning. It's also where she sleeps.

Raine and I have become extremely close over the last seven days. We are all living in close quarters here, but you'd be surprised at how little you can see a person. I don't see Scarlett much and we share a bedroom, but she avoids me on purpose. I still have no idea why.

Raine thinks it's because Scarlett is jealous of me, though jealous of what exactly, I don't know. Raine said it's because I'm beautiful, which just made me blush insanely and lose the ability to speak for what seemed like an eternity.

I hardly see Wes either, as Rory said, he is always in his workshop creating new things for us and trying to find a way to take off our bracelets without killing us. The latter is still unsuccessful.

Wes is Scarlett's twin brother, and they do look very similar. Both with blonde hair and blue eyes, both beautiful, there's no doubting that they are related.

Scarlett likes to fight and scowl at me; this seems to be her favourite pastime. She is always in the workout room training by herself, or with anyone but me.

Rory is the only child down here. He spends most of his time running around and playing with Scamp, as well as turning up when you least expect him. He can get into any room without being noticed, I'm incredibly impressed by it.

He stops by and sees us all every day, learning things as he goes. I think he spends a little extra time with Raine as he seems to like all of the medical equipment.

I'm not too sure how but Rory has also taken care of where Scamp goes to the toilet. He won't tell any of us his secret, but he assures us that Scamp is well looked after, and considering I haven't found any dog poo laying around, I'm inclined to believe him.

Kimya is our cook, and a fantastic one at that. Though more importantly, she is Rory's mother. She was in some kind of accident that caused the three bones in the middle of her ears to dislocate, which meant that sound couldn't be sent to her inner ear, so she became deaf. It's a good thing we learnt signals in school as we use them a lot down here when we are around Kimya, though I think she can read our lips most of the time.

There is a room in the bunker that I was surprised to see. Raine hadn't included it on the tour for some reason, but I was amazed when Kimya took me there.

It's an underground garden, full of plants and vegetables, it's brilliant. I don't know the science behind how it functions, and I haven't asked. For once I like the mystery.

I go to the garden every day and help Kimya in any way I can. I like to feel useful and I enjoy being around Kimya, she has a kind face. Some of the plants down here Raine uses for medicines, that really confuses me when she tries to explain it all, so I just gathered the plants she needed and leave her to do the rest.

Carlo mainly keeps us hidden, alive and safe. He brings us food supplies once a week. Sometimes we get extras, but often it's just the right amount for us to get by. I guess that's the only similarity between living down here and up there, you always have just enough food, never too little or too much. Lucky for us, we have Kimya's garden.

I thought I would see Enzo more but he doesn't come very often, I guess he doesn't want to bring too much attention to himself. He is sometimes able to bring us more medical supplies though, which Raine is grateful for.

If I'm not training or helping Kimya, I try to spend time with Raine, maybe learn a few things from her. Though mostly I feel like I get in the way. Sometimes, I just hide in the shadows for hours with Scamp contemplating the situation and thinking of how I can get out of it. I don't want to spend my life in this bunker.

It's a good turnout for Rory's birthday, and he is positively beaming from ear to ear. Carlo and Enzo have even made it down here for the celebration.

Along with myself, Raine, Scarlett, Wes, Kimya, and even Ajax, it's nearly a full house. Carlo apologises to Rory that Pete couldn't make it, but he needed to stay up top with his daughter today, I haven't heard that name before, I'll ask Raine who he is later.

A hush falls over us all as Kimya brings out a cake from the kitchen for Rory, and we all sing the birthday song.

"Your birthday's here,
Spend it with cheer,
Rejoice with family,
Rejoice with friends,
Spread your smile,
And have a lovely, lovely birthday"

It's a very pitchy performance but I've never seen a child look as happy as Rory does right now, even Ajax produces a wide smile for the boy. He definitely has the love of everyone here, this is his family, and I realise now that I am now a part of this family too.

I've never seen a cake as big as this one before, it's at least four times the size of the usual cakes we receive. Rory's name is written on the top in icing. Kimya is an excellent cook. Rory asks if he can cut his own cake now that he's twelve, he thinks it makes him grown up.

His mother agrees and passes him the knife, then much to my surprise, he starts to cut it into small pieces, eleven in total. Then he announces there is a piece for everyone here, he wants to share his cake with his family.

I'm touched by the generosity of this boy and amazed at his kindness and love for us all. He says the last two pieces are for Pete and his daughter if Carlo could deliver it for him, which he agrees to.

I am incredibly excited to have some cake, especially as I never had my own. I eagerly take my piece. My jaw is really hurting today so I have a tiny bite off of the end.

Instead of my usual taste bud explosions from the delicious sweetness, I find it difficult to swallow. I can still feel the cake crumbling on my tongue, so moist and fresh, but my appetite is gone.

I pass my cake to Raine and tell her to have it, saying I've a sore throat. It technically isn't a lie. I've had it for a few days now when my throat closes up and I find it hard to swallow or my appetite leaves me.

I plaster a smile on my face not wanting to spoil anything for Rory, making a mental note to get Raine to give me a check over in a couple of days if it still persists. Once again, I'm missing out on my favourite treat.

∞

I wake up in the middle of the night with a lockjaw. This is happening all of the time now and it's incredibly painful.

It's been two days since Rory's birthday, and my muscle spasms are only getting worse, though now I seem to be getting the majority of them in my jaw.

I can't take the pain anymore so I go to the medical room hoping Raine can give me some painkillers.

I slowly open the door and see she is sleeping on one of the beds. She likes to sleep in here in case anyone needs her overnight, she wants to be close to her patients and the medicine.

I walk over to her and gently brush aside the hair from her face and tuck it behind her ear. She looks so peaceful and angelic.

I pull my hand away and hold it to my jaw as it throbs and Raine stirs awake. She opens her eyes and looks right at me, a smile spreading across her face.

"Well hello, beautiful, why are you sneaking into my room in the middle of the night, hey?" She's teasing me, and if I weren't in pain I would probably be blushing. She soon notices my hand holding my jaw and jumps out of bed turning the main light on.

She rushes back over to me and asks what's wrong, I manage to get out the words 'jaw' and 'lock' but I sound weird because I can't move my mouth to speak properly. She gets me to sit down as she rummages around in the cupboard for some painkillers for me.

She comes over with some packages as my jaw loosens slightly, though the pain remains. I take some painkillers and just about manage to swallow them, my jaw relaxing with the motion.

"Thank you. Can you run some tests? It's becoming more frequent and really painful," I finally admit.

She looks at me with worry deep in her eyes, I know she's already concerned, but it's the look of worry that scares me. She doesn't say anything either, she just nods and gets her clipboard to start making notes.

She runs through a series of questions, some are a little intimate and would usually be embarrassing, but with her, I don't feel shy.

She checks my knee and there's no sign of the wound reappearing there. She says she doesn't need to take any blood, which is a massive relief for me, she knows I hate needles.

She finishes asking me questions and checking me over physically and stands back looking at her clipboard. I sit there and wait, but she doesn't say anything.

She goes over to her bookshelf and picks one up, starting to flip through the pages. I guess she isn't too sure what's wrong with me either.

She stops turning the pages and stares at the book, not looking at me. She stands there for a few minutes just staring at the page. I get the feeling she isn't reading, and she knows what's wrong with me but doesn't want to tell me, which only worries me more.

"Raine, what is it?" I say as I lift her chin up so she's looking at me. I'm utterly shocked to see that she has tears in her eyes, it must be bad. She puts down the book and holds my hands, looking me straight in the eyes.

"Talise, there is only one explanation I can think of and the book confirms my thoughts." She actually starts to choke up a little but composes herself instantly when she realises her tears are close to spilling. She takes in a deep breath, probably to keep the tears at bay.

"Raine, it's okay, tell me." I'm dreading what she is going to say but I need to know, and she knows I do. She's calmed herself now, she must be realising how scared I am.

"You have tetanus. I'm guessing you got it from the rusty nail as it was such a deep wound. I'm so sorry, Talise." She's apologising like it's her fault, but I still don't understand. I never spent a sixth in the hospital, I don't know what tetanus is.

"Okay. But what does that mean?" I ask.

She looks at me with pain in her eyes, she thought I knew what it was.

"Talise, if you don't get a booster shot to treat it then you're going to die. I used the only booster shot we had five months ago on someone else." She doesn't say anything after that, she just lets me process her words as she always does.

My mind starts spinning, thinking of what I need to do.

I'm dying.

I have an illness that will kill me, and I don't know if there's anything I can do about it.

I can't seem to catch a break lately; my life is falling apart. It takes me a minute or two to think of the most important question I could ask right now.

"How long do I have left to live if we can't get a booster shot?" I know it's a horrible question to ask her, but I have to know. I need to know if I have days, weeks, months or years. I just have to.

She sighs heavily and looks at her clipboard laying on the bed next to me. She leans her head forward so our foreheads rest against one another and she whispers an answer to me that's barely audible, but I hear it loud and clear.

I lay down on the bed, suddenly overcome with a headache. I ask her to hold me and that's what she does.

She turns off the main light, climbs into the bed with me and wraps her arms around me.

I bury my head into her neck and all I can hear going around in my head is the answer she gave when I asked how long I had left.

'I don't know.'

Chapter Eleven

I wake up to an empty bed, my head hurting and my throat dry. I look at my surroundings, I'm in the medical room.

Memories of last night come flooding back to me and all I can think is that I want my parents. I miss them so much that it hurts to think about them. I can't begin to imagine what they are going through right now.

I get up to go to the bathroom, but I need to sit back down immediately. I have a horrible headache, and my muscles are in pain, probably from the way I slept in the foetal position all night.

I take a deep breath and wiggle my limbs, getting some motion back in them. Raine walks in with a glass of water that she hands to me with a small smile.

She goes over to one of the cabinets and comes back with some pills for me, she tells me they are for the muscle sores and headaches, I take them greedily, but my throat doesn't want to swallow them. I force them down.

Whilst I take the medication, Raine tells me that Carlo has his sixth tomorrow. He will be going to the elder's home and asking Enzo if they have any tetanus boosters there so they can steal one for me.

She explains that tetanus isn't curable, I have to receive a booster shot every ten years after the first one, but I need that first one sooner rather than later.

I will also need to be on some antibiotics and medication to help control the muscle spasms, she isn't certain how long I'll need to take them for, just that I need them. The worst part is that I also need two injections.

The day goes by incredibly slowly. There isn't much I can do other than read some medical books and worry about dying before I can get the booster shot.

I spend most of the day feeling nauseous, unable to stop thinking about the injections I need to have. And not just one, but two.

I go to train with Ajax, but Raine stops me. She won't let me go to the garden either, she says I need to rest for the day. I do, however, get a visit from Scamp, which brightens my day no matter what.

After what feels like the longest day of my life, Carlo turns up.

He is brief with what he says to me, he has to get back up top before he's noticed for being in the barn for too long when he isn't meant to be working there today.

He spoke with Enzo and found out that there are a couple of doses stored at the elder's home, but they will be hard to get. Enzo doesn't have access to the specific medicine cabinet they are kept in, only a few people have the keys to it.

He reassured me that Enzo will get the medicine for me as soon as possible. He should be able to bring it to me in a few days' time, he says they have a plan.

It puts my mind at ease slightly, knowing they can help me, I just hope it isn't too dangerous, and I really hope I don't die before Enzo gets to me.

I don't feel like I'm dying, it doesn't actually seem real. If I'm going to die, I don't want it to be down here, hiding. I want to be with my parents.

I spend the rest of the day thinking how I could get to my parents' house, how I can escape this bunker without getting stuck and whether or not my body will take me the distance.

I drift off to sleep at some point, then I'm woken up in the middle of the night by Raine. Enzo has arrived with my much-needed medicine, I don't need to wait a few days, he is here now, to save me again.

Raine gets me out of bed and allows me to get dressed before letting Enzo into the medical room. He rushes forward to wrap me in a great big hug as soon as he sees me, I can see the concern in his eyes.

"I'm so glad you're okay, well, not okay, but you are alive and that's what matters. I couldn't risk your life waiting a few days," Enzo whispers into my ear as he holds me in his embrace.

"I'm okay, honestly. But I'm glad you came, I've missed you." I reply easily because it's true, I have missed him. It's strange, the amount of times I'd seen Enzo at the elder's home and we never had a conversation. Yet here he is, he's saved my life twice already and he's here to do it again. I don't know why I feel so connected to Enzo, perhaps because he keeps saving me, but I feel like I've known him forever.

He pulls back from our embrace and looks me straight in the eyes, a serious look on his face.

"Are you ready?"

I know that I need these injections, but it doesn't change the fact that I'm still terrified of needles.

Enzo insists on administering the medicine for me, he has medical experience. If he does the injections, it means Raine can hold my hand and keep me calm.

I sit on the side of the bed, facing the wall so that I don't have to look at the needles. I breathe through my nose to try and keep the nausea at bay.

Enzo wipes a spot at the top of my arm to clean it and applies the numbing cream. I look away so my eyes are focused on Raine, she smiles at me warmly and gives my hand an encouraging squeeze.

I try to think logically, if I don't let him do this then I will die, I need these injections to live.

I take a few deep breaths to keep myself calm, I don't need to get worked up about this, I just have to sit here.

I squeeze my eyes shut and grip Raine's hand even tighter in anticipation for the pain and whisper for him to do it.

"It's already done," he says.

My eyes fly open and I look at my arm, he shows me the empty needles, though I still shudder at the sight of them.

"How did you do that? I didn't feel anything!" I ask slightly amazed.

"I sure did," Raine says as she flexes her hands and laughs.

I laugh along with her and instantly the tension in the room goes. I can't believe that was it. I barely had time to process my illness and what it meant, but now the worst part is already over. A massive weight feels like it's lifted off of me, I am safe, for now.

I get up and thank Enzo, he has to leave again already. I look at Raine and the knots in my stomach start twisting again. She stands there, so close, smiling at me.

It's then that it really sinks in. I have ten years now before the next booster is needed. I'm so overcome with emotion that I pull Raine in for a strong embrace.

I wrap my arms around her, her body responds immediately, her arms going around me, thumbs rubbing against my back.

I nearly died, so I think it's about time I took another risk.

I pull back out of our hug slightly, so our faces are inches apart. We stand, staring into each other's eyes. Before I can lose my nerve, I push up on my tiptoes and close the distance between us, brushing my lips with hers.

Within seconds she responds to me, our bodies press tightly together, her hand runs through my hair as our lips stay firm on one another.

I get lightheaded but I don't want to stop, she is consuming me with this kiss. Fire spreads through my body and I'm hungry for more, hungry for her.

She moves me back slightly so I'm pressed against the bed, I hold it with my hands and jump up. I'm sitting on the bed with her standing between my legs, my hands fly back to be around her. Our kiss deepens, I've never experienced anything that felt this good before.

"Ahh, amore proibito." A gruff voice says from the doorway. We immediately break apart to see Carlo standing in the doorway smiling at us.

I feel my face burn bright red. I'm so embarrassed for getting caught, and because I wonder if he hadn't interrupted us, how far would we have gone.

"Carlo, erm, hi. What was that?" Raine manages to get her words out easily enough, I admire her, I can't seem to speak.

"I said, amore proibito, it means forbidden love in my native language." He stands there for several seconds smirking at us before he says he came to tell us there is some dinner ready if we are hungry.

I stalk out of the room straight after him, too embarrassed to say anything, or be alone with Raine right after that earth-shattering kiss.

∞

It's been a couple of days since I had the injections and my medication started. My body is feeling better already, the spasms have lessened and I'm back to training every day, building my strength up. I haven't had much time to spend with Raine, she's been really busy.

Since I've been down here, I still haven't had a chance to speak to Carlo and get more information. After Rory's party, with me being unwell and the panic around my illness, it slipped through the net. I will get to him soon though, I'll push him to give me some information.

I've asked Ajax what he knows, but my questions are greeted with silence. I had a chat with Wes too, he can hack the systems they use, so surely, he knows more about 'the others?'

He still couldn't advise me on anything more than what I already knew. He can hack nearly any computer or network system, even the watchers. But he can't find anything, anywhere, about 'the others.'

I've had plenty of time to process.

Everything I have been told makes sense to me, the pieces adding up slowly. Though I still don't know who built this bunker, how long it's been here for, or if there are other people like us that know the truth? So many questions and so few answers.

Rory has just bounced into my room to let me know Enzo is on his way down here, how he knows that I've no idea, but I get changed and go out to see him. I get to the entrance just as the door is closing behind him, I rush forward to give him a hug.

He hugs me back and smiles wearily at me, something is off about him, he looks tired and drained of energy. I drag him over to the kitchen, sit him down with a hot drink and ask what's wrong.

"I think they know that I took the booster shot. The last couple of days they seem to be watching me incredibly closely at work, my every move is monitored. Today I went to spend my sixth with the scientists to see if I could get any intel on what's going on, but they turned me away. They said they didn't need any help today as the workload was small, and told me to go to materials instead." He speaks with such worry in his voice, and that scares me, but I try to not let it show. Other than the finders and binders building, no one ever gets turned away on their sixth, ever.

"You shouldn't go back up there; you should stay here with us," Scarlett says from the doorway. I hadn't even noticed she was here.

"I can't Scarlett, you know I'm more valuable up there, I can get things for you that you need down here." He looks up at her pleadingly as he speaks.

"Enzo, I agree with Scarlett, if they are watching you that closely then it can't be safe. They know something and you could get caught coming here, I think you should stay." I say.

Scarlett seems shocked I'm agreeing with her and actually has the smallest smile on her lips before it disappears quickly.

"I'm going back up there. I came down here to check on you, Talise, and make sure the medicine worked. If I get in any real danger I will come back and stay here. For now, I can't come here for a little while, I need to be a model citizen and keep to the rules. I'll come back when I can, I'll be okay, I promise." He says it with finality, and I know there's no point in arguing with him, his mind is made up.

Other than locking him in a room, there is nothing we could do to make him stay, there's no point arguing the matter. I learnt early on that sometimes it's just not worth the argument, a valid point my father taught me, thanks to my inquisitive side.

"Okay. But you come back if there is even the tiniest sign of danger," I demand.

"Promise," he replies and with that Scarlett storms out of the room looking incredibly hurt.

He has to go back now; he can't be off of the tracking system for too long if he's already being monitored. I give him a strong hug goodbye and head off to bed, silently wishing for him to be safe.

I wake up to Scarlett saying my name, telling me to get dressed, it's time to train. I'm still half asleep and must have heard her wrong, I don't train with Scarlett.

But she shouts at me to hurry so I oblige and rush to get dressed, following after her.

It's very quiet out in the hallways, it must be incredibly early if no one else is up yet. She sets up some equipment and starts by sparring with me. She doesn't hold back in the slightest and manages to knock me down several times.

Every time she floors me, she tells me to get straight back up, I need to be ready for when the danger is on our doorstep. I'm not sure what she means but I don't argue with her, I just train hard.

We train like this every morning for just over two weeks, Ajax joins us when he gets up a bit later with everyone else.

Scarlett and I are a great fighting pair, we nimbly move around one another and seem to predict one another's moves, meaning we always win against Ajax if we fight together.

We haven't seen Enzo since he left two weeks ago, and Carlo hasn't been able to reach him through the bracelet either. I'm managing my frustration with Carlo mildly. He hasn't answered a single question since I have asked since I've been down here. He has only come down here once in the last two weeks, and he said he simply didn't have time for my questions and left. The training helps my frustration come out.

This morning Scarlett seems to be fighting me with more force, hitting harder, I'm guessing she's working through her anger and fear too. We are in the middle of sparring when all of a sudden, she stops and looks me dead in the eyes, panting heavily.

"We have to go out and look for Enzo, today." She says this as a statement, not a question.

"You want us to sneak out in the middle of the day to go and look for Enzo? Where exactly will we look, and how do we get out without someone moving the feed for us first?" I'm not exactly saying no to her, it's no surprise she wants to go out and find him, we all do. But I've already tried to get out of here once, and that didn't go too well.

"Let me handle getting us out, and then you can lead us to his house. If he's not there, then we check the elder's home. There is nowhere else he could be unless the guards have him."

"Okay, so we get out, find Enzo, then what? We force him to come back with us?"

"I'm not saying that, Talise, we just have to try and find him. I can't sit around waiting any longer, I'm going soon whether you come with me or not. I could really use your help, otherwise I'll have to ask Wes where Enzo lives, and he definitely won't let me leave. Please, Talise." She actually pleads with me; I don't know if I'm more shocked that she needs my help, or the fact that she said please.

It's not like we've become best friends since training, but she has certainly stopped scowling at me, except for when I beat her in a fight.

I think about when I needed Enzo's help, he couldn't let me wait even a few days. Now the tables have turned, I can't let his life wait, if he's in danger, I have to save him. I owe him my life thrice over.

"Okay. I'm in," I dive down, swing my leg round to knock her to the floor, and stand back up grinning.

"I win," I say, and hold out my hand to help her up, she's actually laughing.

"I best not let my guard down like that later, be ready to go in two hours." She leaves the room without waiting for my answer, I guess I didn't really have one anyway. I just hope we don't get caught, or worse, find out that Enzo is in danger.

Chapter Twelve

Everyone is busy doing their own kind of work so it will be surprisingly easy to sneak out undetected. As we share a room together, we manage to get ourselves sorted and ready in a short amount of time.

I think about going to see Raine before we go but I wouldn't know what to say, and she seems to have been avoiding me since I kissed her.

Scarlett passes me a plate for the bracelets as a precaution, pocketing one herself. We leave our room and head for the bathroom. I hesitate when we get to the door, but Scarlett gestures for me to follow her inside.

We head to the end of the room, past the shower cubicles on the right, and to a cabinet tucked away in a corner that I hadn't noticed before. She pulls the cabinet away from the wall and I'm shocked to see a small door that is just large enough for us to crawl through.

Scarlett looks back at me and grins, pulling out a key from her pocket. At that exact moment the bathroom door opens and Raine walks around the corner, anger burning through her eyes.

"You're sneaking out! Are you both completely mad?" She fumes at us. I wonder how she knows we were leaving, but then I hear Scarlett swear Rory's name under her breath.

"Look, Raine, we are going to try and find Enzo. Now are you coming with us or are you going to tell on me and your *girlfriend* to Carlo?" Scarlett speaks so matter-of-factly, like she's annoyed for having to wait around in the first place.

Raine looks offended by her words, probably because Scarlett called me her girlfriend. It's no secret we kissed, though I get the impression Raine wished it were.

She looks at Scarlett furiously for a good minute before speaking again.

"I won't tell Carlo, so it looks like I'm coming with you, but I'm not happy about this. You better have a good plan. And if I say it's too dangerous and we have to leave, then we leave. Okay?" She doesn't even mention the girlfriend comment, just ignores it. Maybe she doesn't feel about me the way I do about her.

I turn to Scarlett, a little hurt and embarrassed at the same time. She looks like she's about to argue back with Raine but I shake my head and surprisingly she keeps quiet.

"Let's go," is all I say.

It is a very narrow and dirty tunnel we are climbing through.

It's incredibly smart to have an emergency exit though, I give credit to whoever built this place.

We crawl through the escape tunnel for about ten minutes before it starts veering upwards. About ten more minutes pass and then Scarlett comes to a halt and I stop just behind her, Raine behind me.

A small portion of light shines through above us, but not before a horrible stink finds its way up my nostrils. Scarlett opens a hatch door and climbs out, as I follow her. I'm unsurprised to see that we are still in Farming.

We are standing next to the animal's waste area, which luckily for us is next to the wall, and no one ever spends much time over here. That's why it smells so bad, we are standing amongst animal faeces. I internally groan, not enjoying this part of the plan at all.

As soon as Raine comes up, Scarlett closes the hatch and covers it over with some straw, then we start off towards Enzo's house.

It's quite a nice day out. It's cold, but the sun is shining, it feels like it's been a lifetime since I was above ground.

I take a moment to enjoy the sun beating down on me despite the chill. I'd breathe in the fresh air if the stink wasn't so strong here.

My moment is over quickly, with Scarlett hurrying me away. We can't stand around; we need to find Enzo.

We keep a steady jog towards Enzo's house. Everyone should be finishing work within the hour so we should get to his house not long after he's returned from work. We go in silence. I don't want to talk because of my hurt feelings and the fact I am terrified.

The further we get into Sector Two, the more people we see milling around, walking to their homes. I pull my scarf higher over my face and tighten it so it doesn't slip down my face as I jog. Thankfully the brisk air is good enough reason for me to have the scarf on.

It must have just gone 7pm by my estimation, we should only be about twenty minutes from Enzo's house now.

We slow ourselves to a casual walk so we blend in with everyone. I keep my head down hoping not to see anyone I know, especially my mother, as we are in her working Sector.

I'm surprised at how fit I feel. All of that training we've been doing has improved my stamina massively, and the medication is working really well to keep my spasms at bay.

We make it to Enzo's house with ease, and there are lights on inside. I hope this means he's home.

Raine and I stand at the side of the house as Scarlett goes up and knocks on the front door. We decided it would be best for only one of us to be seen if someone other than Enzo answered the door. And I'm glad we did as I can hear a female voice coming from the house.

"Hello, is Enzo home?" I can hear the smile in Scarlett's voice as she talks.

"Who are you?" This voice must be his mother, she isn't rude, she just sounds curious.

"I'm Hannah, Enzo's girlfriend. I haven't seen him in a couple of weeks, and I can't get hold of him on my bracelet, I was wondering if he was here."

"I'm afraid we haven't seen Enzo for ten days now. We've been quite concerned about him as he had been acting strangely the last few days that he was with us before disappearing. You know, I didn't know he had a girlfriend."

"We are quite a new couple; it hasn't been long. Has he not been going to work at all then?"

"No, he hasn't, we don't know where he is. The guards assured us that he's not in any danger as his bracelet hasn't spiked any injuries or illness. Sadly, they seem to think he is mentally unwell, so I'm afraid even if we did find him, he would need a lot of medical treatment. I don't think you will see him anytime soon sweetheart." A tone of bitterness edges into her voice but it only lasts a moment and then she's blasé again.

"He is not mentally unstable," Scarlett answers defensively.

"I'm sorry, but you just don't know him like we do. I hope we find him so we can help him get better, maybe the job was just too much for him. I have to go now; my dinner is ready."

Before Scarlett can reply, Enzo's mother closes the door in her face. I go around and pull at Scarlett's arm, we shouldn't be standing on the doorstep. We go and stand at the back of the house.

"His mother was acting very strange. Why was she not more concerned about where Enzo is? She didn't even seem worried that she hasn't seen him in ten days and that no one knows where he is." Raine says exactly what I was thinking.

How was his mother so calm? I'm already panicking about it. I heard the bitterness in her voice, but it was only a slight hint, there was no fear. She should be filled with fear.

"The guards have him. It's obvious, and you both know it is. We have to rescue him." She's desperate, and I don't blame her, they could be doing anything to Enzo. They could kill him at any minute, if they haven't already.

I try to come up with a plan, I have no idea where we could even start looking for him. We need some inside information, but I don't know where to get it from.

"We need to go to a leader's house and get the information on where prisoners are kept." Scarlett and I turn to look at Raine, our mouths hanging open. Now she is the mad one.

"Just hear me out. If there is a secret prison hidden somewhere, which is more than likely true, then the leaders would know about it. They would have documents on it and the location, they would have a record of the people in there. The head leader would have everything we need, he could also have some information about 'the others.' There is a chance that we can find Enzo, I think we should go there and try."

It's true the leaders would have the information we need, and Mr Ritton would have everything in his house. But how in 'The Island' could we get in, find the information and get out again without being seen?

"I think we should do it. He lives alone, we could watch the house, see if he's home. If he isn't there then we can sneak in. I think it would actually be quite easy, I say we go now," Scarlett says.

Both Scarlett and Raine turn to look at me, they're waiting for me to agree with them. It's crazy, but what other choice do we have? Enzo has saved my life more than once, and it's about time I returned the favour.

"Okay, I'll lead the way. I know where the house is, and where we can hide without being caught. We have to move quickly though, it will probably take us a good two hours to get there even if we jog the whole way," I say.

"Well stop standing around and lead the way then," Scarlett says and starts pushing me forward to get a move on. I break into a light jog towards the most dangerous place for me to be right now.

We duck and hide behind buildings, factories, schools and fences to avoid being seen by any guards. We get to the horse stables and run straight inside, hiding at the back behind a few bales of hay where we collapse to the floor panting heavily.

We sit there in silence, sharing some water and cooling down from the run. I take a moment to check around me, I don't see anyone here, but I do see Violet standing only five feet away.

I slowly stand up and walk over to the horse, I reach up and stroke her nose, just how she likes it. I nuzzle my face into her neck, embracing her. I'm surprised at the tears that start to form in my eyes, realising how much I've missed her. She starts to snort, an indication that she's happy.

I stay like this for several minutes, just enjoying the embrace of my favourite horse. She reminds me of before the madness happened, when everything was safe, at least, I thought it was.

I'm so focused on Violet that I don't even notice that someone has come into the stable and is walking towards me. I look up just as he comes to stand a foot away from me, his lips forming my name. I jump forward and cover his mouth with my hand, vigorously shaking my head.

He looks confused and stares at me, I take my hand away and signal for him to be quiet, he doesn't say a thing as I pull the plate out of my pocket. I grab his wrist, lift his sleeve and place it on the face of his bracelet. I wait five seconds to ensure it's working, then I throw myself into his arms and give him the biggest hug possible.

"I've missed you so much, Joseph." I manage to say between sobs. I'm now in full tears, but tears of joy for seeing him.

All too soon he's pulling out of the hug, I look up at his face to see he is staring behind me. I turn to see Scarlett and Raine are no longer hiding.

"Joseph, come over here, let's talk, but I have to stay hidden," I say as I'm already walking back over to Raine and Scarlett.

As we approach them, Raine reaches out for me but just as quickly pulls her arm back as if just realising what she was doing. It doesn't go unnoticed, Joseph looks at me questioningly. Though that could be because I've been missing for weeks by now.

We all sit down and make sure we are hidden as Joseph looks at me with deep concern in his eyes. I wonder what I should tell him, luckily for me, he speaks first.

"Talise, where have you been? There were a lot of guards around here looking for you, they only left a few days ago. They questioned us about you, asking where you would hide, who you would be with, all sorts of things. What have you got yourself into?" I can tell how worried he's been about me.

"I don't really know what I can tell you Joseph, but I am okay, I'm safe, and that's what matters." I subconsciously look at Raine when I say I'm safe and a small smile appears on my lips, then I remember how she's ignored me and I bury it away again.

"Talise, can I tell you what they've been saying?" He asks, and I nod.

"They told us that when you went to get your bracelet fitted you attacked the nurse. They've been telling people that you're mentally unstable and a danger to the people. They told us you were struggling with life on 'The Island' and this wasn't your first attack." He pauses for a moment and I digest his words.

"I know they are lying. I don't believe you could hurt someone like that for a second. I trust you, Talise, will you tell me the truth?" He's pleading with me now, he needs to know. He also believes in me, he knows I wouldn't do what they said, Joseph has always been a good guy.

I turn to look at Scarlett and Raine, I see the guarded expressions on their faces, they don't know Joseph and I doubt they want to trust him.

"Do you trust me?" I ask them. Raine instantly nods, Scarlett takes a moment and slowly nods.

"Okay then. Joseph, you were right to doubt them, none of what they told you is true. I have been in hiding because on my birthday I overheard something I shouldn't have, and the guards came for me. They were coming to take me in for questioning, which I now understand means they would have killed me. I was injured escaping and I got really sick, my friend had to steal some medicine for me, and we think they found out about it. He has been missing for two weeks, his parents don't know where he is, and we can't get hold of him via his bracelet. We believe the guards have taken him for questioning, and that isn't a good thing for anyone.

"So, we have come here because we need to find out where he is being kept, we believe that Mr Ritton will have the information in his house. And that's pretty much it."

He is quiet for a moment then he says, "What did you hear on your birthday Talise?" I look over at Raine and Scarlett, I can sense they aren't eager for me to say anymore, but I've told him this much, I may as well say what I heard.

"Mr Ritton said something about 'the others.' There are people living outside of the walls." I keep my voice level as I say this, I really hope he believes me.

"Was it just about 'the others' you heard, or did you hear something else that would put you in danger?" He asks this and looks from Raine to me and back to her again, I don't understand what he means.

"It's okay, Talise, don't worry. I believe you, and I can help, on one condition. You take me with you to this hideout you have, I won't be safe here once I've helped you. I can go into the house and get what you need." He says.

How can Joseph be so confident that he could get in the house and get what we need? I want to say yes so badly because I love Joseph, but I know Carlo will be angry with me for bringing him back with us.

But if Joseph can help us get what we need then we could really use him. I look at Raine first and then Scarlett, they both just shrug their shoulders, I guess it's all on me.

"Okay, Joseph. I don't think the person that protects us will be happy about this, but you're like my brother and we could use your help. Do you really think you can get in and out of there without being caught?" I ask cautiously.

"Don't underestimate me, little sister," he says this with a wink and his half-cocked smile, I've missed him so much.

"But how do you know you can do it? Have you even used a computer before?"

"Of course, I have, we all have a sixth you know. I've been in this Sector my whole life, Talise. I hear things, see things. I know I can do this."

"Okay, but I'm coming in with you," I tell him

"No way. I have to go in alone if this is going to work. Please, just trust me. Be ready to run when I come back, just as a precaution."

"Do you know what you're looking for in there?"

"Yes. Believe me I do. Prisoner information and anything else I can get my hands on that could help us escape this hell." His last statement throws me off. Why would he call this place hell? I didn't know he hated it here, he's always so happy. Before I can ask, he's already moving off towards Mr Ritton's house.

The three of us sit there in silence for at least ten minutes before Scarlett voices her doubt.

"How do you know you can trust him? What if he's turning us in right now and they come for us?"

"He wouldn't do that, Scarlett. Besides, if he had, they would be on us already, there's a guard station is only five minutes away from this stable," I answer in a harsh whisper, wanting to remain undetected by any passers-by.

"Look, I know he is like a brother to you, but I don't think this is a good idea, we should leave now and come back tomorrow. We can't help Enzo if we get captured," she replies.

"No way, Scarlett. He is in there risking himself for us and for Enzo. If we don't get the information now, who knows how long Enzo will have left? We are here for Enzo; we will get the information and save him. Joseph is trustworthy, I promise." I know she will do anything to save Enzo, she clearly fancies him though she'd never admit it.

She looks like she's ready to argue with me some more when a figure appears, running towards the stables, towards us. I signal for her to be quiet and we all crouch down lower behind the hay. I'm relieved moments later when I see it's Joseph coming over to us.

He crouches down next to me and grins as he pulls out a small memory stick from his pocket.

"Is that everything we need?" Scarlett asks as she leans forward and grabs the stick from him.

"Yeah, it's all on there, I found his password and got onto his computer, I downloaded all of his files. Whatever you need, it should be on there. I hope you have a computer, I couldn't get paper copies, there wasn't time." He looks at me at this and I nod that yes, we do have a computer.

"How did you get in and out without being caught? Surely Mr Ritton would have been there. How do we know we can trust you?" Scarlett asks.

"If you trust Talise, you can trust me. I would never betray her," he replies without pause.

Before Scarlett can respond I ask Joseph for the time and he looks at his bracelet, a little shocked that the time and date are visible even though the plate is covering the face. It's 11:03pm.

"Talise, how long will it take us to get to your safe place?" He asks.

"About four hours, if we jog most of the journey," I reply almost apologetically. He thinks this over in his head, trying to come up with a solution.

"Okay, I say we go to my house for one hour, then we can head there at about 12:30pm. That way there shouldn't be anyone outside, only a few guards in each Sector patrolling." His knowledge is quite impressive, we have no other plans, so I nod in agreement and we leave the stables, though not before I give Violet one last stroke.

Joseph has kept the plate on his bracelet the whole time, we figured it would be too dangerous to take it off now. We sit in his incredibly small home whilst he makes us a drink and gives us all the little bit of food that he has.

We have about forty minutes until we want to head off again, so we all sit back and enjoy the little rest. Between the three of us we explain what we know to Joseph, he takes it all on board and doesn't doubt anything we tell him.

He asks a few questions that we don't have the answers to, but he doesn't seem too worried about that.

I'm sitting next to Raine as Scarlett converses with Joseph, about I'm not sure, I stopped listening a while ago now. All I want to do is lean over and hold her hand again, I want to feel her touch, her kiss, and it hurts not being able to.

"I'm sorry I kissed you," I whisper, knowing only she will hear me. She looks at me confused, she has barely spoken to me in two weeks, why would she be confused?

"Why are you apologising?" She asks.

"Because you clearly didn't want me to kiss you, I figure that's why you've been avoiding me."

"I haven't been avoiding you."

"Please don't treat me like an idiot, you could just tell me you're not interested and that I read the signs wrong."

"It's not that at all. I like you, Talise, I really do."

"Then why have you been ignoring me?"

She doesn't say anything to this, just looks at her hands. I've put myself out there and she's giving me nothing, I'm embarrassed all over again. I announce to the room that I need some fresh air and go outside to clear my head.

I open the door slowly and check no one is outside. Though the hour is late I still need to be cautious. I don't see anyone around, so I step outside.

The cold night air hits my face, it feels refreshing and peaceful. I can hear some of the animal sounds around us, this is where I always saw myself living, in Sector Three, happy with the animals.

"Talise?" Raine softly speaks my name as she steps outside next to me.

"Please leave me alone." I don't want to listen to any reasons as to why she doesn't like me, it just hurts.

"Talise, I meant what I said, I really like you. But you are right, I've been avoiding you. Please know, I'm sorry about that, it's only because I'm scared."

"What could you possibly be scared of? I kissed you, it's clear I like you. I'm the one that looks like an idiot."

"You don't look like an idiot, Talise. And I'm scared because I've only kissed one other girl before, and she turned her back and ran away from me, like it never happened. I was terrified that you would do the same."

I turn to look at her, she has tears in her eyes, but I need her to understand that what she did hurt me.

"Raine, you know that's exactly what you did to me, right? You avoided me and kinda pretended like it didn't happen."

"I'm really sorry Talise, I didn't mean to do that. I didn't even realise I was doing it. I'm such a fool. You are so amazing. I just don't want to ruin it."

"You hurt my feelings Raine, you embarrassed me, I felt so pathetic. I don't want to be put in that position again."

Tears are falling from her eyes; she takes my hands and looks me straight in the eyes.

"I promise, from now on, if I get scared, I will tell you. I will be here for you. I want to be with you. I'll be honest and tell you how I feel. Can we just ignore the last couple of weeks? Not the kiss though, I don't want to forget that kiss."

I think over her words and I can't blame her for being scared, I was scared, I still am. I wipe a tear away from her cheek and take her hand back in mine. I don't want to forget that kiss either, I've thought about it so much since it happened.

It was sensational and overpowering, and I want another like it, though not right now. This isn't the time or place, so instead I lean forward and plant a delicate kiss on her lips.

"Amore proibito," she says as I pull back and we smile at one another. I don't want to let her hand go, not now, not ever.

Chapter Thirteen

At 12.:30pm we get our jackets and shoes on and prepare for the journey back to the barn. I take the lead and we start with a light jog, keeping a steady pace so that we don't exhaust ourselves too quickly.

The quickest way for us to reach the barn would be to go diagonally through Sector Two so that we come up near the hospital. If we wanted to be more cautious we could run alongside the wall, but it would take us at least seven hours to do that from where we are.

We risk taking the quick route, if we went the long way people would be heading to work before we even made it to the barn and we would definitely be caught. We leave Joseph's house and start a light jog through the buildings and towards the elder's home.

We get past our first grouping of houses in Sector Two, like Joseph said, everyone is in bed. All of the lights are off in the houses, it's pure darkness outside.

I get the feeling that we are being watched.

I keep turning around and checking to see if there's someone behind us, but there never is. I think the fear is getting to me and making me paranoid.

I just can't get rid of the nagging feeling that someone is there, shadows dancing in the dark.

We are near some of the cages now and I can't help but shiver, thinking about when I was in one of them.

I come to a stop and the others do the same behind me. There is a large empty space ahead, there are no buildings to hide behind, we will be completely out in the open.

We need to cautiously take it in turns to run ahead to the next spot of cover. I signal for Scarlett to go first, followed by Raine, then Joseph.

I take one last look around the space and set out to run over to my friends, when all of a sudden, I fall face first to the ground. There's a tight grip around my waist, pinning my arms against my body.

I hit the ground hard, my face taking most of the impact. My head pounds loudly and my vision is blurred. I feel a wet trickle running down from my nose.

It takes me a moment to realise I am tackled to the ground; someone is diving at me from behind. I try to clear the fuzz from my head, but my body is sluggish, not the way I wish it would.

The arms around my waist let go, instantly I bring my elbow back with a hard thrust. I feel the impact when it connects with the person behind me, a man's voice cries out in pain.

My body is responding to my thoughts now, I push myself up off of the floor and turn to face my attacker. When I see him, I freeze on the spot as I recognise the person in the guards uniform. What is he doing here, and why is he dressed like that?

He's cradling his nose, blood running through his fingers, it takes me a second to realise that I did that. I really hurt someone, I made them bleed.

He looks me in the eyes and whispers my name as if he didn't know who I was until now.

He moves his hand away from his face and fiddles with something in his pocket. I'm too distracted by the sight of him to know what he's doing. I look down just as he grabs my wrists and cuffs me.

I pull my hands away from him and struggle to get free, but he is stronger than me. Even with his blood-soaked hands he doesn't lose grip on me, and before I know it, he's pulling me towards one of the cages.

Now I'm desperate to escape him.

I kick my legs out and one connects with his ankle, but he doesn't fall or let go, he just swears under his breath and keeps moving. Then I'm in the cage and he's slamming the door shut locking me in.

My mind races, I've been captured, but not by any guard, I've been locked away by my best friend! Why has Connelly become a guard? He's always been so kind, gentle, and incredibly intelligent.

I can't believe he attacked me; how could this have happened?

I pace the cage and feel the walls, hoping for an opening somewhere, but I know I won't find one.

I'm in a metal box.

No window, no light.

Just me and these four walls, and they feel tight around me.

I need to gather my thoughts and make a plan. I'm unsure if I should shout out to Connelly or not.

I don't want to draw more attention to myself, but we already would have made noise out there and I need an escape.

"Connelly, why are you doing this? Please, let me out." Silence follows my call.
"Connelly, you are meant to be my best friend. Why have you locked me in here?"

"Say something to me!" I shout and bang on the door.

I'm shocked when the door starts to open, and I quickly get into a fighting stance.

It's not Connelly I see. Raine rushes inside, takes the cuffs off of me and wraps me in her arms. I look behind her to see Joseph and Scarlett carrying my best friend, the guard, between them.

I can see they have put a plate on his wrist, smart thinking, it means the doctors won't be alerted to his injuries. I hope it acted before they spotted the signals his nose injury would have sent.

"Are you okay?" Raine asks as she inspects my bloodied nose.

"Yeah, I'm not hurt, I just, I can't believe it," I say as I look down at my friend, unconscious and cuffed on the floor.

"We knew we might get caught, Talise, I'm just sorry you got hurt," Raine says as she strokes my cheek.

"I don't think that's why she's in shock, Raine. That's Connelly, isn't it, Talise?" Joseph says before I can speak, and I remember that he also knows him. I would have been in Breeding with him before, we had the same sixth.

I look up at Joseph and nod in agreement, still shaken as my best friend has just attacked me.

"Well, do either of you feel like explaining to us who Connelly is before he wakes up?" Scarlett asks from the entrance of the cage, thankfully she left the door open.

"Connelly is my best friend. Before my birthday I had two best friends, Connelly and Jane. I can't believe they've made him a guard, it's not where he belongs," I say staring down at his unconscious form.

"Talise, he just attacked you and was going to turn you in. If I hadn't have knocked him out and taken his keys then you would still be locked up in here. I'm sorry, but I don't think he's your friend anymore," Scarlett replies.

I don't want to argue with anyone about this, but if I could just talk to him, maybe he can help me.

"Please, can I just talk to him? He's still my friend," I ask.

"Talise, we don't have time for this, just take the plate and lock him in, we have to go." Scarlett is starting the argument up and I know she will end up winning.

"It's okay. We can wait for ten minutes, then we have to go. Try to shake him awake, we will wait outside and keep watch. But ten minutes, and then we go." Joseph says this not just to me, but the others as well, I don't know why but they seem to listen to him. Raine gives my hand a squeeze and with a small smile, she heads outside with the others.

"Who are they?" A voice asks from the floor. I spin round and stare down at Connelly. How long has he been awake for?

"They are my friends. Like you are. Or were, I'm not too sure right now," I reply, realising then that I have no idea what I intend on saying to him.

"Connelly, I've missed you, and Jane. But why did you attack me?" I ask him before I lose the chance. He stares at me, right in the eyes, he looks sad.

He shifts around on the floor slightly and manages to sit himself up, I lower myself to the ground and sit across from him.

"They told us you were unwell, Talise. That you attacked the nurse who tried to give you your bracelet, they say you killed her. Now I see that you don't have a bracelet, I'm more inclined to believe them. You need to get help from the doctors. Please, I can help you." He actually believes I could hurt someone, I thought he was smarter then that. I thought he was my friend.

"It's not true. I didn't attack anyone, they tried to inject me with something. They want me dead."

"No one want's you dead, Talise, we all just want to help you get better."

"There is nothing wrong with my mental state, Connelly. I'll tell you the truth, there are people living outside of the walls. There are probably thousands of them, we are not the only people left in the world. The leaders have been lying to us for 79 years and they will continue to lie."

"Talise, can you hear yourself right now? You are not making any sense. That can't be true, it's not possible. I work closely with Mr White, he's one of the leaders and he's a good man, he wouldn't lie to us like that."

"You believe them over me? Your best friend?" I ask, to which he looks lost for words. He looks at the floor, because he can't answer me. I still want to keep trying to get through to him though.

"Please believe me. I need you to believe me." I'm begging him now. He looks up at me and I can see tears forming in his eyes.

"I can't, Talise, I'm sorry. You need help." His words crush me, he doesn't believe me, and he won't. I have to leave, my time must be up by now.

I lean forward and wrap my arms around him, giving him one long last hug. I reach down and take the plate off of his bracelet whilst I embrace him hoping he won't notice. I can't let him know we have them. I let go of him and stand up, tears streaming silently down my cheeks.

"Please, Talise, stay with me. I'll help you; I will look after you. You could be with me, I, I, I need you." His words throw me off, I look at him, he needs me. But he doesn't believe me. I turn back around, ready to walk out.

"The doctors will be here soon to let you out. They will be aware of the injury to your nose. It should be spiking on their system now, and they will know you are in here, they'll come for you," I say without any emotion, as I reach the door about to leave.

"Talise, wait! I love you. I've loved you since we first met. Please, stay with me and let me help you. I promise, I can help you," he practically shouts at me, like he's desperate, like it's his life on the line.

He loves me, how can that even be true? I turn to look at him, his eyes are terrified, he's crying and looks so weak and vulnerable, my best friend.

"If you truly loved me then you would believe me. But you don't. I loved you as a friend, I thought you would always be on my side, I wish you could have believed me. You've just broken my heart, Connelly. Goodbye." I manage to get the last words out even with tears streaming down my cheeks.

I leave the cage.

Joseph shuts the door behind me, no one says anything even though I know they heard everything. I start to run, towards the barn and as far away from my old friend as I can.

It doesn't take long for us to get back to the barn after our encounter. We all run in silence and make it back in record time. We head back to the secret exit we used earlier to get ourselves back to the bunker.

I'm surprised no one else came to stop us. I guess they didn't know where to look, or were too busy searching the area close to where we left Connelly in the cage. We didn't speak the whole way back here and we are still silent as we make our way inside.

I let Scarlett go first, followed by Raine, myself, and then Joseph brings up the rear. I barely even notice the stench this time around as I'm too distracted by what happened with Connelly.

I emerge in the bathroom after Raine and I'm greeted by Carlo glaring at us.

"What in 'The Island' is going on here?" He demands. I didn't think he could look any angrier, but as Joseph climbs out of the secret door and stands beside me Carlo looks like his head is going to explode.

"What is he doing here?" Carlo fumes as he looks directly at me.

"WHY would you bring him here? What are you thinking? I assume it's you that decided to bring him along, wasn't it, Talise?" I'm slightly thrown off guard by the sheer anger radiating from Carlo, he's physically shaking.

"He helped us. I thought it would be okay to bring him, he's a friend and risked his life for us, to get us the information we need to find Enzo." I manage to keep my voice level and not cower from his anger and gaze.

"And why did you sneak out in the first place to try and get that information? Anything could have happened to you out there. Raine, why didn't you stop them? I thought you were more responsible." He actually sounds disappointed in her. Before I can stick up for her, Scarlett speaks out.

"Carlo, it was my idea to go and find Enzo, I wanted to go to his house to see if he was there. I made Talise come with me as I didn't know where he lived, I was scared. Raine tried to stop us but we told her we were going no matter what. She came to keep us safe. Don't be mad at her, or Talise, please, it was my idea."

"Scarlett, I appreciate that you are trying to stick up for your friends, but they have their own thoughts and make their own decisions. You didn't force them to go and I know you didn't suggest bringing back this man, did you?" He asks, and she shakes her head looking at the floor.

It was weird to hear myself being referred to as Scarlett's friend, considering how she's never really liked me.

"I don't see how it's any different, me bringing Joseph and Enzo bringing me. It's probably even safer because I have known Joseph half of my life, he is like a brother to me. So, I don't see what the problem is with me bringing him here to keep him safe after he helped us steal information from Mr Ritton's house." I'm surprised at how firm I am being with Carlo, but I don't like how rude he is being towards Joseph right now.

Carlo stares at me for a long moment then looks over at Joseph, then back to me.

"You don't know, do you?" Carlo asks me.

"Know what?" I reply, confused by his question. Carlo looks at Joseph again who turns to face me, a sorry expression on his face. He looks down at the floor as if defeated, not saying a word.

"Talise, this man is the son of Harold Ritton." Carlo practically spits the name out. I look at Joseph; I don't know anything about his parents and he's never mentioned them. But we've never known Mr Ritton to have any children, it can't be true, can it?

"Joseph, is this true?" I whisper, my hand reaching out to touch his arm. He looks at me, tears forming in his eyes and he nods.

I can't believe it, how could Mr Ritton be his father? It doesn't add up.

"How?" I ask softly.

"My father disowned me a long time ago for who I am. But they won't let me leave Sector Three, I have to stay there until I marry, which I never will. My father killed the only person I've ever loved," he says, as tears fall down his face.

I pull Joseph into a hug, I'm sure he will tell me more when he's ready, I won't push him right now.

"It's how I managed to get the files," he whispers.

"Now do you see what danger you've put us in by bringing him here? He can't stay." Carlo says this like there's no negotiating and a total disregard for Joseph's feelings. No matter who Joseph is, it isn't his fault that his dad is a monster who pretends he doesn't exist.

"He isn't going anywhere, Carlo." I state.

"Excuse me?" He's taken aback by my words and looks at me with a mixed expression.

"I said he isn't going anywhere. Joseph is my brother. As far as I'm concerned, he doesn't have a father. Joseph has nothing to do with that man and I don't think you should send him away for it. He has helped us a great deal tonight, we probably wouldn't have made it back here without him. So, I'm sorry, but he stays." I don't know where all this courage has come from. I just can't let Joseph be cast away by more people.

Carlo scrutinises me but says nothing. I don't know what is going through his mind, but he turns his back on us and walks to the door.

"Just know this, Talise. If we all die because of him, it will be your fault." And with that he leaves the room.

∞

I've been locked in the cage for eight days and no one has come to see me. The door opens and Connelly stands in the doorway, he tells me that I'm crazy, and walks away laughing. My father then stands in his place, tells me what a disgrace I am, that I should never come back, they are happier without me.

The room changes and I see Mr Ritton, he's holding a baby over a cliff. He says he doesn't want this son and throws the baby over the edge. I scream out Joseph's name and wake up in a sweat.

I'm lying in a bed, but it's not mine or a medical bed. I look to my right and see Joseph is asleep in the bed next to me. It was just a bad dream, and he is here, he is safe with me.

The clock on the wall tells me that it's 8:16am, I've only had two hours sleep, but I'm wide awake now. I couldn't get back to sleep if I tried.

I get up and head to Wes's work room, maybe I can take a look at the memory stick Joseph stole for us and get some information on where Enzo is.

I'm not surprised to find Wes there, looking at multiple computer screens, no doubt going through the new data.

"Hey, Wes, what are you up to?" I ask as I walk into the room.

"Oh Talise, hi. I'm just looking through the memory stick, there is so much information on here. We really need to do something about what happens up there." His reply is monotone, no hint of sadness or anger in his words. I dread what he's found.

"I know we do, Wes. Hopefully this memory stick will give us the answers we need, have you found anything on Enzo yet?"

"Not yet, but I think I'm close to it. Talise, I should tell you, when Rory told me that you had left through the secret tunnel, I contacted Carlo and told him. I was concerned about my sister, I don't want anything to happen to her," he says and I can't really be mad at him.

"It's okay, Wes, I understand. I'm sorry we didn't tell you that we were going. Do you mind if I look through the information with you? I have a feeling everyone else will be sleeping for a while longer." I laugh, trying to ease up the atmosphere.

"Of course. Pull up a chair and I'll hook you up to your own monitor and send you some files I think might have information about Enzo in. Everything is coded on here so it's not clear what you'll find in any folder, we just have to keep searching. I'll send you some of the ones I haven't looked at yet."

When Wes said he would send me 'some' of the files, I didn't realise it would be so many, 48! It makes me think about how many files are on that memory stick in total, how many awful secrets we will uncover.

I sit there in silence with Wes as we both read through the files looking for Enzo.

Time seems to fly by, I hadn't even noticed Wes get up and leave the room until he calls my name from the doorway and waves a sandwich at me. He walks over and hands it to me, I look at the clock, it's 1:35pm and it's still quiet in the bunker.

Rory is around here somewhere playing with Scamp, he tried to come in here a few times, but Wes was firm with him, today, he couldn't be in here. Thankfully, Rory listened, after a short sulk he went off to play with Scamp and left us to it.

I make small talk with Wes whilst we eat, but it's very one sided on my part. Within minutes, we've finished our food and we are back looking at the files again.

I'm briefly aware of people coming in and out of the room throughout the rest of the day. I see how Wes can stay in here all day, I'm lost in the work, desperately looking.

Most of the files have important things that we need to know, some aren't too immediate, so I make a note on some paper the names of those files we need to discuss.

I am learning a lot from these documents. I've even found out why the bracelets don't come off. If the bracelet is removed with force, I know that we would die, but this tells me how. A poison is released into the body immediately through the small needle. No matter how fast you pull, it won't work.

There are tendrils that have snaked in through the bracelet and wrapped around our veins. If you pull, you pull your veins out and bleed to death. As if poison wasn't enough. There is a video attached to this document, it's called 'test runs'. I don't need to watch that, it's pretty clear what will be in it.

I find a 'compliance' folder. This one I mark as something to look at immediately after we find Enzo. It turns out that the bracelets release 'Nanobots' into our blood stream, these are manned by a special group of watchers. The Nanobots can control people's thoughts.

They pick up signals in our brain waves and transform undesirable ideas and thoughts into something more 'appropriate.'

Is this why no one questions the leaders? Because they are controlling people's thoughts? I don't even know where to begin with all of this madness, how can we stop them?

I don't understand the science behind all of it, but I understand the severity of the situation. I'm alarmed by all of the things I'm reading, of how deep this all goes, and I wonder what kind of information Wes has too. This is just too much, but I can't stop, I won't. I have to keep going, for Enzo.

It starts to feel like I'm never going to find anything to help Enzo when I spot something in one of the files. I open it to find another bunch of folders within, just like most files I've looked through today, but this one is different. There are far more folders in this one than any other, and they're all numbered. These ones don't have names like the others did, they're just numbered 1 to 6994.

I open up file number 1, inside there is just one readable document, so I open that. It starts with a paragraph of writing about the leaders and their right to be charge. Then it starts to talk about disobedience, and how people that undermine the leaders should be punished according to the laws.

I see the name 'Frank Stenning' written in large bold letters along with 'Sector Two.' Underneath it says 'crime; questioning the leaders right to take control of 'The Island.' Then it says 'Punishment; execution.' At the bottom of the page, in large green letters, is the word 'Completed.' There is nothing else written on the page.

I close this page and open file number 2, again there is one document inside containing a single, readable file. The same paragraph is written at the top of the page, followed by a name in bold, though this one says Sector Three. The crime was stealing bread. Punishment was execution, completed.

I start opening file after file, scanning through them all. I'm horrified by what I'm reading, the leaders have killed this many people so far, and kept a record of it, it's disgusting. After I read a file, I amend the title of the document and put in the person's name next to their number, they deserve that much at least.

I start looking towards the end, opening random ones. There seem to be more men in these files than women. I do come across one that particularly disturbs me.

Number 3286. 'Florence Morella, Sector One, crime; disrespecting Mr Ritton. Punishment; execution.' And at the bottom of the page, in that bold green lettering, it says 'Completed.' It makes me wonder, what in 'The Island' she could have done to disrespect Mr Ritton that would equate to murder.

I can't read much more of this right now; they are making me feel physically sick. I skip to the end to what I guess to be the more recent files and I open up number 6994.

My fears are confirmed when in bold letters I see the name 'Enzo Cardelous. Sector Two. Cage 6. 'Crime; helping fellow criminals by stealing vital medical supplies and withholding important information from the leaders. Terrorist activity and a strong threat to 'The Island.' Punishment; execution.' My heart starts to beat harder with every word I read, I scroll to the bottom of the page praying it doesn't have those haunting green letters there.

I take a deep breath and search the bottom of the page, there are no green letters, and a wave of relief covers me, he is still alive. Then I notice the words written in bold red; 'Currently in captivity, daily questioning until April 1st. If the criminal does not cooperate, he will be executed with immediate effect on this date.'

I sit there and re-read those words over and over. Enzo is alive, but not for long. I look up to the wall where the clock hangs, it's 5:39pm on March 29th.

"I found him," I say, leaning back in my chair, staring at the screen, not quite believing my own words.

"I found him," I repeat, letting it sink in and making sure Wes hears me.

I turn to look at Wes, he's staring at his screen, I don't think he heard me. He has a mixed look on his face of horror and intrigue, all rolled into one.

"Talise, I haven't found anything about Enzo, but you have to see this." He turns to look at me as he says this.

"I found him, Wes." I say for the third time, though this time he actually hears me. He moves his chair over so he can look at my screen, but he doesn't get too close, he doesn't like being in close proximity to others. I stand up and walk away, not wanting to look at the words anymore.

I stand at the back of the room and stare at the little table in front of me with all sorts of gadgets, wires, metals, bracelets, and things I don't even recognise. After a minute I turn around and Wes is looking at me.

"We will need to rescue him," he says. I nod, not sure what to say. Wes stands and announces he will bring the others in here and instantly leaves the room.

I walk back to the computer I was at and sit in front of it again. I close Enzo's page and bring up the page before, I need to look at something else. If there are more people we can rescue, then I plan to get them all.

'Number 6993, Talise Crane, Sector Two and Three; border. Crime; terrorist activity, murder, assault and stealing medical supplies. Punishment; severe questioning, judgement on execution ruling. This individual is considered extremely dangerous, she could ruin everything. She does not have a bracelet. Measures are being put in place to capture the criminal. Be cautious if approaching this individual, she's suspected to be conspiring with others.'

I sit there staring at the utter lies I just read. I knew they wanted to question me, but I didn't know how badly they wanted me. How am I such a threat to them? Even my best friend didn't believe me when I told him about their lies.

I hear voices and realise Wes is coming back to the room with some of the others, so I close my file. I don't rename it, I can't, not yet.

I reopen Enzo's file and move away from the computer as Scarlett and Carlo head over to read it, shortly followed by Raine, Ajax and Kimya.

I'm surprised to see Joseph standing in the doorway, he looks at me and smiles. I walk over to him and he wraps me in a warm hug. I tell him what I found on the computer about Enzo, I don't mention my own file to anyone.

"When do we go and rescue him?" Scarlett asks from the other side of the room, tears brimming in her eyes.

"Tonight," I instantly reply, there's no need to even question it. The safest possible time to get him is night time, and I don't want him being in the cage for another day getting 'questioned.'

"Yes, tonight. Wes, can you find out where the cage is that he's in, and what the security is like?" Carlo asks as he gestures to the computer.

"Actually, there is something else I need to tell you all first. Before Talise told me she had found Enzo, I actually found something of importance in the files I looked through." Wes says this and looks around at us all as if expecting permission to continue. When no one says anything, he sits back down at his computer and types a few things in before he continues.

"There are some files here about security around the bunker and the cages, so we will be able to make a great plan to get Enzo back. But I also came across a prisoner file. There isn't a name of the prisoner and it doesn't give too much information. Usually, they imprison people in cages, but this person is in the secret bunker prison. It's one of 'the others,' from outside of the walls."

No one says anything, we all stand and stare at Wes, mouths hanging open.

"So, what you're saying, is that one of 'the others' has been captured and is being held in a secret bunker prison?" Joseph asks, because no one else seems to be able to say anything.

"That's exactly what I'm saying. From the records here, it doesn't seem like this person is being questioned too intensely but I think they are going to change their methods pretty soon, as it's not working for them so far. We have to rescue this prisoner as well as Enzo." Wes says this as a statement, no question about it.

For the last forty-five minutes everyone has been discussing and arguing over the plans of rescue. Scarlett thinks we should focus all of our efforts on getting Enzo out, but Wes insists we rescue the other prisoner.

It's a tiring process listening to everyone argue, and Carlo isn't taking charge as he usually does, he's distracted with the files I renamed, he won't stop staring at one of them.

Whilst the others argue I look over some other files we have. They listed Enzo being in cage 6, so I want to find out the location and security detail of the cages. I find the file easily enough, there are 1000 cages in total. They are positioned throughout each Sector, 200 in Sector One, 600 in Sector Two and 200 in Sector Three. There are currently 280 cages in use and one of those is occupied by Enzo.

I can't see anything in the plans about extra or hidden cages other than the ones we are all aware of. I guess the bunker holds their only secret prison. Cage number 6 is located in Sector Two, it's close to the cage I was put in briefly by Connelly.

We were at cage twelve. I can't believe how close we were to Enzo and we never even knew. But it's a good thing, it means we can get him out and back to the barn within an hour if we have someone strong to carry him back.

The plans start to form in my head, everyone else behind me is still arguing about what to do. I check the time, it's 6:46pm, we have to move soon.

"Everyone just be quiet already!" The room falls silent as everyone turns to look at me, I guess I shouted a little louder than I had intended to.

Carlo is the only person not looking at me, he's still staring silently at the screen. I reach over and touch his shoulder giving him a little shake, he looks up and stares right through me.

"Carlo, I have a plan," I speak gently to him, he is clearly upset about something, but we need him right now, he is our leader. He looks at me and nods once, pulling himself away from the computer.

"I know where Enzo is being kept, I found his cage on the map, it's actually only a few over from where we left Connelly in the early hours of this morning. Ajax and Raine, I think you two should go and rescue Enzo, he will be weak, so Ajax will probably have to carry him. Raine, you can deliver any immediate medical attention that he may need before bringing him back here."

Scarlett looks like she's about to say something, but I signal for her to be quiet, I need to finish telling them my plan, so they hopefully agree to it. I know Scarlett will want to get Enzo herself, but I need her for the second rescue.

"Scarlett, Carlo and I will go and rescue the prisoner from the bunker prison. It is vital we save this person; they may be able to help us get outside of these walls. I plan on escaping; I can't live here in this system anymore. With the prisoner helping us, we can meet with 'the others' and ask for their help."

I take a moment's pause and let that sink in for everyone. We never mentioned escaping the walls of 'The Island,' but I've just declared, to them and to myself, that I am leaving. I've wasted too much time down here without any plan or idea of what to do, now I have it, escape.

"The security plans for the bunker are on the files. We use them, we go in, get the prisoner and get back here. And we go tonight. Raine, you and Ajax should go at 10pm, myself, Scarlett and Carlo will leave at 9pm because we have further to go."

The room is silent as everyone runs it over in their heads. Ajax is the one that agrees with my plan. Raine also quickly agrees, that's Enzo's rescue sorted. I hope that Carlo and Scarlett will agree to come with me, otherwise I'm going alone.

"What if an alarm sounds whilst we rescue the prisoner, or the security has changed because they know we have their plans? What if it's all a trap and we get caught?" Scarlett voices her concern, though Carlo remains quiet.

"That's another part of the plan, Wes." He looks up at me then, shocked that he's part of the plan. He isn't a fighter, and the worry has become apparent on his face.

"Wes can stay here, hack into their system and monitor any alarms that go off. He will be able to guide us back to the barn safely using the trackers on everyone's bracelets. We can communicate via those bracelets you made for us all as well, I see you finished them."

Wes nods along as I speak, agreeing with me. He knows that as soon as he hacks the system he can access everything the watchers have, he can track all bracelets, hear communications, everything.

Everyone looks to Carlo, he is our leader after all, and he should be the one agreeing to the plan. He seems to notice everyone staring at him, he looks over to me and sighs.

"My wife was number 3286. According to this they killed her because she disrespected Harold Ritton. She did nothing of the sort. She questioned him about the bracelet and its purpose, we didn't know how dangerous that would be. He liked her though and made her an offer; he would forget all that she said if she married him. She turned him down and it angered him to be rejected so he had her killed. I can't let them carry on killing innocent people, so we go tonight. Everyone get ready for another long night. We go ahead with Talise's plan." Carlo finishes what he says and then walks out of the room in silence, managing to deliver a hard glare towards Joseph.

His wife was number 3268. I try to remember her name but it's not coming to me, I need to focus on the missions and get prepared.

Rory comes bouncing into the room with Scamp at his heels, we are all still standing in silence. Scamp runs over to me and I bend down to give him a stroke. He jumps right up on to my knees and licks my cheek; I can't help but giggle a little at his affection. I scratch behind his ears and just about hear Rory say something about food over the happy moans from Scamp.

I stand up and walk over to Joseph, he looks angry.

"My father is a terrible man, Talise, I hope you know that I hate him."

"I know Joseph, it's not your fault who your father is. Give Carlo time, he will come to learn this too."

"I know. I will keep my distance as best I can, especially now that I know my father had his wife killed."

"I'm sorry, Joseph, we can talk about it if you want?"

"Maybe tomorrow. You have a rescue mission to prepare for, I'll be okay Talise. Go and save that prisoner."

He gives me a sad smile and I walk off to prepare for the mission.

The next couple of hours go by too quickly with most of us preparing to leave. I feel bad leaving Joseph here, but I don't want to risk him coming with us, and he seems able enough to stay and help Wes, so I leave him to it.

Wes hands out all of the bracelets to those of us going out on a rescue mission and gives us a quick explanation of how they work. They're very simple, luckily these ones slip on and off, so we don't have to be stuck with them forever.

The bracelets have the time on them, and a basic message and call function, that's all. They are all battery powered and charge up through the computer, they should stay on for ten hours before they need to be charged again. Wes kept the design similar to the bracelets everyone above ground has, just to ensure if they are spotted, they hopefully won't be recognised as different.

Those that already have bracelets from the leaders have to wear these bracelets on the other arm so that the plate doesn't affect the signal.

I pack a small bag for my group with help from Raine. Water, bread and some basic medical supplies in case our rescued prisoner needs some aid. Though I hope I won't have to use the medical supplies on anyone.

Kimya comes around and gives everyone a hug. She signals for us to all be safe and then holds her hand over each of our hearts individually, to signal 'love' to us. I feel bad that she can't come with us, she is a great fighter, but without her being able to hear, it could not only endanger her life, but it could also jeopardise our mission. She must know this as she never complained. It is probably best for her to stay here with her son anyway, Rory needs her more than anyone else here does.

It's 8:55pm, I have to leave in five minutes, so I spend those last minutes with Raine.

"Please be careful and come back in one piece for me," she whispers into my ear as we're wrapped in one another's arms.

"I promise to be careful if you do too." I lean back as I say this and smile as she stares into my eyes with such warmth.

"Amore proibito," I say and then I lean in and kiss her. Our lips lock and it sends fire through my body, her hands wrap in my hair and I hold on to her, not ever wanting to let go.

I'm so insanely happy in this moment being with her.

"Hey love birds! It's time for some of us to go." Scarlett's voice calls out from the doorway, making us pull apart and end our kiss.

I take Raine's hand in mine and hold it up to my lips, leaving a gentle kiss there. Then I pick up my bag and leave the room, turning to wave goodbye to the girl that's stealing my heart, hoping we both make it back here alive.

Chapter Fourteen

It should take us two hours and twenty minutes to reach the bunker where the prisoner is being kept. Raine and Ajax will get to Enzo, rescue him, and make it back to the barn by the time we reach the bunker, providing all goes well for them.

It's dark out and there are a few people around, though not too many. We thought it would be best for Carlo to keep his plate on his bracelet, Wes will be able to keep people from noticing Carlo's absence from the system whilst on the mission, so it should go unnoticed when he reappears in his home tomorrow morning.

The three of us keep a steady walking pace on our way, we go in silence with the occasional message from Wes. He keeps us updated as to whether or not there are people near us so we can stop and allow them to pass, just to be safe.

After an hour we aren't making enough progress with all of the stopping, so I suggest we start jogging to ensure we can get there on time.

Wes found us an open window of time where guards swap over from evening to night shifts, the corridors should be completely empty for approximately fifteen minutes.

Once we are inside, we will have a clear path to the prisoner. As soon as we open the door to the cell, we will have to get the prisoner and run. The prison isn't hidden too deep within the bunker, the leader's arrogance benefits us.

But we will still be at high risk of being caught and it's extremely dangerous, so we will need to keep an eye on the time.

After an hour of jogging and weaving between houses and factories, we reach the finders and binders factory. It's a secure building which we can't get into, only the workers are able to access it.

It's such a delicate (and sometimes dangerous) job, so people aren't able to work there on their sixth, only workers and the leaders are permitted entry.

This is the closest factory to the bunker that offers us cover from the guard's station. There are some houses ahead, but we have to run through the open space to get to them with no cover. We have to be really careful here, we don't want to be seen by any guards in the station. Luckily the finders and binders is a massive building and the walls offer plenty of cover.

We wait a few minutes, then Wes's voice comes through Carlo's bracelet, he speaks in a hushed whisper and we all crowd around to listen. We have to wait for two minutes, then one by one, run to the houses on our right. They are the last bit of cover until we run through the bunker entrance.

Carlo goes first. Once he disappears into the darkness of the houses ahead, my bracelet beeps once, meaning it's my time to go. I reach the houses and find Carlo instantly; we wait in silence until Scarlett joins us.

I check the time on my bracelet, it's 11:13pm, we made it in time. In two minutes we need to run together to the bunker entrance, all of the guards are already inside to do their change over.

We stand in the shadows and wait for our signal that it's safe. None of us says anything, we just wait as the minutes drag.

Wes sends me a message, 'they're back, all 3, alive.' I sigh with relief, Raine and Ajax got Enzo and they made it back to the barn already, they're alive and safe. It fills me with more confidence to complete my own mission now.

Even if we fail rescuing the prisoner, we've managed to get Enzo and he was the priority. Though having this prisoner on our side may be the exact thing we need to escape safely.

All three of our bracelets beep in sync, that's our cue to get to the entrance. We all run forward, within two minutes we are at the door, and walking inside. Lucky for us the leaders are arrogant and don't think the door needs to be locked, there are usually guards inside to provide security.

What the people don't know, is that there are usually guards on the inside of the door so if someone were to wander in, it wouldn't be long until they were questioned or made to leave.

Wes sent a false message to the guards who were meant to be guarding the door right now. I wonder what he sent to them to get them both to leave, not that I mind, it got us in easily.

The corridors inside are silent. I take the lead as Wes talks to me through my bracelet, giving directions. We take a right, a left, another left, then stop. Wes has gone silent; I whisper to my bracelet asking if it's left or right now.

I'm met by silence.

I tap my bracelet screen, nothing happens. My heart beats faster with every silent second, I'm about to turn to ask Carlo what to do when I hear Wes's voice from behind me. I turn and see that Scarlett has her bracelet up and Wes is saying something about the connection on mine being faulty.

I let Scarlett take the lead now, we seem to fly through too many doors, running down multiple staircases and corridors, I could never remember the way back out again.

After what feels like too long, we come to a stop in front of a large metal door. I hear Wes say that this is the one and we need to be quick, we are behind schedule, we only have seven minutes to get the prisoner and get out of here.

Scarlett takes a small, silver, square plate out of her pocket and places it over the keypad lock. She says 'go' to her bracelet and instantly numbers are flying across the screen. One by one they stop on the display; Scarlett puts those numbers in to the keypad and it lights up green. We've unlocked the door.

She grabs the handle and pulls the door open towards her, I stand in the doorway, and take a step into the dimly lit room.

The prisoner is sitting on a thin mattress in the corner of the room, he looks up at us with utter hatred in his eyes.

He has darker skin than me, and matted, shoulder length black hair. His eyes are a bright green, they make him stand out. I can tell even though he is seated that he is well built and clearly tall. He looks to be in his 40's, possibly 50's, I wonder how they captured him, he looks like he could fight.

He looks me straight in the eyes and his features seem to soften, he looks happy. Amazement spreads through his face and he climbs to his feet, smiling at me as he croaks out "about time."

"You were expecting us?" I ask, perplexed. "No. But if anyone was going to rescue me it would be a rebel group, you don't exactly look like guards. Now, shall we get out of here?" he asks as he stands up and rubs his hands together as if fighting off the cold.

"Well, aren't you a treat." Scarlett says with sarcasm dripping off of her.

Suddenly Carlo and Scarlett's bracelets beep in unison, I look down at Scarlett's screen to read 'meeting over. RUN.'

Carlo swears under his breath and asks Wes for directions out. I look up at the prisoner, and he's eyeing me curiously, though it's quickly masked.

I don't need to say anything to him, he walks out of his cell and we all start to run with Carlo taking the lead.

We round a corner to find three guards walking towards us. Scarlett takes advantage of their ignorance of us standing there and runs towards the nearest one, punching her square in the face. Within seconds a guard is advancing on me as a third goes for Carlo.

The prisoner blocks the third guard's attack and manages to floor him instantly.

I aim a kick at my attacking guard, but he easily blocks it. I quickly thrust my hand up against his nose and hear a loud crack. I look over to quickly check the others and turn back to my attacker just in time to see the punch that knocks me to the ground. I land awkwardly on my right arm, pain shooting up to my shoulder.

My head is spinning and then someone is above me, hitting my ribs with some form of metal weapon. The guard is leaning over me with one hand balanced on the wall, the blood from his broken nose dripping onto my chest. I thrust my knee upwards and it lands in the gut of my attacker. He staggers back and the hitting stops for a moment.

My ribs are screaming with agony as another figure looms over me, I turn to see Scarlett struggling back to her feet as the guard she was fighting comes for me.

I try to push myself up from the ground, but my right arm can't take any of my weight and I fall back down. I put all of my strength into my left arm and push myself up.

Just as I get to my feet, the prisoner leaps forward and knocks the advancing guard into the one I just got in the gut.

He lands a kick to her face whilst the other gets to his feet and tries to jump on his back. But he's too fast for them, he spins around connecting his elbow with the guard's jaw, who drops to the floor, instantly unconscious. I knew he looked like he could put up a fight.

The prisoner goes over to Scarlett, who is on the floor again, and helps her to her feet. I lean against the wall and catch my breath, my ribs are putting me in huge discomfort, and my arm is useless, I think I've broken some bones.

We have to get moving again, people will be coming here soon to check on the three unconscious guards, their bracelets will be sending signals to the watchers and doctors right now. Unless Wes blocked them.

A screeching sound blares out through the hallway, one long, high pitch sound that lasts about five seconds. It makes my ear drums feel like they're splitting, and I can't help but hold my hands over my ears to try and block it out. The movement sends pain through my right arm again, I can't get it up to my ear, it looks like it's bent the wrong way.

When the sound cuts out, Wes's voice comes from Carlo's bracelet, he's not whispering anymore, he's shouting. I can hardly hear through the ringing the noise still going through my skull, but I can make out the words 'alarm' and 'run' clearly enough. I guess he couldn't block all the signals.

Carlo takes the lead again and we follow behind. It's hard to run now with my beaten body but I know it will be one hundred times worse if I don't get out.

I recognise the corridor we are in now; it was one of the first ones we came through, we are near the exit. I know the next corridor on the right will take us out of the bunker, but Carlo stops just before we reach it.

"There are guards reaching the entrance, they are about to come in and see us. Wes says they have weapons he has never heard of before, but from the transmissions he's listened to it won't be good for us. That is the only exit, we can't get out any other way," Carlo tells us in short sharp words.

We are trapped. They are going to catch us all and probably kill us, there's nowhere we can go.

"Wes says the room just behind us on the left is a storage room, there's no one in there, we can hide and hopefully escape later once the guards are all inside." Carlo doesn't sound very hopeful even as he says the words. The guards will eventually check all of the rooms, he knows as well as we do, we aren't coming out of here alive.

The storage room is better than standing in the hallway waiting for the guards, so we all rush over and bundle inside. Carlo stands in the doorway of the room but doesn't come in.

"Please look after my people. You will find all of the information in my room, where the other hideouts are and anything else that I know. I'm sorry I never told you sooner, but I'm a stubborn old man. You are so brave and intelligent, Talise, I'm glad you found your way into our lives. It's my time to be with Florence now." He reaches down and takes the plate off of his bracelet and hands it to me along with the bracelet Wes made for him, and a small silver key. I give him a questioning look, but he just smiles at me, a warm, genuine smile.

"Be strong and trust your judgement. Goodbye," he says.

Then he closes the door on us all with tears in his eyes.

I'm not too sure what happens next, all I know is that someone grabs me around the waist as I lurch for the door, saying the word 'no' over and over again. He can't go out there, it's suicide. He will never make it back, we can't just leave him, I have to go and get him.

I tap my bracelet and call Wes, he doesn't answer. I try again, and again but nothing happens. I go to ask Scarlett to call him when she shows me a message on her bracelet, 'when I tell you to run to the exit you do it.'

I'm ready to argue back that I will not go, we need to save Carlo, but the sound of multiple running footsteps sounds come from outside of the room and we collectively hold our breath. It sounds like a stampede out there, the guards are running past us like they're chasing something, or someone.

"GO!" Wes shouts through Scarlett's bracelet and I know that I can't go back for Carlo, we have to run now otherwise we will all be caught. Scarlett opens the door and the three of us run as fast as we can down the corridor and towards the exit.

There are no guards in sight. Wes speaks as we run, saying that we need to go to the nearest grouping of houses and take cover, we can't stop running, we have to sprint.

My ribs are screaming at me, the faster I run the harder I breathe, and it's incredibly painful. I have to hold my right arm against my body, keeping it in place with my left, making it harder for me to run fast. But I don't slow my pace, none of us do, we all know what it would mean to be caught.

The cold air hits us hard as we come out of the bunker entrance, but we don't stop. I head straight for the houses, taking lead so our rescued prisoner can follow us.

We make it to the houses, I wind through them, still running, wanting to be buried deep in the cover they provide.

I'm extremely out of breath. Once we are deep in the houses, I take a minute to stop and catch my breath. I still have Carlo's plate and bracelet clutched in my hand. I put the plate in my pocket and manage to slip his bracelet over my wrist, so I have working communication again.

I call Wes and ask him what's happening inside the bunker, but he won't tell me. He says Carlo gave him strict instructions to get us all back safe, he can be saved later. I try to argue with him but he won't let me, and I know he is right, but I don't like it.

We've stopped for too long, Wes tells us that more guards will be coming from the stations soon, our safest option is to get up to Farming. As soon as we are up there, we can run in a straight line to the barn, and we should avoid all of the guards that are heading to the bunker through Sector Two.

So, we run, and we don't stop running until we reach the barn in record time. We run inside and wind our way to the back where the secret entrance is waiting for us. Just as we start moving the feed, I realise there is no one above ground to cover the hatch after us.

I message Wes but he says not to worry about it, he has someone that is going to cover it back over as soon as we go down. I don't like the idea, but we really are out of options now, so we climb down into our bunker.

I never thought I would struggle down this ladder as much as I had the first time I came down it, but it's even harder this time with only one useable arm.

I have to use my chin to hold myself on the rung whilst I quickly fumble for the next rung down with my good arm.

I'm very slow at first but manage to pick up the pace as I make my way down. I'm glad I've been training so hard these past few weeks, I never would have been able to do this before, I didn't have the strength.

As soon as Wes opens the door for us, I rush to the medical room, knowing that's where Enzo will be. I need to see him so he can help me plan a rescue for Carlo. I push open the door and I freeze, disturbed by what I see.

Someone is lying on one of the beds, sleeping, I think. This person is too thin, they look skeletal, like they've been starved.

Their face is covered in bruises, the right eye is swollen and purple, sitting on their sunken face. It looks like someone has hacked away at their hair with a blunt knife, it's all patchy and there are cuts all over their scalp.

Their small amount of facial hair seems to be caked with dried blood. They are covered in a blanket, but their arms are out on either side of their body.

I'm nearly sick when I look down at this person's hands. They are severely burnt, the skin is bright pink and misshapen, but that's not the worst part. This person is missing two fingers on their right hand and the thumb on their left.

What kind of monster could do this much damage to a person, it's horrifying. I stand there and stare at this person, I don't know who it is, but it isn't Enzo.

I spot Raine leaning over the person, starting to clean and dress their hands. I can see how delicate she is being, her hands work with such precision. When she's finished on the hands, she comes over to where I'm standing and motions for me to go outside.

I walk out and she follows me, I turn around and it nearly breaks my heart to see the look on her face. Her eyes are haunted with the horror she's seen. I wrap my uninjured arm around her despite the protest from my body and I stand there, holding her as best I can.

We stand there for several minutes until she pulls away from me and notices my appearance. She seems to panic and asks me what happened.

I don't know what to say about my own mission, I don't even know what's happened to Carlo.

"I'm fine, Raine, but who is that in there? Where's Enzo? Wes told me you rescued him." I look at the door as if I can see through it to the person inside on the bed. I need to see Enzo, I need to know he is okay.

Raine takes my hand in hers and gives it a squeeze.

"He's in the medical room, Talise." She says.

"Oh, I didn't see him. I only saw that other person whose hands you were dressing," I say, confused. I look in her eyes and see the tears there threatening to spill.

"Talise, that is Enzo in the bed. He suffered some really bad injuries; I don't know what they did to him, but he is hurting. He hasn't said a word since we found him, I don't think they fed him the whole time he was in there. He has endured some horrendous torture, physically and mentally, but I think it might help for him to see you." Raine says all of this whilst keeping hold of my hand and looking in my eyes.

I don't understand her words though. That isn't Enzo in there, it can't be him.

The pain and suffering that person has been through, it can't be Enzo. Because if it is him then it's all my fault and I can't handle that level of guilt.

"Talise, where's Carlo?" Rory asks from behind me.

I turn to see that Kimya and Rory have come out to join us. Scarlett and the prisoner are still standing by the front door and I look around for Joseph, but I can't see him. I look over at Rory who has Scamp asleep in his arms.

I don't know what to say, I don't know where Carlo is, I don't really know what happened. Everyone is looking to me for an answer I don't have.

"Carlo's dead." Wes's voice rings out loud around the otherwise silent room.

No one says anything. Kimya lets out a little cry as her hands move to embrace her son, tears stream down his cheeks.

I don't move, I just stare ahead, seeing nothing. He's dead.

He sacrificed himself to save us and now he's gone. His death is on my hands. I had the plan to rescue the prisoner and I made him come on the mission, it's all my fault, all of it.

His last words ring in my head. I didn't think Carlo even liked me, yet he said he was so happy I was in his life. I'm so confused.

Ajax walks off to the training room and within seconds you can hear the thump of repeated punching on the bag.

I stand there, frozen, as I remember what Carlo said. 'It's my time to be with Florence.' I didn't understand at the time what he meant, but now I realise, it's the name from the file, Florence Morella, Carlo's wife.

Chapter Fifteen

I wake up in pain.

My ribs, arm, head, eye, legs, muscles, just about everything hurts. As the fog starts to clear from my mind, I remember why I feel like this, and I realise I deserve it. Carlo died because of me.

Raine is lying next to me in bed, she's sound asleep. I look at her face for a few minutes, taking in her features and admiring her. I won't be selfish and wake her for pain relief, I'll let her sleep now and ask later when she's up. Instead, I get up and try to distract myself.

Ajax is at the punching bag again and likely wants to be alone, so I leave him to it. Joseph and the rescued prisoner are sleeping, and I don't know where Rory is. I imagine Scamp will be with Rory and they'll be with Kimya somewhere, probably grieving.

None of us have really spoken to one another since the news about Carlo last night. Everyone has been keeping to themselves, dealing with it in their own way. After Wes announced it, we all drifted off to separate rooms to grieve alone.

I've yet to go back to the medical room to see Enzo, which I'm feeling incredibly guilty about.

I go to Wes's work room. I know he would have been up all night looking through files, trying to find any information to help us out of this situation.

I think I need the distraction as well.

I can't bring myself to go into Carlo's room yet. Even though he told me that I should look at it all, I just can't face it, not when it's my fault he died.

Wes is sitting at a table at the back of the room fiddling with the bracelets he made for us, I guess he's fixing my faulty one. I can see why the others admire him so much, he is the smartest person I've ever met and an impeccable inventor.

Wes stops working and looks to the ceiling with a deep sigh. I knock on the already open door, but he doesn't turn to me.

"Wes, can I ask you something?" I ask from the doorway.

"They announced it this morning," he says, still staring at the ceiling.

"His death. You can read the report if you want, I found one on the computer. As none of us have the daily news reports on our bracelets, I've been keeping up to date with them here." He looks to the computer and then to me, indicating that I should look.

"Old age, they said. Natural causes." He drops a piece of metal on the table and I don't say anything. I feel he is talking at me right now; he needs to say it but doesn't need a response.

"You wanted to ask me something?" He says without looking at me.

I decide it's best not to mention what he just said, I'll look at the report later, maybe in a couple of days when I can bare to look at the lies they've written.

"I was just wondering how you learnt so much about, well, everything. The hacking, your inventions, it's all so incredible, and I don't really know anything about you and how you came to be here. I was hoping you would tell me?" I hope by asking him this it will take both of our minds off of what happened last night, even if just for a minute.

He turns to me then and points to one of the chairs across from him, so I take a seat.   He runs his hands through his messy, blonde hair, and over the recently grown stubble on his chin. Even when he looks exhausted and defeated, Wes is still quite handsome.

"We were born in Sector Two. Technically I am one minute older than Scarlett, though she would deny it if you asked her. We may be twins, but we couldn't be more different if we tried.

"On my sixth I would always try to go to the metal finders and binders, but they never let me in. They also wouldn't let me work with the production of the bracelets, so I mainly went to the scientists, going to a different lab every week. The thing about me is that I always want to learn more. School wasn't enough for me, I wasn't using enough of my brain. I needed more knowledge.

"I'd always be reading books on how to build things, how metals and magnetics worked, and anything on computers I could find. I knew that computers would have all of the knowledge I needed, and I wanted to learn it all, so I started practising hacking. I would look for coding, ways to get into a device undetected. There was always something new to learn.

"On our 18th birthday, I was assigned to work with the scientists in Sector Two, and Scarlett was assigned to be a guard in Sector Three. We both excelled in our new jobs within the first week. You've seen how great Scarlett is at fighting, so it wasn't a surprise that she was chosen to work with the Lieutenant after only two weeks of service.

"The work with the scientists was mediocre, it wasn't challenging, and I grew bored quickly. They didn't know what to do with me, so they put me on updating reports on the computers just so I was out of their way. That was a mistake, I was put in a room full of computers with my curiosity always getting the better of me.

"I was looking through files and thought I'd look up how the work was going on testing the rest of the Earth outside of 'The Island,' but I found nothing. The folder that was meant for updates was empty, not a single person had reported any findings, because no one had gone to look.

"Turns out they have a room buried deep in the bunker where they have an endless supply of poisoned soil. That's what they are running the tests on, they get the soil and take it to the lab every so often, claiming it was obtained from outside. So, when it's checked over by scientists, everyone believes the outside world is still damaged.

"I didn't understand why they weren't giving us real findings and I couldn't find the reason behind it either. They had a folder with dates saying when scientists went out to obtain the samples, but they didn't match up with any other documents. I erased my internal footprint and I left the lab. No one even noticed I had left early; I think I was just an annoyance to them. The next day was my sixth so I went to the watchers, I knew I needed to hack their systems next."

He pauses for a moment and takes a sip of water.

"That's where I found out about them listening to us constantly. The watchers sat me at a computer and told me to look out for spikes in someone's adrenaline which could indicate an injury. They left me to it and I found a way into their system, I downloaded all of the information and some of their software onto a memory stick.

"I got through all of their blockers and through all of the digital walls they put up. They have a device they created to listen for key words that could relate to an uprising or defiance towards the leaders. There are a whole team dedicated to listening to people's daily lives through their bracelets without their knowledge.

"Anyway, I erased my footprint again and finished the work for the day, when I went home, I looked through the rest of the information. I found confirmation that they could track us, and I learnt why we would die if we took the bracelets off. I had no other option, I had to create something to block the signals from the bracelet to the watchers. I stayed up all night creating the plates you all use now. I made three in total that night, I didn't sleep. I was ready to go and get Scarlett when guards burst into my home and knocked me out.

"I woke up in a cage. I was left there for three days before someone came to take me in for questioning. You should know that when you are in the cage and the door is closed, the engineers have designed it so that you are cut off from all communication on your bracelet. They are enabled once you leave, but until then, you have nothing, only the time and date.

"I would usually talk to Scarlett every day via the bracelets, even if it was just a quick hello. But it had been three days and she hadn't been able to contact me. They brought her into the room when I was questioned. They told her I had broken into the system and stolen information I didn't have the authority to have. She had to say her goodbyes to me as I was a terrorist, and my actions had endangered the lives of everyone on 'The Island.' I still don't know how they found out what I did."

They were going to kill him for hacking the system. The lengths they go to in order to hide what they are really doing can't continue.

"Scarlett gave me a hug and said she loved me. Told me how she had been to my house to look for me but couldn't find me anywhere, and that I was still as messy as ever, which was a blatant lie. I knew then that she had found what I had found, she'd read the files, found the plates, she knew. We couldn't risk saying anything more as we knew they would be watching and listening to us. I told her I was sorry, and then she left the room, and they took me back to the cage.

"Scarlett came to get me that night. She had flirted with the idiot guard that had the key to my cage. She opened the door, and just held the plates in her hand, she didn't quite know what they were for. I put them on the faces of our bracelets, and I hoped they would work, having not yet tested them. We didn't wait around, we ran. I told her we needed to go to Farming, I knew it would be safe.

"We ran into a few guards on the way, but Scarlett took them out easily enough, we all know I'd be useless in a fight."

Wes has joined very few training sessions with us, and he can't even land a punch.

"We reached the barn, and Carlo was there, waiting. I put a plate on his bracelet and told him everything I had learnt. He said he would hide us, so he brought us down here and it became our home. I created the beacon blockers and placed them around the bunker, so whoever is down here is always hidden from the system without having to have a plate on.

"That was three years ago, we were the first people to live down here. It was already kitted out and fully stocked, Carlo had a lot of materials for me to work with. We could tell he'd been preparing for something like this. Carlo knew before anyone else; I don't know how, he just knew."

We sit in silence for a few minutes, both deep in thought, Wes doesn't say another word. I feel a pang of sympathy for Wes and Scarlett, he didn't mention anything about his parents, I assume they are still alive. I know the pain of having to leave your family behind.

"Wes, when Scarlett rescued you from the cage, how did you know to come here, to Carlo?" I ask after what I deem to be a long enough silence.

"As you probably figured out, I'm not all too great with conversations. This is easy, I'm telling you facts, but when it comes to the present, I struggle with the right things to say in a social scenario. My parents thought it would be good to come to Sector One on my sixth sometimes, my dad actually works up there, right above us. They thought it would help me being in that kind of environment. I met Carlo when I was here, I was hiding out in the barn because I didn't like being outside all day. He was always kind to me; he would tell my dad I was helping him so I could stay in the barn away from all of the people. He told me I would always have a safe place here with him. It was a risk, anything could have happened, but it was the only place that I could think of as safe," he says and stares at the wall.

I walk over to give him a hug, but as soon as I get close his whole body clenches up and he seems to cower in on himself.

It's my fault he's lost Carlo, the man who had saved him and Scarlett. He saved all of us and now he's gone.

I feel so guilty.

"Talise, you should go and see Enzo," he says which takes me by surprise. Now it's my turn to stare at something, the floor.

"I'm scared," I whisper.

"Well, I don't why, and I won't pretend to understand it either, but he has been asking for you. I think it would be good for his welfare if you went to him. I'm not sure how, but Raine suggested if we all see Enzo separately it would help him heal."

I look up at Wes. I know he's right, but I'm scared because it's my fault Enzo is in there. All of the bad things that are happening are my fault, and I can't handle the guilt of it all.

"Scarlett is there with him now, so you won't be alone." I think he wants his sister to have some support from me, it's not like Wes to get involved in these sorts of things usually.

We all need each other right now; I can't hide from it any longer. I need to own up to what I'm responsible for and be there for my family. I stand and offer a small smile for Wes before I leave and head to the medical room.

I stand outside of the medical room for at least ten minutes building up the courage to open the door and go inside. I know I need to; I just can't make my body move. I've never been so scared.

I take a deep breath and force myself to move. I need to forget about myself, I need to do this for Enzo, he needs me to be strong. I gently push the door open, hoping to go unnoticed.

The room is empty other than the one occupied bed with the stranger in. Scarlett is sitting in a chair at the side of it, holding a part of the person's arm in her hands.

I stand there, staring at them. The person looks no different to when I first came in here.

Scarlett looks up and sees me standing there. I'm not too sure what expression is on my face, but it causes her to get up and walk over to me.

I look at her face as she stands before me, gesturing to step back out of the room, closing the door behind us. I do so almost too eagerly, then instantly hate myself for being happy to leave the room.

She looks so tired; I don't think she slept last night. I imagine she has been sat at Enzo's bedside constantly. Her eyes don't show any signs of tears, she is so strong, and I admire her for that. I wish I could be as strong as her.

"Talise, you know it's still Enzo in there, don't you?" She asks me gently, but I can't say anything. I don't know what to say.

"He's still the same person. You should talk to him; he's asked where you are. He really cares for you, Talise." She almost looks sad as she says that, and that's when I finally realise why she had disliked me when I first came here. She thinks Enzo fancies me.

"You love him, don't you?" I ask and she smiles, looking at the door as if she can see him through it.

"From the moment I met him. And I'll never stop loving him, regardless of whether or not he wants me. No matter what he looks like, I'll love him for the person he is," she says as a single tear slips down her cheek.

I take a risk and step forward, wrapping her in a hug, which she awkwardly returns. It's brief, almost instantly she pulls away and tells me to go in there and face him before she walks away.

I look at the door, it's time to go in there now, he's alone and I should be there for him. I open the door and step inside of the room, my eyes immediately lock with the person in the bed and they smile at me.

"I was wondering when you would come to see me, I've missed you." It's Enzo's voice that speaks from the bed. And now I know, this is Enzo, beaten and hurt, it really is him.

I burst into tears and collapse in the chair next to him, my head resting on the edge of his bed. And for the second time today I repeat the words 'I'm sorry' over and over because his suffering is all my fault. And he

lays there, battered and broken, whispering that it's
okay, which only makes me cry harder and longer.

∞

I come out of the medical room and shut the door
behind me, leaning on it and taking a deep breath. It
sends pain to my ribs, but I push the pain out of my
mind, it's nothing compared to what Enzo went through.

I spent two hours talking to him in there. I
managed to stop crying after a while once I realised how
selfish it is of me when he has suffered so much. Raine
popped in briefly to give us both pain relief, but then she
left us alone again. Enzo hasn't told me what they did to
him, and I didn't ask, I'm terrified of the answer.

Scarlett had told him about Carlo's death and
stayed with him to keep an eye on him. I was grateful for
this, as it also meant that Raine spent those nights
sleeping by my side, and I really needed her there.

Scarlett is now sitting with Enzo again; I don't
think she could stay away for too long. She came in with
some food for Enzo, I thought I would leave them to it as
I need to see the rescued prisoner and find out what I can
anyway.

Enzo made me promise to go back and see him
later this evening, which I agreed to easily. Though I'm
still struggling to come to terms with what's happened to
him, it helped to talk to him.

I know I can be strong for him now. But it's hard,
and the guilt eats away at me.

I make my way to the room the rescued prisoner
is in and I'm relieved but cautious to see he is in there,

sitting on the bed and staring at the wall. I knock on the wall as there is no door to this room, he looks up at me, a small smile appearing on his face though his eyes remain sad.

"Can I come in?" I ask.

"Please do. I was hoping to talk to you, but I thought I would be respectful and wait for you to come to me. I know you are all grieving for the man that died rescuing me. I am sorry for that, although grateful you helped me," he replies, sounding sincere.

I can't look into his eyes when I reply so I make my way over to the empty chair and take a seat as I talk.

"Thank you, I appreciate that. But I do have some questions for you, I'm sure you have some for me as well." I look up at him now that I'm seated.

"My name is Cray Junior, named after my father. Joseph tells me your name is Talise. I was born in Sector One, and I escaped this place when I was 18, before I got the bracelet."

"Why did you leave? And how did you escape? When were you captured by the leaders?"

"That's a lot of questions and I will answer them all. Can I ask first though, do you know if my mother is still alive? Her name is Karon Mytis. Can we find out? She should be 86 now."

"Yes, she is alive." I'm surprised I know this, but I'm certain Karon Mytis is friends with my grandma, she lives at the elder's home.

The happiness that radiates from him is heart-warming. He has gone so many years without his family, he must be desperate to see them. I hope I get to see my parents again soon.

"Okay then, Talise, let's go and see my mother," he says and jumps up, rubbing his hands together, a grin plastered over his face.

"Cray, it's not that easy. There are guards all over the place looking for you and me. I don't know if we would make it." It's tough saying these words, knowing how painful this is for him. But I don't know if I can risk it.

He looks a little deflated and sits down on the bed again, looking at the floor. He seems to decide on something as his head snaps up and he looks me straight in the eyes.

"Please, Talise, take me to see my mother."

He is desperate and I understand why. It's been weeks since I saw my own parents and I'd give anything to see them right now.
I know I have to help him, but I need information from him first. Especially if the worst happens and either one of us get caught.

There will be many risks taking him, but I can't deny him this. It would be too cruel.

"Okay. I can take you to her, we can't go out until it's dark. So that gives us some time for you to tell me what happened to you, how you got out and then captured. I need to know about 'the others,'" I tell him sternly, standing my ground.

He eyes me for a long moment, not giving away anything, then he breaks into a grin.

"You are definitely the daughter of my best friend, stern and stubborn just like her." I'm thrown off by this, but before I can ask what he means he starts to answer my questions.

"'The others,' as you call them, are survivors. 3862 of them landed on 'The Island' when everyone else did, but they landed further north. The 'top of The Island,' as they say, and there was nothing around for them. They grouped together and scouted out the surrounding area. There wasn't enough space on the ships for everyone to sleep, so they all started looking for resources. They didn't know why they were here, what happened to all of the other ships, where was the safe place they were promised?

"Something they discovered early on was that the water here is safe, someone volunteered to test it. When they didn't die, they became the leader of the group. The person willing to die for everyone seemed like the smartest choice. The leader took charge, moved them all closer inland where they found buildings, all deserted but still standing."

"One of the search parties they organised came back with a woman, her wrists bound, confusion all over her face. She spoke with the leader and told of how there are thousands of survivors south of 'The Island,' right at the bottom, living behind the tallest walls you've ever seen.

"The escaped woman was questioned by the leader. She told them that she was a scientist who was working for the leaders behind the walls. But once she learnt their plans, and what they were going to do to their people, she had to leave. She couldn't be part of it, so she ran. She told the leader of the plans from within the walls, and everything that had happened since the evacuations.

"They welcomed the woman. She became part of the community, and worked alongside our leader, giving all of the knowledge on how they could best protect themselves. The community was spread out, taking up houses that were close to the walls but far away enough to be hidden. Patrols began along the walls day and night, to keep the people safe. Now it's our main work. Protecting the population from the leaders within the walls.

"After the scientist gave the information and they relocated the people to surround the walls, the leader realised there needed to be someone in charge at each section. They created a council, there were, and still are, five members.

"A few years after the scientist escaped, there was another escape from within the walls. They thought this person came for safety from your leaders, but they were wrong. They killed twelve people before anyone managed to stop them.

"Now anyone coming out from behind those walls we are ordered to kill. We must never hesitate, we never ask questions. We shoot before anything can happen, to keep our people safe. And that's how they've survived. We are planning ways to help everyone in the walls and trying to implement them, but we haven't succeeded. There aren't enough people or the technology, not even now, after all these years."

I'm shocked at how bluntly he spoke about killing people coming from inside the walls. How could they shoot us without speaking to us first? It's so cold.

I have so many questions, his story only gave me more to ask. Mainly I need to know about the plan that the leaders have for us all, what did the scientist say that could be so bad?

"What are the plans for us?" I ask tentatively.

"I cannot say, Talise, I only told you my story because it was part of the deal to see my mother. I cannot tell you anything else," he replies.

"My parents are up there. Will you not help me save them? I know you can understand the importance of that."

"I do, but I'm afraid it's too late, we can't save them. If the plan is going as we believe, then there are not many people left within the walls that we can save."

"But there are a multitude of people here, how can you say that?" I demand.

"One day you will understand. But I cannot tell you, it is not my place. Now please, I know it's frustrating, but can you put it aside and take me to my mother?"

I think on his words and I refuse to accept that my parents are beyond saving, it doesn't make any sense. We didn't find anything on the files that would risk the lives of everyone above us, otherwise we would have planned a way to stop it already.

"Okay, just a few more questions. How were you captured?" I ask.

"I was too close to the wall for too long."

"Why were you close to the wall?"

"I can't say."

"How long have you been held prisoner by our leaders?"

"Four days."

"Would anyone come to rescue you?"

"No."

His answers puzzle me. He was so open earlier and gave so much, but now he's cagey. He was only in the cell for four days, he looks well, especially compared to Enzo. Something isn't right here, but I can't place it.

"I know 'the others' shoot first. I heard our leader discussing it, that's why I'm hiding down here. They want me dead because I know about you, I know about 'the others.' So, I need your help as well. If I can get us out of these walls and on to the other side, I need you to make sure we don't get shot by 'the others' first, by your people," I say.

"Talise, I don't know if that would work, they may think I've been compromised and kill me and anyone with me as a safety precaution."

"You've already managed to escape these walls once without somehow getting murdered instantly like everyone else. So surely, going back out there when you are part of the community will be easy. They are your people after all, your family." I stare him straight in the eyes, waiting for the next challenge.

I don't know what it is, but something shifts behind his eyes, he never breaks eye contact and replies.

"Okay. If you just take me to my mother, then we can escape. You get us out of the walls, and I will *try* and hold off the immediate shooting." He must realise it's a death sentence if he stays here, he's better off facing his own people. They won't shoot him; I know they won't. The leaders captured him for a reason, and I don't think it was because he was too close to the wall.

Seeing how they treated Enzo in those two weeks and seeing how Cray came out untouched rang an instant alarm for me. He isn't just one of 'the others,' he has a purpose and I'm going to use it to our advantage.

"Deal," I say and hold out my hand to shake on it. As he grabs my hand and shakes it, I lean in and whisper to him.

"I know we won't be shot when we leave, Cray, your people would never shoot you, you are one of their leaders after all." And with that I drop his hand and leave the room, but not before I see the alarm in his eyes.

He didn't expect me to figure that part out. Good.

Chapter Sixteen

I don't know if I can trust Cray.

I want to, but something is stopping me. The way he carries himself and speaks, he acts like he's in charge, regardless of him having been captured.

But he isn't daunting like Mr Ritton, there's just something there, something off. I will figure it out, me and my questions will get to the bottom of it.

For now, I must stick to the deal. I need to take him to see his mother.

I figure the best person to give me advice about getting in and out of the elder's home would be the person that has worked there.

Surprisingly, Scarlett isn't in the medical room when I get there, Enzo is in there by himself. He seems to be awake, so I go in and sit myself in the chair next to his bed, managing to keep my nausea at bay if I keep my eyes off of his hands.

Thankfully, someone has put a woollen hat on his head, I imagine it was to keep him warm, but it helps me a great deal not being able to see all of his injuries, and I know I'm weak for that.

"You're back soon, you've only been gone for an hour." Enzo says as he looks at me and smiles. I realise he must be counting the minutes in here while he's alone, and guilt washes through me again, I try to fight it back and plaster a smile on my face.

"I knew you'd be missing me already, so I thought I'd pop back in," I laugh.

"As much as that is true, that's not why you are in here right now. So, what is it?"

"Damn you, Enzo Cardelous, you know me well. I came here looking for Raine, I'd forgotten you were even here," I say with a laugh and before I can move out of the way, he's thrown his empty cup at me, but he's laughing too.

He has to lower his arm back down slowly and I can see the pain in his eyes from the movement, it must have really hurt him to throw that cup. I give him a minute to settle back down and don't say anything.

"Talise, you came in here to ask me something, so you might as well do that now before I throw the plate at you, and that won't bounce off." He grins at me, but his smile doesn't reach his eyes, it hasn't since we rescued him.

"Okay, I don't know how much you know about when Raine and Ajax rescued you, but we also rescued a prisoner from within the bunker." He doesn't seem surprised, I guess Scarlett has already told him.

"The man we rescued is called Cray, he told me that 'the others' ship landed on the northern part of 'The Island,' right at the top. They found a scientist that had escaped our walls who told them of some awful plans the leaders had for us all. She couldn't be part of it, that's why she left, and 'the others' welcomed her with open arms. They all have orders to kill anyone that comes out of our walls, I don't know why exactly, but they do. They have us surrounded and watched every hour of every day, there are thousands of them out there. He said that one of our people killed twelve of theirs, and that's why they are so careful, but something doesn't add up.

"Cray has agreed to help us escape. When we get on the other side of those walls, with him in our group, they shouldn't shoot us. He is one of them, we should be safe. But he wants to see his mother first, just one last time, her name is Karon Mytis. I cannot deny him that, especially as it's his only condition to help us." I finish and look in Enzo's eyes, I wait for him to speak before I say anything further.

"So, you're here because you want to know the best way to get into the elder's home, right? That is where Karon is, isn't it?" He asks, almost angrily.

"That's right, I need to know what time would be best and where she will be. I'll take him there, let him see her, then we will come back here to plan our escape, for all of us," I say, and reach out to put my hand on his arm. I don't want to take his hand due to how much pain that would cause him. It should be Scarlett holding his hand, not me.

"Talise, do you know why I cared so much about you and your life from the moment we properly met?" His question throws me off, I wasn't expecting that at all.

"Erm, because you're a good person?"

"No. It's because you remind me of my sister. I'm sure Raine told you that she died in the same accident that killed her parents." I nod at this, not wanting to say anything.

"I thought so, and I don't mind her telling you. She was my younger sister, she was only there because it was her sixth, and she wanted to spend the day with her friend. It was my sixth too, I could have been there, I could have saved her. But I wasn't and I couldn't.

"Then I started seeing you when you visited your Grandmother, and it was like seeing her all over again. That's why I wanted to help you so badly, why I can't let you die or be in danger. That's why I didn't tell them anything when they tortured me. I couldn't save my sister, but I can save you." He chokes up at the last part and he has tears silently streaming down his bruised face.

I'm not too sure what to say, I never realised he felt that way. I just thought he was a decent person who wanted to help a scared girl. And now I know why he didn't tell them anything when they mutilated him, whilst they did unthinkable things to such a kind person. Because of me, because he wanted to protect me.

"Enzo, it's not your fault she's dead. Please don't blame yourself for the misfortune of a work accident. If you were there, you probably would have died as well," I say gently.

"You can't honestly still believe it was an accident, Talise. Not after everything we've learnt about the leaders. That explosion was no accident. They murdered those people."

I'm surprised by his words, but they do make sense. Knowing everything the leaders have done, it does make me wonder. But why, what reason could they possibly have for killing those people?

This isn't the time to figure it out though. I have somewhere I need to be, and Enzo needs to help me get there.

"Enzo, I'm sorry your sister died and I'm sorry they tortured you because of me. I will never forgive myself for that. But if I don't take Cray up there, we won't be able to escape. And no matter how good it is down here, we can't live here for the rest of our lives, we need to get out. We need to stop the leaders from hurting any more people like your sister.

"I have to take him tonight. Then I can plan an escape for all of us, they'll never be able to touch you again. Please Enzo."

He doesn't look at me, just keeps his head down, crying silently.

"Be there for 9pm. There will only be two staff on until 9:15," he says, then closes his eyes with tears still falling.

I'm sad that he's mad at me but I'm also a little relieved. He should be mad at me, it's my fault he's in that bed right now, I deserve his anger.

I get up to leave and I hope one day he will forgive me. Just as I reach the door, I hear his voice from behind me.

"If you see a guard, or anyone, anyone at all, you run Talise. You run faster than you ever have. I ran, but they caught me. They have a new weapon, it's like a whip but it stretches out much farther, it wraps around your ankles, tight. Then the guards can pull you to the floor and you can't get your feet out, only a button on the handle releases you. Then they use it as a whip once you're captured. So, you run, okay?"

"I'll run. I promise. Faster than ever," I say and smile at him before pushing open the door.

"Talise!" He shouts before I'm out of the room. I turn back to face him.

"Yeah?"

"There's one more thing I should tell you. Before they captured me, I figured something out at the elder's home." He looks down at his body and hesitates.

"What was it?" I ask wearily.

"I was looking into the deaths of a few elders, I was suspicious because the few that had died, to me, weren't sick enough. I contacted Wes and he did some digging and read some messages.

"Talise, some of the guards are tasked with killing the elderly. The ones that can't help in any way, not even looking after the babies or toddlers. Apparently, they see them as a waste of resources, so they inject them with a drug that sends them to sleep, for good. It appears as if they go peacefully and naturally in their sleep." Tears are still spilling from his eyes. These are people he cares for and there are guards killing them. It's outrageous. But that means…

"Why are you telling me this now?"

"I think you know, Talise."

"You're saying Cray's mother might already be dead. This whole trip could be wasted, and we may get caught for nothing."

"Yes, but it's not just that, Talise. Think about it, they kill the elderly that can't help. Your Grandmother is losing her memory rapidly, there is no cure for her. There is nothing she can do to help 'The Island;' do you see what I'm getting at here?" He half asks because he knows I know.

Anger burns through me, and fear. So much fear. I have to save my grandma too, she needs me. This mission just got a lot more complicated.

I don't say anything to Enzo, I give him a curt nod and turn to walk out of the room.

∞

I nearly hit Joseph in the face with the door.

Lucky for me he steps back before the door can hit him and manages to avoid a nosebleed for himself. I feel silent tears rolling down my cheeks from what Enzo said, the thought of them whipping him crushes me. And the idea that my grandma might get murdered soon is unthinkable. These actions are unjustifiable.

Joseph puts his arm around me and asks if I'm free for a chat. I nod and let him pull me along. I know I should go to Carlo's room, but I've got some time before I have to leave with Cray, so I enjoy the detour and the comfort of Joseph.

We go to an empty room and take a seat. I manage to compose myself and stop the tears, looking up to Joseph.

I wonder what he wants to talk about, I feel like he wanted to talk to me before he saw the tears. There could be a number of things though, our list of discoveries and challenges seems to be growing daily.

We both sit silently for a few minutes.
I tell Joseph that I'm fine and ask what he wants to talk to me about.

"I wanted to tell you the full story about my father," he says.

"You don't have to, Joseph. I trust you, and it's not your fault that man is your father."

"But I do have to tell you, Talise, because it concerns you." This throws me off. I look at him questioningly and decide to sit back and let him talk.

"I was in love with a man when I was younger, and he loved me back. I still love him now. We knew we had to hide our relationship from everyone. Somehow, my father found out about us when I turned 18. I guess now at least I've figured out it would have been because of the bracelet, of course he would have me listened to and watched closely at all times."

"My father took away my lover, Daniel, and he had him killed."

He takes pause to wipe the tear that's threatening to spill over his eye, and he clasps his hands together to stop the shaking. I doubt he's ever told anyone this before.

"My father left me in the cage for two weeks. I nearly died; it was torture. But nothing compared to the pain of losing Daniel. When my father let me out again he told me that he would spare my life because I am his son, but that was all. He wanted nothing more to do with me, I was a disgrace.

"The other leaders wouldn't allow me to move Sectors and have a home to myself as I was unmarried, and my job was in Breeding. So, much to my father's distaste, and mine, I had to stay living in Sector Three until I married. Of course, I would have to marry a woman, anything else is forbidden.

"You need to know this because it is still the case. If they cannot force people to marry the opposite sex and reproduce then they have them killed. I was spared because my father has the smallest part of humanity left in him, and he couldn't have me killed. But I've had to suffer every day because of it. Sometimes I wish he would have killed me."

I can't believe his words, that Joseph could even wish his life away pains me deeply.

"No, Joseph, never say that. Please don't ever wish you were dead, I'm happy you are alive, you are my family. We can escape this place together. We can both be who we are and love who we want, I will save you from him." My words are true, I must save him, and everyone else.

"Talise, it's okay. I don't want to die, not now when there is so much hope for us. I know you can do it; I believe in you. I just wish Daniel's life could have been spared, I wish he could be here with us right now. I miss him every day. But you need to know, you need to know it will be hard for you and Raine out there."

"Thank you, Joseph. But it's already hard for me out there. If they find me, I'm dead regardless of who I love. That's why we must escape, to build a new life outside of these walls where we are free. I have hope in the future, and it's what gets me through the days," I say and take his hand in mine, giving it a squeeze. He has been so brave and suffered so much pain that I wish I could take away.

I know there could be danger outside of the walls, we don't know what their rules are. We don't even know if it's safer than here. But right now, I might have a chance of survival out of these walls. I don't have a single hope within them.

Joseph leans over and wraps me in a long, silent hug. I hold on to him, it helps me think of home. After a few minutes he pulls away from me and offers me a half-cocked grin.

"Isn't it about time you did whatever mission you are trying to plan already?"

"How did you know I was planning something?" I ask, bewildered.

"Oh please. I think I've known you long enough to know when you're up to something. Whatever it is you are doing, be safe, little sister." He plants a kiss on the top of my head and walks out of the room.

I sit there for a few minutes thinking over what he told me.

I think about the girl Raine had first kissed, how she had ignored her the next day, and that she is now married to a man and expecting a baby. I guess some people can hide their true selves. If it was my life on the line, I wonder, would I deny my feelings in order to survive, or would I have died up there regardless?

I can't think of it too much because I have to tackle one last battle before I leave for the elder's home in a couple of hours. I must go to Carlo's room.

Even though it's not been that long since Carlo died, his room feels oddly cold, as if no one has been in here for weeks. I think a small part of that is true though, Carlo never slept down here at night, he couldn't risk being off the radar for so long, or even being seen in the barn overnight.

His bed is perfectly made, I wonder if it has ever been slept in. I know that no one else has come into this room yet, I am the first. I have to push the guilt I have into the depths of my mind, so I can focus on my task at hand.

I go over to the table in the centre of the small room and start looking through the scattered pieces of paper. I'm not even sure what it is I'm looking for, I'm simply just looking, because he wanted me to.

I spend about an hour in Carlo's room reading through the papers on his desk. Most of it is things I'm already aware of, 'the others,' suspicions about their life, what the leaders are doing to people that find out about them.

There are various folders lined up next to the wall, about twelve altogether. I make a note to myself to come back and read those tomorrow, there isn't enough time now to get through them.

I come across what I think in the back of my mind I was searching for, the other hideouts. Carlo had never told us anything about other people he was in touch with. There isn't just one bunker, there are five.

The details are written in some sort of code that I can't understand, but I have a feeling Wes will be able to figure it out soon enough. I pocket the sheets and pile up the rest of the papers on the table, leaving it neater than when I came in.

I head to Wes's work room and I'm unsurprised to see him in there, sitting at his desk, looking at the computer and tapping away at the keys.

"Hey, Wes, I've found some information about another four hidden bunkers, I was wondering if you would take a look at them and find out where they are?" I ask as I hold out the papers, he moves to take them, breaking his intense stare at the computer.

"How do you know they are secret hideouts?" He asks, not even looking up at me but already studying the paper.

"Don't worry, I see why. It's coded but you can make out the basic letters. I'll figure it out, give me an hour or two." He still doesn't look at me when he talks.

"Wes, I'm going above ground with the prisoner we rescued, I need to take him to see his mother. Can I have two of your bracelets? And would you mind just keeping an eye on the area for any extra guards for me, just as a precaution?" As I speak Wes stops reading the paper and freezes, he stands there staring ahead for at least sixty seconds.

"I don't think you should go, Talise. Since our last rescue mission, the leaders have implemented some new rules. There is a 9pm curfew. No one is allowed to be out after 9pm other than the leaders and guards. If you are, you are immediately put in the cage for one week. People are only allowed to leave their homes to go to work, all social aspects have been cut off. Children aren't even allowed to leave school; they have to wait for a parent to collect them and take them home. Security is incredibly strict out there; you won't be safe.

"But I'd wager a 98% chance that you are going to go regardless. So, yes you can take two bracelets and I will keep watch for you. Remember it's a ten hour battery life from when you turn them on, but you should be back here in four if you are going to the elder's home." He says in his usual emotionless tone.

I know Wes is looking at this statistically, and my chances of getting back have just dropped, but I need to get us out of here. To get us outside and safe from these walls.

"Thank you, Wes, I appreciate it. Are the bracelets ready now?"

"Yes, go ahead and take two from the table. I'll start on this map, tell me just before you leave so I can get in the system and have my eyes on everything before you get out of the hatch. I'll get Pete to move the feed just in time for you to get out, but then you have to cover it back over yourself." He's already looking back at the coded paper I gave him and making notes.

I leave the room and head to get a bag ready. I pop my head into Cray's room and tell him to be ready by 8pm, that's when we'll leave. I know he has the strength to jog the whole time so I'm positive we can get to the elder's home by 9pm. I would rather be there a few minutes late than be caught waiting around.

I pack a bag with some water and medical supplies, just in case. I find Raine and spend ten minutes sitting with her in silence, just holding her. I check the time on the wall and see it's 7:58pm. Time to say goodbye and tell Wes I'm heading out.

"I'll be back in time for bed, I promise," I say as I lean up and plant a delicate kiss on her lips.

"That will be a very late bedtime, but okay. Be safe and careful. Make sure you come back to me please." I can hear the worry in her voice.

"I'll be back in one piece, and you'll get me all to yourself again." I grin and stand up, grabbing my bag from the floor and heading toward the door, I stand in the doorway and turn back to look at her.

"Amore proibito," I whisper and leave the room.

Chapter Seventeen

It's 8:01pm and I'm heading out of the door with Cray.

I decided it best not to tell anyone about my grandma. I will take Cray in to see his mother, and five minutes before we have to leave, we will get my grandma. I'm hoping he will carry her for me, if not, I will have to manage.

Cray hasn't said anything about my accusation of him being a leader out of the walls, I guess that confirms the truth of it. I still don't trust him, but I need him.

Just as Wes said it would, the feed has been moved off of the hatch, so we can get out easily enough. I go first, when I come out in the barn I look around, I'm unsurprised to see that there isn't anyone here. I wonder if I will ever meet this 'Pete' that helps us, maybe it's safer that I don't.

As soon as Cray is up and out of the hatch, I immediately start moving the sacks of feed from against the wall to cover the hatch again. Within seconds he follows suit, and we have the hatch covered in minutes.

We weave between chicken coops and tools towards the entrance of the barn. We stay low to the ground the whole while, keeping ourselves as hidden as possible, though it is quite unnecessary, there is no one here.

We get to the door and I turn to Cray and signal for him to wait, he looks at me bewildered. I stare at him confused for a minute, maybe he doesn't know how to signal.

As there's no one around I just whisper to him to wait, and I move forward to poke my head out of the barn.

I look outside and absorb the surroundings. It is dark outside but not pitch black, so I still have good visibility. It takes me a moment to take in what I'm seeing; how different our Island is from what I saw days ago.

It looks deserted out here, I can't see a single person anywhere. At this time there would usually be people walking around, kids playing, people laughing and having fun. But there isn't a person in sight.

Wes was right with what he said about the curfew and that no one would be outside, everyone wanting to get home in time. I wonder if people are scared and confused about what's happening, I would be if I was them. I'm scared myself, but for a whole other number of reasons.

It will take us over an hour to get to the elder's home, if we keep a fast pace then we can get there quicker, giving us more time with Cray's mother. I go to signal him and remember he won't understand, so instead I just wave him over.

"Ready for a run?" I whisper.

"Let's go," he says and smiles at me, I know how eager he must be to see his mother.

I take the lead and step out of the barn. I head diagonally towards the wall, weaving in-between the few obstacles separating us.

I know that the wall is where we can get our best cover and it's a direct line towards the elder's home. If we get separated or something happens, at least Cray can figure his way back to the barn.

We press ourselves flat against the wall and wait, covered in darkness. I scan all around me, I still can't see anyone in sight, no workers or guards. I imagine we will see some guards the further into Sector Two we go, as that's the bigger Sector. I hope we don't see any.

I start walking towards Sector Two, slowly at first, one hand on the wall, then I pick up my pace. I walk faster, then start into a light jog. I can hear Cray behind me, so I don't turn around to check on him.

I suck the cold night air into my lungs as I start to run. A quick glance behind me tells me Cray is right there, matching my pace. My ribs still hurt, but it's manageable. I can block out the pain.

I still can't see anyone around, I know there is a curfew in place, but this doesn't feel right.

I imagine it feels that way because I'm always expecting someone to jump out and arrest me. The lack of people should make me feel at ease, though it only fills me with more fear.

It doesn't take us too long to get to the elder's home, we keep a good pace the whole way. I run faster at times, enjoying the freedom of it, no matter how brief it is.

We stand up against the wall and catch our breath. I spy on the exit of the elder's home ahead of us, I think it will be the easiest way in. There are lights on in some windows, but I don't see people moving around inside, though my view is limited.

Enzo ensured us there would only be two members of staff until 9:15pm. It's 9:07pm, we have seven minutes to get to Cray's mother room and out again without being seen. He will have a couple of minutes with his mother at best.

Cray looks at me and gives me one short, curt nod. It's now or never, we run towards the door.

We reach the door and I pull on the handle, of course it's open, doors are hardly ever locked. I open the door slowly, and check inside, when I see no one there I step in, shortly followed by Cray.

We close the door behind us and stand there, only for a moment, as if waiting to be jumped on by a herd of guards, but nothing happens.

There's no point waiting around anymore, we are inside and on a time limit. We head towards room 138 as Enzo advised, that's where Cray's mother should be.

We jog through the corridors, only stopping at corners to listen out for any sound of a person and to have a quick look. When I see the way is clear, we go again. It doesn't take us long to reach the room, we step inside quietly and I see the frail old lady in her bed. I rush over to gently place a plate on her bracelet. Cray stands in the doorway, frozen.

I whisper to Karon gently so I can wake her from her sleep with minimal scare. She opens her eyes and stares at me for a moment, saying nothing. I don't know if she knows me or not so I speak to her.

"Hello, Karon, you may not know me, but I have someone here to see you, he's come a very long way to find you," I say, and turn to see Cray still standing by the door.

"It's okay Cray, come and see her, there isn't much time," I say.

He doesn't take his eyes off of his mother, I don't know if he even heard what I said but he takes a step forward, and then another. Within a few strides he's at her side and holding her hand, the room is silent for what feels like too long. When I check my bracelet it's only been thirty seconds.

I take a step closer to the bed, walking to the other side so I'm facing Cray. Silent tears are falling from his eyes. Karon looks up at me confused, then back to her son.

Another moment of silence.

"Am I dead?" She asks.

"No, Mum, no. You are alive, and I am too, I am here," he says, and kisses his mother's hands, his tears falling on to them.

"But you never made it. The accident, I thought you were dead."

"I never died; I've been hiding. I'm so sorry. They were going to kill me. I had to run, to protect you, I had to leave."

"My son, I can't believe you are here, oh, my son." She's in tears and pulls him in for an embrace. She holds him there tightly before letting go and looks to me. She takes hold of my hand in her left and holds Cray's in her right.

"Thank you. Thank you so much," she says and kisses my hand, then let's go to grab Cray's hand with both of hers.

I can only imagine how much this means to her, seeing the son she thought had died a long time ago, holding him in her arms once more.

"Thank you for coming to see me one last time. I love you very much my son," she says.

"I'm not leaving yet, Mum, I'm still here."

"I know darling, I know. You aren't going anywhere, I am. I've been holding on for you, for so long, but I'm tired now. So very tired, my son. I can finally sleep now, knowing you are okay and having said goodbye."

She releases her hand from his grip and lifts it up to touch his cheek. Her hand rests on his face and he holds it there, tears coming heavily. Her eyes are full of tears too, and she doesn't take her gaze off of her son, she stares straight into his eyes with a smile on her lips.

"My son, I'm so proud of you. So very proud you survived so long. Keep fighting the bastards." The last part of her words fade to a whisper as Karon Mytis slips away into death's grip.

Cray lays his mother's hand down, so it rests on her stomach, but his eyes are wide with shock.

"Mother? Mother wake up. Please. Wake up." He lightly shakes her shoulders, trying to wake her up. But you can't wake someone from death.

I stand there silently, unable to say anything.

Cray leans over and cradles his mother's lifeless body.

She's gone.

Oh no, she's gone. Karon Mytis is dead, she has a bracelet, guards will be coming. Panic sets in and all of a sudden, I know we have to leave immediately, or we will be caught.

I don't know if the plate Wes created blocks out the death signal or if it's just for tracking and communication, but I don't want to wait around to find out.

Will I have enough time to rescue my grandma? My heart is tearing apart, if I run now and get her, surely, I can make it out? They must expect deaths here, they wouldn't send many guards to investigate.

I'm only fooling myself here. I know the guards will be on us in minutes. We have to leave. I will get us back safely and return for my grandma, I'm not abandoning her forever. I will come back, and I will save her.

"Cray, I'm so sorry but we have to go. The guards are coming, they will kill us. Grab the plate, we have to leave." He doesn't respond to me, just carries on holding his mother in his arms.

I can't imagine how much pain he is in right now, but I need him to be strong. I have to be hard on him. We must leave.

I walk round to him and take his arm in my hands, giving him a little pull. He doesn't budge.

"Cray. We. Must. Leave. NOW!" I didn't mean to shout but he isn't hearing me, he needs to hear me.

For the first time since we entered the room, he looks at me. His eyes look like a little boy's who is experiencing pain for the first time. He is crushed, he just saw his mother die, and is holding her limp body in his arms. I've never seen such pain in a person's eyes before, but I know he can cope, he has to.

"Listen. Anytime someone dies their bracelet sends out a signal to the watchers. Guards are then sent to the location. They always send a group of guards just in case there was foul play in the person's death. If we don't leave right now, guards will catch us, and we will die. Please Cray, we have to go." There are too many tears threatening to overcome me right now, but I banish them into the darkest parts of me.

I pull on his arm as I speak, pulling him away from his mother and towards me, towards the door and our escape. Away from his mother and away from my grandma.

He breaks his eye contact with me and looks to his mother. He leans forward and leaves a kiss on her forehead before turning back to me and delivering another short, curt nod. I open the door and run, hearing the heavy footsteps behind me.

And I run like I've never run before.

We burst out of the door and head straight for the wall, knowing it's the quickest way back to the barn. It's probably the safest way which benefits us greatly. As soon as we reach the wall, we both dive to the floor and lay flat against the wall for a few moments.

I look around and Sector Two is alive with people. Not just people though, guards, everywhere. I don't know how, but I have a feeling they know I'm here, and they want me, badly.

I'm so stupid for not thinking they would watch Cray's mother. I just assumed that in captivity he didn't tell anyone who he was, and that they wouldn't know she was his mother. How could I be so blind?

There's no way we can run to the barn now, the two of us together won't go unnoticed, not with this swarm of guards, we have to split up.

The best way for Cray would be to go to the secret exit in the manure pit that Scarlett showed me. He will be safe going straight there, it's closer and safer than getting to the barn. He said he grew up in Sector One, so he should still remember where it is if he follows the wall, and the smell. I'll have to take a different route back, but I know 'The Island,' I can get myself around and hidden, whereas he can't. He needs the quick, safe route.

"I have a plan," I whisper to the dark night, praying no one is nearby to hear me. He moves himself round to face me and gets closer so we are inches apart and can hopefully remain unheard.

"There are too many guards out there now, we have to split up. We have a better chance if we go on our own. There is a secret exit from our bunker that you could use to get back there. All you need to do is follow this wall all the way down to the manure pit. Forget about going across to the barn, just keep going forward, you'll reach the smell before the place. If you get lost, use your bracelet to call Wes for help but be careful. I'm sure you'll remember where it is when you see it."

"Talise, I'm not leaving you out here alone, it isn't safe," he interrupts.

"It isn't safe if we go together, trust me, it's better this way. Now when you reach the manure pit, there is a little wooden hut. Next to it you will find a hatch door, though you may need to move a few things around to get to it. There is only one way through the tunnel. Before you go down, tell Wes what you are doing, at the other end there will be a locked door. Let him know when you are there, and he can let you in. Okay?"

"Okay, I understand, but what will you do? You must keep yourself protected."

"I will. I know this Island like the back of my hand. I can get around more easily than you can, plus, I'll have Wes if I need him. I'm going to take the long way around back to the barn, it should take me about five hours. Don't call my bracelet, no matter what. I will call if I need to, but do not call me and do not let Wes or anyone else call or message me, okay?"

"Okay," he says, and I start to think that he's only agreeing with me because his mother just died, and his brain is probably scrambled, he isn't thinking straight. But I can't risk someone calling my bracelet if I get caught, it's too dangerous.

"Be safe, head for the manure pit. Keep your head down, stay close to the ground if you can. Do not contact Wes until you are about to go into the tunnel unless you absolutely have to. I'll see you later, okay?"

"Okay. Be safe, Talise."

"I will. Now go!" I say and pull myself up off the ground and head out towards some of the cages, away from Cray and away from my family. I take off my bracelet whilst I run and hide it in my under top, if I'm caught, I don't want them finding it.

The sadness washes over me then as I realise that I probably won't make it back to the barn, there are just too many guards.

∞

I weave in and out of the cages, some are occupied, some empty. I don't hear anything from inside them, I don't hear anything near me at all. I stop running and lean against a cage, panting heavily. I strain my ears to listen out for any kind of noise, but I hear nothing.

I don't like this silence; I need to keep moving. There may be some hope of me getting back to the barn, and back to Raine, after all.

Just as I'm about to move off there is a crunching sound not far away. The only sound anywhere near me. I run in the opposite direction, not waiting to see what the noise was from.

Another crunch behind me and a bright blue light radiates by my feet, not quite touching, but very close.

I take a sharp left and run harder and faster. I make my body move in ways it's never known, the pressure is on, I'm being chased.

Another crunch, this time ahead of me, I dive right just as the blue light flies over my head. I don't know what weapon it is they have, but I really don't want to find out.

I can get lost in the houses soon, 400 metres and I'll be masked by them, I can make it.

I have to run across open ground, but it sounds like my pursuers are right behind me, I've got no choice.

I sprint out into the open, pelting forward. I see the gap in the first two houses and focus on it, I need to get there. I can't stop, can't look behind me, I just run.

CRUNCH! A searing pain shoots it's way up from my wrist, all through my arm and into my body. My feet stumble and I fall to the floor in a writhing heap as the electricity soars through me. My arm convulses and my body trembles trying to fight the pain, it's excruciating.

My vision is blurred, I can't see anything around me.

I look at my wrist; all I see is blue. I blink a few times and breathe in deeply through my mouth trying to centre myself, I need to get up and get moving again.

I look again at my wrist; my vision clears and I'm shocked. Wrapped around my left wrist is a metallic cord shining with bright blue light. I pull at it and try to release my wrist but it's no good, it does nothing. The cord is tight on my wrist and whoever has the other end is keeping a firm hold on it.

I get in a steady position on the floor, my right hand now supporting some of my weight against the ground.

I take a deep breath and yank my left hand in one smooth motion towards my chest as hard as I possibly can. I hear a thud and a cry from behind me, I don't wait to look. I pull the cord closer and closer to me until I have the end my captor held. It's the whip Enzo told me about. I search the handle for a button, there's one at the base and one at the top of the handle. One button must send the volts through me, I take a guess it's the one at the top, that's where a thumb would rest. I don't have much time to think about it, so I take the risk and press the button on the bottom.

Instantly, the line around my wrist weakens and falls away, I'm free. I roll the cord up and hold it in my hand, getting to my feet, ready to run again. I know this wasn't my only pursuer, but now I have one of their weapons which gives me a sliver of hope.

I stand and stumble slightly, my body still in shock from the electricity that went through me. I drag my feet forward, one in front of the other. I know I can pick up the pace, I will my feet to go faster, I must keep moving. I'm practically at the houses.

I look to one of the houses and see a woman standing in the window. She was staring at me until I caught her gaze, now she's gone, probably hiding.

I reach the two houses, I'm just about to disappear between them.

CRUNCH!

Another cord has fastened around my left wrist again, I drop the whip I was holding and reach round ready to pull the cord from it's wielder. Before my hand can match my thoughts there's a WHOOSH from the right of me.

I scream out in pain.

Searing hot pain.

My hand is on fire. Not like the fire from my fever, this fire is real. My hand is actually on fire, burning.

I look down at my hand and there is an arrow through it, an arrow! It's covered in flames, licking over my hand. I can't even see my hand anymore. The smoke working it's way into my lungs. I start coughing and stumble forward, I still have to escape.

The pain is unbearable, and my vision is completely distorted. I have to keep going though, I must escape.

I'm pulled by my left wrist and fall to the floor. Another jolt of electricity runs up my arm and through my body, this one more intense than the last.

My whole body convulses on the floor. Everything within me is on fire, the pain is indescribable. All I can do is look at my right hand, the fire engulfing it. I can actually see my flesh melting, the skin on my hand is melting!

I feel nauseous and I vomit in my mouth, but I'm lying on my back and I start to choke.

Someone rolls me onto my side, so I spit my vomit onto the floor, heaving and retching. I can't catch my breath, I'm suffocating.

Someone has placed a shiny blanket over my right hand. The fire is out, but the pain is still there.

I can't say anything, I can't do anything, I lay there, lifeless.

Hands are all over me, grabbing me under my arms, my legs, my back. Hands that pick me up and start carrying me. I don't know if I can stay awake much longer, the pain is too much to bear.

I need the darkness to consume me now, I don't want to face the pain, I can't. The back of my mind is pulling me, willing me to slip away. I don't need to be here now, I can leave, I know I can. And so, I let myself slip into the darkness.

Coldness.
My hand is cold.
My back is cold.
Where am I?
I peel open my eyes. A grey ceiling above me.
I lean my head to the right, a door a metre away. To the left, a wall. I'm raised above ground, I try to feel what's underneath me, but I can't feel my right hand.

I remember fire and pain; I must be in a cell.
They caught me.

I ran but they still caught me.

I look down at my hands and I'm immediately worried. There is a strange black glove on my right hand, though my left hand is uncovered. The fire, they burnt my hand.

I'm wearing the same thing I was before I went to the darkness. They haven't changed me; I should still have my bracelet.

I wonder what the time is. I look at the walls around me, nothing but a camera.

I still can't move my right hand; I think they've numbed it. I can see it but it feels like it's not there. Why would they put me through all that pain to then numb my hand so I can't feel it?

It's strange. I doubt they gave Enzo any numbing agents.

First step, I need to check if I still have the bracelet in my top. I pull my legs up, checking they both work; they do. I use my left hand to push myself up, taking all of my weight. I slowly get myself to a sitting position.

No matter how much I worked out with Ajax and Scarlett, it still takes a lot out of me to even sit up. I've lost my strength. I guess that happens when you've had electricity burning through your body and a flaming arrow through your hand.

I take a few deep breaths, then get myself to stand. I take a few steps towards the door, then lean against it for a moment when I get there.

It's cold.

Everything in this room is cold, it's all metal.

I look at the bed I was lying on, just a metal board, no mattress to soften it, no blanket, just a slab of metal.

The camera is above the door and facing the bed, though I know it will cover the whole room, it probably has sound as well. I walk back towards the 'bed,' and just before I reach it, I intentionally stumble and catch myself with my left hand on the floor.

I stay there for a few moments and then pull my knees up so I'm crouching in on myself. I lift my left hand off the floor and reach under my shirt to check for the bracelet. I feel the bump of it with my fingertips and a wave of relief washes over me.

If only my right hand was working this would be easier, I'm not left-handed. I stay crouched over on the floor and manage to wiggle the bracelet out. I take it in my hand, keeping it under my shirt, and look straight down so I can make out the screen.

I type out a quick message for Wes, I know I need to be fast as someone could come in at any moment. I make my message short but clear.

I clumsily type 'Captured. U listen. B silent.' I send it to him instantly then move around a little, making it look like I'm trying to get up again.

I slump back down into my crouch and call Wes; the screen shows me that we are connected but he doesn't say anything. I hastily get the bracelet back into my undershirt and make a show of attempting to get up two more times before managing on the third.

I imagine they have the same barrier on these walls as they do the cages. I wonder if they didn't turn them on for me because as far as they're aware, I don't have a bracelet. Or perhaps Wes's design is so advanced that it can still get a signal within the barrier. That wouldn't surprise me, Wes truly is a genius.

I know people will be watching me right now, so I make myself look weaker than I am. I saw the time when I messaged Wes, it's 2:04am, there are four hours of battery life left on the bracelet. I just hope someone comes for me before it cuts out and I get some information that Wes can overhear.

I don't know how much time passes by, but I sit on the bed and focus on moving my body. I struggle with my right hand a lot, but there's nothing else for me to be doing here, so I put my full effort into it.

My legs are steady again, my left hand has no issues, it's just my numb right hand. I go to take the glove off multiple times, but I'm scared of what I will see underneath.

Images of Enzo keep flashing in my mind and I remember what they did to him, how burnt his hands were, and how mine will probably look the same.

I talk to myself a couple of times, though it's more for Wes. I make it sound like I'm asking the guards questions though.

I ask why I'm in a metal room, why they had to burn my hand. I ask when someone is coming to see me, I ask for water and I ask them for the time. All of my questions go unanswered, but I know that Wes is at least getting a small description of what happened.

After what feels like a day of waiting around, I decide it's time to take off my glove. I loosen the base that's tight on my wrist and just as I'm about to pull it off the door to my cell opens.

Two guards walk in, one with a black bag in his hand. The guard standing in the doorway looks down at me smugly, the other moves to put the bag on my head. I look him straight in the eyes as he does it, I want to seem brave.

He actually looks a little apologetic as he slowly puts the bag over my head, I catch a glimpse of his bracelet as he does so, it's 4:48am, I've been awake in this cell for nearly three hours.

Once the bag is secure on my head, the guard takes my arm and lifts me up so I'm standing, I feign a slight wobble and his grip remains strong. He steps forward whilst holding my arm and I take that as my cue to walk with him. As soon as I'm out of the door the second guard takes my other arm, and they march me away together.

I try to count the number of turns we take and stairs we go up or down, but I lose count quickly. They really wind me through the building, we must be hidden very well in this bunker.

I make sure to comment on all the turns they are taking and ask them if they are aimlessly walking me around in circles. I need to make sure no one tries a suicide mission to rescue me.

I'm taken somewhere and sat in a chair. My hands are lifted, and then cuffed to a bar on a table. The bag is finally taken off.

The guards leave the room and I sit there by myself, observing and waiting. There are four cameras in this room, one in each corner.

They keep me waiting in the room, probably watching me, trying to scare me. I ask how long they will keep me in this room for and ask them to uncuff me because my burnt hand hurts. I ask if four cameras are really necessary, I'm unsurprised I get nothing in return.

At least Wes will know, I just hope they don't wait too long before talking to me, the battery will die.

The door opens and I look up to see the Lieutenant from my 18th birthday, the one that escorted me to the hospital and then no doubt gave the nurse the mysterious injection for me.

I can't think of anything to say so I try to smile at her, but it probably comes out as more of a snarl than anything. She doesn't react to me at all, just takes a seat across from me with an electronic device in her hand.

"Who else are you working with, Talise?" She asks me outright and I don't know why but that annoys me, this woman annoys me, everything about this situation annoys me.

"What, no 'hello, Talise, how are you?' Your manners are poor, Lieutenant."

"We know you are working with Enzo Cardelous. You helped him escape our custody. But don't worry, we will find him again soon, and he will be put to death," She states plainly.

"I'm not worried. You should be worried." I don't know why I even said that.

"And why should I be worried, Talise?" She asks, leaning forward.

I lean forward to mimic her.

"You'll find out, Lieutenant, but not until it's too late," I say and then lean back in my chair, smiling. I have no plans that should make her scared and nothing to go on, but I can't sit here and be bullied by her. I need it to look like I have some sort of power, even though I'm weak and defenceless.

"This isn't a game, you know. There is no escaping for you. We know about your little hideout at the barn. It's only a matter of time before we go down there and arrest them all. So why don't you tell me about the other people you are working with above ground? That way I won't have to question your friends too hard."

Panic seeps back into my body. Every part of me is riddled with fear, how in 'The Island' do they know about the barn? It's impossible. Carlo never would have told them anything, how do they know?

Before I go into a complete meltdown, I take a moment to collect myself and think about her words.

Wes is listening so it will be okay. She said it's a matter of time, that means they haven't gone there yet, they aren't even there right now. Wes can gather them together and get out of there before the guards arrive. He can save them.

"You won't find them," I say, and the Lieutenant laughs.

"Oh, but we will. You see, we know about your special little inventor friend, and those plates he made. You left one on Karon Mytis. We examined it and we were amazed to find out what it could do. Now we have a way to look through the system and find anyone who disappears, even if just for a fraction of a second. So, you see, anyone working with you, and not in hiding, will soon be found when we get through all of the data. Even those in hiding will be found once we get the engineers to work on the plate and reverse it. They will all be arrested and questioned, just like your friend Enzo was, and it will all be your fault, Talise."

My breath catches in my throat. They know. They know everything.

I can't believe I didn't get the plate off Karon; I was so stupid. I told Cray to, but honestly his mother had just died, he probably didn't even hear me ask him. I've put everyone at risk because of it. I must warn them, I need to escape, to save my friends, my family.

"What is the time, Lieutenant?" I ask.

That's the first time I've caught a glimpse of an expression other than hatred on her face. She's surprised, then confused, then the mask is back on and she glares at me. But she also lifts her sleeve slightly to look at her bracelet and the time.

"It's 5:57am," she replies, and I can't help but smile.

The bracelet has three minutes left before the power cuts out, Wes would have heard everything she just said. I know he will already be putting a plan in place to recuse everyone and save as many lives as possible.

"Thank you. Is there anything else you wish to share with me Lieutenant, or should I go back to my cell?" I ask bluntly.

She actually smiles at that, a genuine smile, like she's impressed.

"You know, Talise, I can't decide whether you are brave or stupid. You can go back to your cell, but you will be executed. Tonight. I think 9pm would be as good a time as any. It's 5:58am now, enjoy your last fifteen hours of life," she says all too smugly.

"Oh, one last thing, Lieutenant. That whip you caught me with, it electrocuted me, right?"

"Yes. Did it hurt?"

"Sure did. Not as bad as the flaming arrow through my hand though. Goodbye, Lieutenant," I say and smile, though this time, it's a sad smile, because I'm hurt, beaten and captured. I am going to die, and I won't have anyone to speak to again before they kill me.

The Lieutenant looks at my right hand, still covered in the glove and she looks angry. It's hidden away again within seconds, but I'm sure I saw it there. She must be annoyed they wasted a glove on me, or maybe she doesn't like the flaming arrows.

She waves her hand and guards come in, un-cuff me from the table, cuff my hands in front of me and start to walk me back to my cell.

"Goodbye my friends," I whisper to my chest in hopes they hear me.

A single tear escapes me, but I manage to hold the rest back. There is a tiny vibration from where the bracelet is under my top and I can only assume that means the battery has died.

The only positive I get from this imprisonment is that I helped my friends. Wes would have heard all of the information he needed.

I hope he got the last part about the electrocution in the whip. I think if he has enough time he could probably create some form of clothing to keep us safe from the electrocution.

No. Not us, them.

He can keep them safe and give them the advantage. Because tonight I'm going to die.

<u>Chapter Eighteen</u>

Back in my cell I lay on the cold, hard metal. I still can't feel my right hand. I don't know if that's a good or bad thing, but I guess it doesn't really matter.

I've been up for so many hours now, I can't recall the last time I had a full night's sleep. There's nothing I can do in here now. I already checked my bracelet and it's dead, but I still keep it hidden.

I drift in and out of sleep, nightmares creeping into my unconscious mind and tearing me awake. Time is a mystery.

I feel like I've slept for hours, but I know it could have just as easily been twenty minutes. There is no indication to show where we are in the day, where I am in this bunker, or when my end will come.

I think about everyone hiding at the barn and pray Wes managed to hear everything. I know he would have a plan to get everyone out quickly and quietly. I just hope it wasn't too late. All I can do is pray they are safe, all of them.

I can feel everything about to rush over me, ready to break me. I'm going to shatter and fall into the depths of grief, never to surface. But I can't cry now, otherwise I'll never stop, and I'll die here alone in my tears.

I miss my family so much.

I miss Raine. I'm never going to see any of them again.

I can't help it now; the tears consume me and steal my breath from me.

I cry for hours, feeling the loss of my loved ones. I feel their deaths and I feel the guilt. I cry for Enzo and what they put him through, I cry for Carlo and his sacrifice. I cry for my parents.

My tears run nowhere, they can't be soaked up, so they gather on my 'bed' and stay there. I wipe my face on my shirt numerous times, but I give up eventually, there's no point now, it's soaked.

I don't cry for myself though.

When some of the tears have stopped, I sit on my bed and face the door, staring into nothingness. After an unknown period of time, the door opens and in steps the head leader, Mr Ritton, the king of lies.

"Ahh, Talise, you caused us so much trouble. I'm glad we can finally put an end to it." His gruff voice speaks with pride, he sounds happy that I'm here, happy that he can finally have me killed. He is a disgusting human being.

"Why can't we know about 'the others?' Why the big secret? We could build a bigger and better world together, with them," I question him. My tears are long forgotten, my anger taking over.

"You don't understand what needs to be done, Talise, and you never will. This is all out of my control, it's what must happen," He replies coldly.

"I don't believe anything you say. You are a liar, torturer and murderer. You make me sick." I don't know where my courage is coming from, but I have nothing to lose now, my execution imminent.

"I confess, you are right. I do tell lies, but only to protect everyone. I want us all to survive, I do it for 'The Island' and the people in it. You know too much, so you are a threat to the people. If everyone found out then it would cause panic, people would turn on one another and our world would crumble once again. You already have death on your hands, do you really want more people to die because of you?"

I don't say anything. Death is on my hands already and it's haunting me every second of every day. I don't know what to say back to him, he has me defeated and he knows it. "Your execution will be on the stage tonight, in front of everyone. For those unable to attend in person, like your little friends in hiding, they will see the execution projected on their bracelets, not only will they see you die, they will hear you die. Everyone on 'The Island' will witness your execution," he says smugly.

I pray that Wes's plates will stop the feed from showing. I can't have them watch me die. They can look away from the projection, but they will still hear it, they will hear me die.

My parents, my parents must watch my execution. They probably think I'm crazy, a terrorist and a murderer, but they still can't want to see me killed. Their own daughter.

There is nothing they can do. I feel the need to cry for my parents now, but I hold it in, I'll wait until I'm as alone as I can be with the camera watching me.

"You're a bad man, Mr Ritton. Why do you hide the fact you have a son? He is an incredible man, and you've disowned him." That's all I have left.

"I have no son," he spits out.

"That man disgusts me, the way he is, it's not right. I spared his life when he was younger, but I made a mistake, I should have killed him along with that other man. Joseph is a traitor. I wouldn't think twice about killing him now. I have no son." His anger grows with every word until he's shouting.

How he says those words hurts me, but I won't show it. I just look at him with as much hatred as I can muster, and I stay silent.

He paces the room for a few moments, I never take my eyes off of him. He turns to face me and displays one of his fake, white smiles for me.

"It's been a *lovely* talk, Talise. I will see you at your execution." He leaves the room without another word or glance in my direction. I take a few deep breaths to calm myself and try to hold back my tears a few moments longer.

But they come regardless, and the grief returns. I sit there for however long it is crying alone again. That's all I can do. I cry until someone comes back to my cell.

Connelly walks in holding a tray with food and water. I meet his eyes and all I can see is heartbreak in them. I'd almost forgotten about our confrontation in one of the cages. He looks so pained; he looks me over and I see the sorrow in his eyes.

"Hi, Talise." He coos at me, setting the tray down next to me. I say nothing, just glare at him.

"I'm so sorry. I'm sorry I couldn't help you with your illness. I wish I knew sooner; I could have saved you." He still thinks I'm unwell.

He is so blinded by the leaders! How can he believe them and not me, how can he stand by and watch me get murdered? Tears start to fall from my eyes again,

I cry for Connelly now, and how he's hurt me all over again.

"This really is goodbye, Connelly," I choke out.

"It doesn't have to be, maybe I can ask Mr White to let me take responsibility for you. I can look after you, we can marry, I can keep you safe, Talise." He begs me. He's down on his knees in front of me and holding my hands, begging me with everything he has, but it's pointless. And it just makes me angry.

"Connelly, what do you think is happening here? I am going to be executed tonight. You cannot save me now, you never could. And even if they let me out, I wouldn't marry you, Connelly. You never believed me, you still don't. I'm in love with someone else, a forbidden love that would get me murdered all over again if they knew about it. There is no safe place left for me, Connelly, I'm going to be executed no matter what."

He looks confused at that; did he not know I'm being executed? Or maybe it's because I said I have a forbidden love, maybe that confused him. But he doesn't say anything. He lets go of my hands and leaves the room, his gaze on the floor the whole time. The door closes behind him and just like that, I'm alone again.

I look at the tray next to me. A sandwich and a cup of water. I may as well have it, I'm starving. I start to eat the sandwich and think how strange it is that they are feeding me when they're going to execute me.

Enzo was starved for weeks, they never feed people they are going to kill, it's a waste of resources, so why me? What's so special about me?

I sip the water and look at the sandwich again, opening it up and looking for anything unusual. But it's normal, nothing wrong with it. I feel tired again, maybe I should sleep.

I didn't realise how tired I was, my eyes are feeling droopy and my body lacks energy. I lower my hand to my lap, no longer having the strength to hold it up.

The water spills from the cup and all over my lap, my body going limp.

I've been drugged.

Maybe they are killing me now, to get it finished sooner rather than later. I fall to my side and lay on the 'bed.'

Once again, I slip into the darkness.

∞

I hear her voice.

She's calling to me, through the fog, the clouds, she calls me. I must be dead and Raine is guiding me, she's pulling me through, towards the light.

It's a harsh light though, shining right into my eyes. I feel a grip on my shoulders, shaking me.

I open my eyes and I'm met with a small light shining in them, I move my arm to swat it away, but my limbs won't respond.

I hear her say my name again, it's Raine. I look around the room, there's just the two of us in here. Where are we? This isn't my cell. She's still saying my name, calling me to her, to focus.

I look at her and see the worry in her eyes and focus.

I focus on her and her beautiful face that I want to touch. Her lips I want to kiss, her hair to stroke. The fog starts to clear but my body doesn't want to move, my arms are dead weights.

"Raine." I whisper her name, then repeat it several times over to make sure it's her, and she's here, with me, wherever we are.

"Hey, beautiful. You were drugged in your cell, try and focus on me, we only have a few minutes."

"Did you rescue me? Are we in a safe place?" I ask her, still trying to clear the fog, not quite understanding.

"I'm so sorry, Talise, I tried, we all did. But they came for us, we had to run and hide. I was outside when a guard saw me, it was Connelly. Instead of capturing me, he let me in to see you, he said it's his apology. But we don't have long."

That surprises me and I'm thankful for Connelly then. I can forgive him, because he brought Raine to me, he gave me a chance to say goodbye. I know there is no chance of escaping this bunker cell. They seem to have moved me to another room, I can't quite feel my body properly, my legs are numb. There is no hope of survival.

"Are you here alone? Did Cray make it back okay?" I ask.

"Yes, he made it back to the bunker in time before we had to evacuate, and yes, I'm alone," she replies sadly.

"I'm so happy to see you, but you have to leave. You have to save our family."

"Talise, no. I've got to save you. I can fight the guards; I'll get you out of here."

"No, Raine. You can't do it by yourself and I'm in no position to run. Connelly may have let you in, but he won't fight the other guards to help us escape, you can't save me this time. You have to let me go."

"Talise, that isn't an option. Can you try to stand? We can go right now." She barely gets the last words out because she starts crying, the tears choking her.

I try to reach for her to comfort her, but my arms don't work, I can't move any of my limbs.

"Please don't cry. You can take our family and Cray, run, escape these walls. Go and live out there, be free from the fear in here. You can use my execution as a distraction, everyone will be focused on me. You'll have an open window to run, don't waste it. Let me sacrifice myself so you can be safe, please Raine, for me. You have to run. You have to survive."

The tears stream down her face as she clutches my left hand, her grip firm and unfaltering. I'm surprised I can feel her touch and it warms me, I have that at least.

I can see the torment in her eyes, and I hate how I'm leaving her alone in this world. But it is the only way to save her, the woman of my dreams, the person I've fallen in love with.

I didn't know it was possible to love someone so much in such a short space of time. This is what I've always wanted, a love like my parents, but now it's bringing me the highest level of pain imaginable.

Pain that could never be physically impacted upon someone, no, this pain runs deeper than that.

"Please," I whisper. At this, she looks up at me, tears spilling too fast from her eyes. I know I won't be able to say everything I want to without choking up, or at least passing out from the drugs they pumped me with.

I'm going to put all my strength into these last few minutes with her. I can stay strong, for her.

"Promise me you will remember the good times. Remember our smiles and laughs, our stolen kisses in the medical room. Remember me from when we were happy, remember everything good," I plead.

I wish I could tell her how scared I am, but she needs me to be strong right now, I can't be selfish.

But she can live, I must focus on that, she will live, and that is more important to me than my own life.

"You should go now. It's time for you to run. My end is inevitable." My eyes feel heavy and start to drop slightly.

I look at her eyes, her piercing green, beautiful eyes and I smile.

She sweeps the hair back from my face and smiles back at me. She kisses my forehead delicately then pulls back a little and stares into my eyes.

"I love you, Talise. I know you won't ever leave me. We will always be in each other's hearts and nothing can ever change that. You may be gone for a little while, but we will find our way back to each other, even through death."

My heart races, beating faster than ever before. This is the first time she has said she loves me. If I wasn't fading so fast, I would be drowning in my tears.

I realise then I still have the bracelet in my top, I can't let the leaders get that from my corpse.

"Bracelet, in my undertop," I say so faintly I'm not sure she heard. Within seconds though she is removing the bracelet from me and tucking it into her pocket.

My eyes are closing now, and I smile, I smile as widely as my slack face will allow. I wish I could keep my eyes open, so I could look at her beautiful face some more, but the drugs are too powerful.

Just as I'm slipping away from my own consciousness, I force myself to say something, one last thing.
I want to tell her I love her too, but I know I can't, my mouth won't allow it. It's just two words and she will know. Just our two words.

"Am," I'm struggling to fight the darkness. "Aa, amo," I feel the strong pull, I'm about to go.

"Amoooor," slurring.

"Sssssh, ssssh, it's okay, I know, I know. You love me too," she whispers as she strokes my hair.

And then I slip into the unknown, hating the fact I couldn't tell her 'Amore proibito' one last time.

Chapter Nineteen

Voices.

So many whispers.

Hands under my arms.

I feel my legs again; my feet are dragging against the floor. I'm being half carried, half dragged somewhere.

I try to lift my head to see who has me but it's too heavy. My limbs are dead weights, the drug has started to wear off, but it's still in my system.

I know where they are taking me though, it's time for my execution.

We come to a stop and I'm pulled up between two guards, lifting me up slightly so I'm not as slumped in their arms.

The bunker doors in front of me open and I'm cast in light. I hear the rain falling, a small gift for me in my last few minutes.

I'm walked towards the stage, that's where I will be executed. I hear Mr Ritton talking through the speakers, he is at the front of the stage.

He has a mask of sadness plastered all over his face, acting as if my death saddens him. More lies.

I focus on the details, hoping it helps the drug wear off quicker. There are three chairs on the stage, two of them are occupied. I look at the people sitting there and see that it's the other two leaders, Ms Keller and Mr White.

I'm unsurprised they are here; they are required for all big announcements. Neither of them looks at me, they keep their eyes fixed on Mr Ritton the whole time, their faces without expression.

I'm taken to the back of the stage and walked up the steps, towards a wooden block.

They are going to decapitate me.

The guards carrying me push me to my knees in front of the block, and one of them cuffs my hands in front of me. I look down, my right hand still has the glove on, I guess they forgot to take it off.

I look up and out over the crowd, and I tune in to what Mr Ritton is saying.

"A criminal, a terrorist. This woman has threatened us all for too long now. She has murdered people, broken into my home, raided other facilities on 'The Island.' She has stolen food and water supplies for herself, leaving us all with less. She has lied and hurt us all. We tried to help her, but we fear she has become unstable and dangerous. She murdered the nurse who tried to give her the bracelet."

He turns and points straight at me as he delivers those words, shaking his hand as if overcome with rage.

"She has oppressed us for too long now. There is no help for this woman, we must execute her so we can be safe once again." I can't believe the lies he's spinning, and the fact the crowd are listening to him, I see some of them nod their heads in agreement.

It makes me sad to see what control this man has over the people, I wish I could have done more to stop him and the other leaders. I just hope Wes and the others can do something to help. I hope they escape; they should be going over the wall now.

"It is with a heavy heart that we have to do this, but we are left without a choice, she is simply too dangerous." Mr Ritton finishes his speech with his hand on his heart, looking out across the crowd, allowing the silence to spread.

I take one last look at the crowd before I die.

There are disgusted looks, some questioning ones and some sad ones. I don't know if it's sadness for what I've supposedly done, or sadness at seeing a young adult getting killed. It's weird to think of myself as an adult after everything that has happened over the last couple of months.

I see my parents, they're holding hands, silently crying. I try to tell them to look away, but I can't signal or speak.

Mr Ritton walks over to me as one of the guards lowers me forward, leaning my head on to the wooden block. Mr Ritton leans down and brings his lips to my ear.

"I win," he whispers then steps away.

Someone with heavy boots walks towards me, I can see the axe hanging down by his knees, I quickly look away to the floor.

This is it, the moment I die.

I should have headbutted Mr Ritton while he was close, that would have been cool.

I picture Raine, along with Wes, Carlo, my whole family in the barn. I keep their faces clear in my mind and I imagine Rory's laughter ringing through my ears. I smile to myself at the memories of them all and wish for their safety.

The sound of the axe being lifted next to me takes over from Rory's laughter in my ears. I force myself to look up. I hold my breath and focus on my parents. I stare into my father's broken eyes and refuse to let tears leave me.

THWACK!

Everything goes dark.

Acknowledgements

Thank you for taking the time to read my book, I really hope you enjoyed it! I want to thank every single one of you for joining the adventure of this series.

Firstly, to Kelly. Thank you so much for reading, re-reading and re-re-reading my countless drafts. You are a fantastic friend and I appreciate you so much.

To my sister, Tara. Thank you for helping me in the weaker areas and sharing your big brain with your little sister.

And lastly, to Cooper, my dog. You were no help whatsoever and actually got in the way more than anything, thanks boy.

Please join Talise as her story continues in the second book of the series; The Fall of The Walls, coming soon.

Printed in Great Britain
by Amazon

74949073R00159